ABOUT THE

Simon Van Booy grew up in
of London. He is the author
The Secret Lives of People in Love, and the international
bestseller *The Illusion of Separateness*. He is the editor of
three philosophy books and has written for the *New York
Times*, *Guardian*, *Telegraph*, *Financial Times* and the BBC.
His work has been translated into seventeen languages.
He lives in Brooklyn with his wife and daughter.

PRAISE FOR *FATHER'S DAY*

'A strong voice full of poetic, timeless grace.'
San Francisco Examiner

'Deftly portrays his characters' raw emotions.'
Wall Street Journal

'Van Booy charms us with the struggles of this unlikely
father-figure.' *Sunday Herald*

'In this novel, Van Booy is at his most poignant, showing how redemption can arise from heartbreaking
circumstances.' *Boston Globe*

'There's so much to enjoy along the way, from Mr. Van
Booy's muted lyricism to the profusion of quiet domestic
moments rendered in the strangely captivating way of
Andre Dubus.' *East Hampton Star*

'In *Father's Day*, Van Booy again deftly demonstrates that
he is a master at the craft of storytelling.'
Portland Press Herald

'A moving, redemptive new novel...The third-person narrative gives both characters their own, distinctive voices that nonetheless change over time. Van Booy creates refreshing, humorous, yet poignant childhood milestones that the two reach with emotional honesty.'

Publishers Weekly

'Van Booy's great triumph comes in using a family secret to underscore the message that family is as much a choice as a blood tie. Although any reader will find something to love here, someone who has benefited from a perfectly imperfect family will wear the widest smile. This little book with a big heart is suitable not just for Father's Day, but for any day.'

Shelf Awareness

'[Van Booy's] facility with word choice and sentence structure can leave a reader swooning...[a] movingly understated drama punctuated with moments of quiet reflection.'

Arizona Republic

'The moving account of a unique relationship between a parent and child, thrust together under the worst of circumstances. With fine, nuanced prose and much tenderness, Booy guides this unlikely father-daughter pair into a beautiful maturity, showing us with great heart what it really means to be a family.'

Elizabeth Crane, author of *The History of Great Things*

'Van Booy writes like Hemingway but with more heart.'

New Hampshire Public Radio

Also by Simon Van Booy

FATHER'S DAY

SIMON VAN BOOY

ONEWORLD

A Oneworld Book

First published in Great Britain and Australia
by Oneworld Publications, 2016
This paperback edition published 2017

Published by arrangement with HarperCollins Publishers,
New York, New York, U.S.A

ISBN 978-1-78607-031-9
ISBN 978-1-78074-970-9 (eBook)

Printed and bound in Great Britain by Clays Ltd, St Ives plc

Oneworld Publications
10 Bloomsbury Street
London WC1B 3SR
England

For Joan and Steve

Sometime too hot the eye of heaven shines.

—William Shakespeare

FATHER'S DAY

I

HARVEY WAS BORN in a redbrick hospital on a hill. It was the hardest day of her mother's life and she cried for a long time after.

There was a park near the hospital where children went on swings and ran away from their parents. Harvey's mother used to go there when she was pregnant. She sat on a bench and ate little things from her purse.

There was also a duck pond that froze in winter. People came early, in twos and threes. They held hands going around in loose circles. There was no music, just human voices and the clopping of skates.

When Harvey was old enough to feed the ducks, her parents brought her to the park with a stale loaf. Her father put his hand inside the bag, tearing the bread into small pieces.

"You were born here," he told her.

"In the park?"

"No, in a hospital," her father said. "But in this town."

Some of the ducks came right up to Harvey. They tilted their heads to one side and opened their beaks. When the bag was empty, her father shook out the crumbs.

Harvey wanted to see the hospital where she was born, but her mother said next time, for sure.

Harvey asked how many babies are born in the world on one day.

"Thousands," her father replied. "Maybe millions."

Harvey imagined the babies in her room. So many it was hard to open the door. Some of them were crying, their faces red and glistening. Others crawled around touching things, or just lay on their backs. Harvey imagined sweeping the babies up with her play broom.

"When can I have a baby, Daddy?"

"When you get married," said her father. "When you're in love."

"I only want two. Two little sisters."

At lunchtime, they went into town. Harvey clambered into her stroller. She knew how to get in without making it tip. Her doll Duncan had been waiting for her. He was just a baby and needed looking after.

Sometimes on long car trips he threw up doll pizza.

The crackle of stroller wheels on the sidewalk. Winter salt not yet washed away. Town very busy. Lines of cars at red lights. People inside the cars looking at them. Harvey reaching under the seat to poke the shape of her butt. It was like a big tummy. A big tummy with a person inside.

She put Duncan under her shirt. "Look," she said. "I'm married, and this is my first baby."

Harvey's mother laughed but then felt hollow and afraid. Her husband's arm came around her.

"Everything we're feeling, they said we were gonna feel," he told her.

THE RESTAURANT IN town was famous for a life-size statue of a donkey. Everyone coming in had to touch it for good luck, even Duncan with his plastic doll hand.

Harvey watched her mother's face when their orange

soda arrived in glass bottles. She couldn't read but knew what writing was. Harvey would get soda for being good— which meant not talking, or at Easter—after giving up candy for Lent.

Harvey plopped Duncan on her mother's lap. It was a sacrifice to let him go, but sudden generosity made her feel safe. Her mother sucked down the orange liquid, tipping back the bottle, the pop fizzing as though angry, making her lips shine. Harvey wanted to wear lipstick too, but wasn't allowed. She wanted to touch it with her tongue but was definitely not allowed. It was like the skin of a red apple. *Poor Snow White,* Harvey thought. *She had to sleep for a million years, all because of fruit.* At McDonald's she some-times painted her lips with ketchup, using a french fry, but then retched.

Harvey's mother patted Duncan's head, then cupped her daughter's hand inside her own as though it were a secret she was keeping. Two waiters in fancy hats brought a cart to their table and mashed avocados in a stone bowl. They all watched. The waiters were getting it on their hands.

"It's like green poop," Harvey said.

HARVEY'S FATHER OWNED a jewelry store at the mall. He left early in a gray two-piece suit. Aftershave made him feel important.

Sometimes he came home with a bag of food from Mc-Donald's or Burger King. (Other restaurants didn't put toys in the bag.) Her father's business did well during the holidays. One of Harvey's first memories was watching a woman try on a gold necklace. It was around Christmas, so the shop was decorated. Harvey and her mother were waiting for him to close, but then a man and a woman came in holding hands.

The necklace was brought to the woman on a red cushion, the way Harvey had seen things carried at church. Her mother said that people liked gold crosses at Christmas because Jesus had died on one. Harvey once saw a picture of Jesus dying. His head hung low like he was upset about something. There were spikes too. People stood watching in sandals and bathrobes. Harvey knew there were bad people who hurt others. She had seen them on TV. They had guns and rode motorcycles and came for you at night or in the city.

The woman looked at the necklace on the cushion, then at her husband.

"Where was Jesus born?" Harvey asked her mother.

"You should know that."

"I forgot."

"In a stable," her mother reminded her. "With animals watching and presents from three wise men."

Harvey wished she had been born in a stable on Christmas Day. Santa Claus could have been her wise man. Santa could have given the animals a chance to fly with magic dust. Jesus too if he wanted.

Harvey's father watched the man fasten the necklace around his partner's neck. When the woman felt his hands, she closed her eyes and stroked the cross with her fingers.

Harvey wondered how something that had hurt Jesus could make people happy. Sometimes she would lose count of the things that didn't make sense.

When Harvey was a little older, the mall got bigger and other jewelry stores opened up. Harvey's father tried to drum up business with coupons in the *Penny Saver,* radio ads, and a man outside the mall in a Statue of Liberty costume. The man was supposed to dance and get everyone excited, but whenever Harvey and her father drove by, he was sitting on the curb.

When Harvey was four years old, her mother had to start working.

Harvey was sent to day care and wept uncontrollably when her mother came for her in the evening.

"We've never seen her cry like this," the caregivers used to say.

Harvey's mother made a face. "Don't you love your mommy?"

But that wasn't it. She hadn't been able to cry all day because the people there didn't love her and she was afraid of them.

Her father said the food they served was trash.

At home, Harvey's mother made pasta sauce with canned tomatoes, garlic, and onion. She said sugar was the secret ingredient. She also made fresh mashed potatoes. Harvey poured in cream, then watched it gloop in the mixer. On television, she saw a commercial with a girl doing the same thing. Years later, Harvey wondered if it was only that she was remembering, because all life is pieced together from memory where nothing is certain, even feeling.

In late January, icicles formed outside Harvey's window, dripping into a shallow pool. In winter, nothing grew under the hard leaves that clawed the flowerbeds.

Harvey remembers taking off her mittens to palm the frozen earth. Her hands then were small and fleshy. Garden tools left out were drained of color by winter; the cold handles of a wheelbarrow she used to ride in barefoot, when it was hot and the air rang with green grass.

Sometimes she helped her mother plant bulbs. Eyes that would open in the earth once a year. She had on a cable-knit sweater that came up to her chin. Her mother would press on her hands—press them into the soil and laugh. "Let's grow a Harvey tree!"

Sometimes worms nosed through the grass, strings of flesh that had neither eyes nor mouths but lived and moved through light and darkness, recognizing neither one. If a worm got chopped in half, her mother said, it would have to grow another piece to keep on living.

THERE IS A book of photos somewhere, of Harvey when she was five or six. In one picture she is standing in the driveway with a backpack, her hair pulled back in a ponytail. On another page, she poses on the front step in a red sweater and gray wool skirt. She was told to smile because in pictures it's how you're supposed to feel that counts.

The night before Harvey's first day of big-girl school, her mother cut her hair in the kitchen. She first wet it under the faucet, then spread a towel on her shoulders.

Harvey's father got upset watching his wife sweep the fallen pieces.

"It's only first grade," she told him.

"I know," he said. "I can't believe it."

II

ONE CHRISTMAS HARVEY'S father gave her mother a diamond necklace. Harvey got Barbie's Dreamhouse.

Sometime around then, she built a snowman in the yard. Her grandparents were visiting from Florida and said they didn't miss the cold. It was the last time Harvey would see them alive. They all wore heavy coats and drank hot chocolate from Christmas mugs. Harvey couldn't hold the cup with her mittens, so it fell in the snow. Harvey laughed, because what could snow do? But when she looked, the mug was cracked. At first her mother was annoyed, and Harvey was afraid she had ruined Christmas.

When she stopped crying, her father strung flashing lights along the side of the house. Harvey looked at them and imagined Santa trying to land his sleigh.

A few days before her grandparents arrived, they got the house ready. They had bought the Christmas tree at Home Depot and tied it to the top of the car. It was almost too big to go through the front door of the house. Harvey thought it was funny and wanted to draw a picture.

As they were unpacking ornaments for the tree, Harvey saw a photo album at the bottom of a box. She took it out with both hands and peeled back the cover. Some of the photos were yellow, and it was hard to see who anyone was. Some pages were stuck together and wouldn't open at all. When her father saw the book on his daughter's lap, he shouted to his wife: "Come and see what Harvey's found!"

Harvey said her father's face was the same now as in third grade. His wife regarded the likeness. "That's right." She laughed. "It is the same."

Harvey's mother said she had never seen these pictures. Harvey's father remembered the name of the street he'd grown up on, *Sycamore Avenue*; the sort of car they'd had, *Buick Regal*; and even the name of a dog they'd found wandering along Queens Boulevard, *Birdie*.

"It was a young Lab," said her father. "And it came right up to us and started licking my brother's hand."

"You have a brother?" Harvey said.

Her mother reached over and closed the album. Her bottom lip was shaking. Then she stood suddenly and looked around. "Let's get this house decorated for Christmas!"

Harvey turned to her father. "What's his name? What's your brother's name?"

"Jason."

"No, Steve!" Harvey's mother snapped. Then she went into the bedroom. The sound of the door slamming made Harvey jump.

Harvey's father just sat there fingering a branch of the Christmas tree, as though it were the most precious thing ever.

LATER ON, WHEN Harvey's father was doing things on the roof, Harvey asked her mother if Jason would be alone for Christmas. She rubbed her hands on a paper towel and knelt down so their eyes were level. "Jason is not a part of our family anymore," she answered softly.

Harvey looked at the paper towel in her mother's hands. It had softened and she wanted to grab it.

"He's not a nice man," her mother said. "Very angry."

Harvey asked if he would hurt a child.

"I don't know," her mother said. "I hope not. But I guess he could do anything."

Harvey said she couldn't imagine it.

"Some people are born with bad in them," her mother explained.

"What bad things did he do?"

"Well, he almost killed someone," she said. "Thankfully, the police got there to break it up."

Harvey pictured Frosty in the Christmas movie, getting killed by the thermometer because it turned red and made flowers pop up. Not even his best friend had been able to stop Frosty from melting.

"He'd still be in jail," her mother went on, "if the police hadn't come in time."

A bird drew Harvey's eye to the window. A garden stripped of leaves by winter revealed a pink egg left over from Easter.

"Can I finger paint?" Harvey said.

Her mother busied herself at the sink. "Your father's family wasn't very happy," she said, wringing out a cloth. "It's a wonder your dad turned out so well."

Harvey hoped her mother wouldn't say any more, and asked if she could go outside.

"It's too cold," her mother said.

"Can I finger paint then?"

"I'm trying to tell you something serious—so stop thinking about finger painting for a second, okay?"

Harvey made a face like she was going to cry.

"Let's just feel lucky that Daddy is not like his older brother or his father."

Harvey shrugged. "Okay."

"Can you believe, Harvey, that one night Steve's father tried to set their house on fire—can you believe it? While his own wife and sons were sleeping."

Harvey felt the lick of flames.

"That's what alcohol can do to a person, Harvey."

"If our house was on fire, would my dolls get burned?"

Her mother stopped what she was doing.

"Would my dolls be on the news, Mommy?" Harvey said, straining to lose herself in the feeling that Duncan was lost forever.

"Really, Harvey? I'm trying to be honest with you. You want me to be honest with you, right?"

Harvey nodded.

"Well, this is serious," she said. "Nobody's house is getting burned down. But your father and his brother had a tough time when they were boys. They even spent a few months in and out of foster homes."

"What's foster homes?"

"It's like an orphanage, Harvey."

"What's that?"

"Remember *Annie*? That movie you saw with Grandma and Grandpa when they visited from Florida last time?"

"It was boring."

"No, it wasn't," her mother insisted. "You enjoyed it. It's a movie for children."

. . .

When it got dark, they hung the rest of the ornaments and watched Christmas shows. Harvey's mother made a pot roast for dinner, and her father went out to Dairy Barn for apple cider to drink with it.

When Harvey was in bed, voices entered her room.

She sat up and looked through the darkness at her dolls lined up on the dresser. The dolls were listening too, Harvey thought, absorbing everything in their stillness.

"It's our home, Steve!" her mother screamed. "It's our home, and your daughter lives here! *Your* daughter!"

"Don't use Harvey as an excuse."

"Are you kidding me? Are you fucking kidding me?"

Something fell and rolled around on the floor.

"He's a *convicted felon*!" her mother screamed. "Who knows what he might say, or try and do to get what he wants?"

Then her father raised his voice. "Don't start judging! Jason is a part of our family, whether you like it or not."

Her mother was really crying now. Harvey felt bad for her.

"Haven't we done enough for him?" she said.

"He's still family. He's still flesh and blood."

"Please—*please* don't bring him into our lives. Just imagine what could happen."

Harvey pulled the cord on her pink dragon and listened to a song play from its belly.

A week later, at Chuck E. Cheese's, Harvey and her father were shooting ducks with plastic rifles. When a cartoon dog appeared on the screen with their scores, Harvey asked her father what had happened to the dog he found with his brother.

"We only had him a few weeks," he said. "Then he ran off and we never saw him again."

On the car ride home, Harvey asked if his brother lived on Long Island, and if he was mean when they were kids. Her father put the radio on, but Harvey spoke over it. "Why won't you tell me about Jason?"

Her father caught her eyes in the rearview mirror. "I love you," he said. "Do you know that? Do you feel that?"

They found a pizza shop in a strip mall and sat in a booth with fountain drinks, waiting for the pie to cook.

"It could get me in major trouble with your mother that we're even thinking about him."

"I really want to know," Harvey said. "Is he your little brother or your big brother?"

"He's my big brother."

"Did he try and kill someone?"

"Who told you that?"

"Mom."

"Did she also mention that he's disabled?"

"What's that?"

"He has a fake leg, but he thinks I don't know because we haven't spoken in such a long time."

"How long?"

"Almost ten years."

"Mom just said he was always fighting."

"It's true he got into arguments sometimes, but the victims were not innocent."

Harvey didn't get it.

"What I mean is, Harv, he never got into arguments with nice people or people who couldn't fight back."

"Yeah, like kids."

"Exactly. One time he got in a fight with a real bad man. They both got hurt, but the other man was much worse."

"Did the other man die?"

"No," Harvey's father said. "But he was blinded."

III

WHEN JASON FINALLY got on top of the other man, pieces of broken bottle were sticking out of his motorcycle jacket. Blood sprayed from the man's nose with each blow, and it was like hitting a bag of raw meat. Then the door swung open and cops charged in. People were screaming that the man was dead.

Officers swung at Jason with their nightsticks. They cuffed him, but he wouldn't lie still, so they dragged him out into the parking lot. People leaving the strip mall with boxes of leftovers hurried to their cars. Jason lay on his stomach in the rain, his tongue padding dumbly over the gum where a tooth had broken off. Swelling had closed one of his eyes, but the alcohol numbed him to anything but rage.

Then paramedics came and rushed to get the other man on a gurney. His face was a mask of blood. His shirt was ripped open and his shoes had come off.

The bartender tried to tell the police how it started, but the officer taking the statement kept asking if any weapons had been used. The bartender said both men were drunk and had broken bottles. Other police walked around putting things in plastic bags. The bartender kept trying to explain that it wasn't all Jason's fault.

By the time paramedics got the other man in the ambulance, he was in a coma.

The stragglers in the bar had sobered up and were giving their accounts. The cops nodded and wrote everything down.

When a second team of paramedics arrived, they asked the police to uncuff the suspect. Jason remembers the sensation of being lifted up, and the kind face and voice of a woman about his age who held his hand in the ambulance and said her name was Julie.

When the police had gone and things were quiet on the street again, the bartender slid the deadbolt and turned off the neon bottles that flashed in the window.

When he called his girlfriend, she put on some clothes and drove down. She couldn't believe the mess. "Oh my God, Sam, what the hell," she said.

The bartender threw sawdust on the floor, then swept up and put the splintered furniture in a plastic bin. His girlfriend sat on a barstool and watched him fill a bucket with hot water and disinfectant.

"You know I'll be called to testify," he said.

"You should keep a gun under the bar."

The bartender shook his head. "I'd sell up before I did that."

As he was locking the register, the bartender noticed Jason's black custom motorcycle in the parking lot. He cursed out loud, then looked for something to prop open the door. When they got out there, the bike was heavy and impossible to move because the front wheel was locked. In the end, the bartender had to use a dolly he kept in the basement for shifting furniture around.

NEITHER JASON'S MOTHER nor brother nor any of his friends had enough money to make his bail, even with the quick sale of his motorcycle.

Jason's attorney argued that the terminal cancer of his young client's alcoholic father, a few years before the incident, had certainly played a role in the uncontrollable emotions of an otherwise promising young man.

The trial took place a few days before Jason's nineteenth birthday. The attorney found Jason a shirt with a high collar to cover the tattoo on his neck. His sentence was mitigated by the fact that the other man did not die, and had a prior criminal record that included aggravated assault with a motor vehicle in Queens County, and a felony assault in the state of New Jersey.

The judge took into account the time Jason had served awaiting trial, and imposed a sentence more lenient than the prosecution would have liked on account of the defendant's age, and because the bartender had rallied his customers to write positive letters about Jason to the district attorney.

Harvey's father was sixteen when his older brother went to jail.

He visited once with their mother a week after sentencing. He wasn't prepared for how skeletal Jason looked, or for the heavy bruising.

"Oh Gawd, Jason," their mother had said. "What have you done to yourself?"

That night Steve had a dream he was going to die, and wanted to visit the prison again.

But then a few days later received a letter in the mail:

> Don't come looking for me. No visits, no phone calls, no letters, no cards, no prayers, no nothing. I

blew it. Take over for me at home, live as best you can.

Do all the things I never will.

Your Brother

Steve wrote back several times, but his letters went unanswered.

While Jason was incarcerated, their mother took her own life. She had tried several times over the years, mostly with pills. Steve went to live with Mr. Rosenbaum, his high school math teacher. By the time he was ready to graduate, Jason was out on parole, but no one could find him.

Graduation day was sunny and warm for a late-spring day. Chairs had been set up on the soccer field to make sure all the parents and grandparents and friends and visitors had a place to sit and listen. The night before, the graduating seniors got together at the Pancake House, just off the Sunken Meadow Parkway. School was over and their real lives were about to begin.

When Steve's name was called over the loudspeaker the next day, he stepped up to the podium and shook hands with the principal.

Mr. and Mrs. Rosenbaum stood to applaud. Some of the other teachers stood too. As he was leaving the stage, Steve scanned the crowd one last time, but it was all strangers, people he didn't know, on an afternoon of general happiness.

HARVEY ASKED HER father if he remembered any happy times when they were young. He told her about riding the Queens Q111 bus in summer for three hours to swim at Jones Beach, and sneaking out at night to the twenty-four-hour diner—and how, when they were walking to school along Kissena Boulevard in the melting snow of late winter, Jason would take him into a washroom at the gas station and hold his socks under the dryer, then stuff paper towels in the soggy ends of his shoes.

And, of course, there was the dog they found.

"Birdie," Harvey said.

When the dog ran away, Harvey's father remembered, it was the only time he ever saw his brother cry.

Harvey's father hadn't heard from Jason in about ten years, but five years ago he saw his address on some court records and, on the spur of the moment, signed him up for something called the Diner of the Month Club.

When last he checked, most of the year's gift certificates had been redeemed at diners all over Long Island.

"So he eats," Harvey's father said. "At least we know that."

Then the pizza arrived and the cheese was bubbling and they looked at it.

Twenty Years Later

IV

A FEW DAYS before Harvey's father arrived in Paris, she sent an email, reminding him to get to the airport four hours early in case there were lines. She also advised him that packing liquids in hand baggage would delay him at security.

Sophie had given Harvey two days off from work and told her to come in for only an hour on the third day to look at proof sheets, introduce her father, and show off the projects she was working on.

On the Métro home, Harvey watched a woman rip clumps of bread from her shopping bag. The woman got off at the same station but went in the opposite direction.

Harvey stopped at Murat's grocery to see if her apartment key was ready. Murat's was open all night, and only a short walk from Harvey's apartment on the rue Caulaincourt. On warm afternoons, elderly men and women stopped there to chat. At night, it was bright inside the shop, and there were fruits and vegetables stacked in cardboard boxes. Murat sold everything from cakes to cleaning supplies, and there were tubs of sweets, windup toys, and pocket flashlights on the counter, with prices written out on orange paper that Murat had cut into stars.

The concierge to Harvey's building, Monsieur Fabrice, had warned her when she moved in not to lose the key to the front door, as the lock was an obsolete make and no locksmith in Paris could copy it. But it was important to Harvey that her father have his own key when he came to stay, so she had sought Murat's advice.

"It will have to be cut entirely by hand," he had said, holding it up to his eyes. "But there is someone I know who can do it."

He told Harvey to leave it with him one morning, and he'd try to have it ready by the time she came home.

As promised, Murat had the original and the copy waiting for Harvey when she stopped in. "It looks different," he said as she held them both up. "Because only that round barrel part is necessary. The rest is for show. Very French, huh?"

Harvey paid Murat for the key and bought gnocchi, basil, olive oil, cake mix, cookies, and three bottles of alcohol-free beer. She had bought much the same only a week before. Her cupboards were full, and the refrigerator smelled like oranges and cheese.

Harvey told Murat that her father was coming in a few days and she needed to stock up. Everything in the apartment was cleaner than it had ever been, she told him, and Murat said he now understood why Harvey had bought Old Spice shower gel. Then he held up a bottle of the alcohol-free beer from her bag of things.

"I thought maybe you had a nice Muslim boyfriend—but am pleased to hear it's your father. A girl only gets one father in this world."

V

HARVEY COULD NOT speak French when she arrived in Paris two years before, so her company paid for lessons. Her tutor's name was Leon. He was from South America and taught French, Spanish, and Italian from his apartment in the République section of the city, where he lived with his six-year-old daughter, Isobel.

Isobel's mother lived in Chartres, and Leon took his daughter there every weekend on the train from Gare du Nord.

Sometimes Isobel sat with her father and Harvey during the lesson, scrubbing away with a crayon. Sometimes she folded paper and cut bits out to reveal an accordion of faceless bodies.

In the last ten minutes of each lesson, Leon would give Harvey a short passage to translate by herself so he could run a bath for his daughter. Once Harvey asked if they had bubble bath in France, and Leon told her that shampoo was just as good.

"But I want bubble bath!" Isobel said.

HARVEY SPENT THE day before her father's arrival on the sofa with a French paperback novel called *Outre-Atlantique*. The story was about an old man who didn't know where he was born or when. Harvey lay back with a blanket pulled over her body. She closed her eyes for long periods. The writing was dense, and the rhythm of words, like a current, dragged her out to sleep.

Everything was ready for his visit, including the gift she'd been preparing for Father's Day. It was a box of objects from childhood, and each one stood for some vital moment of their lives.

The most important piece was an envelope containing official documents. She would show these to her father on the last day, and free him from the secret he had been keeping for almost twenty years.

Harvey had discovered the secret by accident. Some minor issue with her French work visa had required her to contact the office of births, marriages, and deaths back home on Long Island. If the Nassau County Clerk had sent the documents directly to her French lawyer, as requested, Harvey still wouldn't know.

She suspected that her father had kept the truth hidden to protect her. There was no other explanation.

IN THE AFTERNOON, Harvey watched a black-and-white film that crackled and made the walls flicker. Women in the film went to bed with makeup on. Men wore dressing gowns with their initials under the pocket and smoked over breakfast.

It was gray outside, and keeping the lights on made Harvey feel safe. Around six, she drew an early bath, then put on her pajamas and pushed a piece of salmon around the frying pan.

Closing the curtains before bed, she could tell it was raining by the sound of traffic five stories below her balcony. It was a busy street—a steady climb through Montmartre that was dangerous in winter when snow dusted the roads, and people huddled in the windows of the bakery, watching for the dazzle of a bus.

Some weekends Harvey invited people over or stayed out at cafés drinking wine. When her friends left to catch the last Métro sometime before midnight, Harvey liked to linger at the table and watch people out late in the darkness. Some strolled with a dog, or walked quickly with bags of food from Murat's, or picked through an early Sunday newspaper, stopping to discard sections of little interest.

Harvey had made some good friends since moving to France. Most of them worked with her in the art department of a media company, which took up three floors of a building that used to be a school. There was a cobblestone courtyard where the executives parked cars or scooters—and where people could go out to smoke or make private calls. Harvey was the only American in the department, and from mid-July to mid-August she spent most of her weekends at colleagues' family houses in the country, returning to Paris with packages of honey or local wine or tiny strawberries that grew wild and didn't last more than a few days.

She often went in on Saturday morning when the office was empty, then spent the afternoon window-shopping along the rue Saint-Honoré, once the main route for prison carts taking people to the guillotines on Place de la Concorde. Harvey would picture the grim, dirt-streaked faces. The pull of the wagon. The echo of horseshoes on cobblestones. People on the street listening to the cries of those who called out for help or mercy or prayers.

There was a café Harvey liked with seats near the window,

and she often went there. The café was expensive, sandwiched between Lanvin and Hermès, but one of the few places to eat near her office. Harvey sometimes looked out past the tourists choosing cakes from a glass cabinet, and with each bite of her meal imagined the dry mouths of people who were long gone from this world, but whose innocence had somehow persevered. They were remembered now, Harvey thought, not for what they had done but for what had been done to them.

She would tell her father about it when he arrived. Watch the expression on his face as she explained it.

Being so far away made Harvey feel their closeness. The physical separation was harder for him because he knew she would never live at home again. But in the two years since Harvey's departure, he had never once complained about her leaving, nor emailed asking her to come back. She used to think he was too proud, but had come to realize that it wasn't pride at all.

So much of her own life had resurfaced on those evenings spent hunched over a language textbook, studying French at Leon's apartment, watching him sharpen Isobel's crayons with a kitchen knife, or clean out her school bag, or wash some favorite item of clothing in the sink so it might dry in time for school the next day.

Like her own father, Leon was always tired and on the verge of some small crisis that could not have been anticipated but which Isobel thought was exciting.

The toilet is leaking. Isobel: *Do you want me to build a boat in my room in case there's a flood?*

The carbon monoxide detector won't stop beeping. Isobel: *If you die in your sleep tonight, do I still have to go to school?*

The elevator randomly stops between floors. Isobel: *Shall we leave cakes and yogurt in there for anyone who gets stuck?*

One evening Leon fell asleep in the middle of Harvey's lesson, so she tiptoed Isobel into the next room and ordered pizza with her cell phone. While they were waiting, Harvey helped Isobel draw a cartoon cat on her iPad. When Leon woke up, he was angry with himself, but Harvey said Isobel was fed, in her pajamas, and had been teaching her French expressions.

Later that night, Harvey took out a photograph of her own father from years ago. She touched his face. Could tell he was happy, despite a reluctance to smile.

After brushing her teeth and getting into bed, Harvey opened her laptop and composed an email to her father, saying she had a free round-trip airline ticket that had to be redeemed soon. She suggested that he look online for times. Perhaps try to make it for Father's Day in a few months?

HE KEPT A photo of Harvey on his bedside table.

She was on her bike at the baseball field. Moments before the picture was taken, Harvey had ridden without training wheels for the first time. She was hot and out of breath. Everything looked dusty. He'd been trying to keep up and was out of breath too.

That bicycle still hung in the garage at home. It had stickers on the seat and a silver bell that Harvey used to ring with her thumb. Sometimes her father would set it upside down, let her spray oil on the chain. He used to carry her bike to the car with one arm. She marveled at that.

Harvey imagined him back at home, watching television in bed to fall asleep, or drinking coffee in his socks under bright kitchen lights. She sensed the emptiness she had left behind, a future animated by past—and how the best years of her father's life had only been the beginning of hers.

VI

THE NIGHT BEFORE her father's arrival, Harvey had a bad dream. Everything she cared about in life was gone.

In the shower Harvey pieced together what she could remember of the dream: She had somehow slept through her alarm, then arrived at the Charles de Gaulle Airport hours late to find it completely abandoned. Taped to the walls in baggage claim (the way she taped things above her desk at work) were photos of her as a child with her father. They were doing things she had forgotten about. But in the dream it was all happening for the first time.

Then, at the empty airport, Harvey remembered that the airplane her father was on had crashed into the sea, or had never taken off, or never existed—and when she looked outside, realized the airport had been closed for years. A runway cracked and overgrown with weeds. Birds circling the control tower.

In the dream she had lived always *there*. Had never been born in the same way she would never die—and the details of her life conjured from emptiness and longing—her father's death as much a fantasy as his life.

Then she was in the hospital.

A child is being born.

First a head. Then a glistening shoulder. A film of blood across the body. A clear, sticky liquid over the mouth wiped hurriedly by a nurse.

Inhalation, then screaming.

The baby is weighed. Her limbs flap because she doesn't know what they're for. She is alive but sees nothing and will remember nothing. This is a world we call *the* world.

BY THE TIME Harvey was out of the shower, the remaining fragments of her dream had come apart like tissue in water. She stood in its wake at the kitchen window, taking mouthfuls of cereal.

Across the courtyard, figures moved between parted curtains. The white corner of a nightgown. The gleam of a pan. A single hand turning, then steam from a tap.

If Harvey wanted coffee before six A.M., she had to hold a blanket over the espresso machine to muffle what sounded like a heavy truck passing through her kitchen. She had learned early on that otherwise affable Parisian neighbors were intolerant of any noise not made by the human voice.

She drank her coffee standing up. Then she rinsed the cup out.

The closet in Harvey's bedroom had a sliding door with a mirror. She dressed carefully, then looked at herself. She had a pair of new ballet flats that some friends had helped her pick out at Galeries Lafayette. She took them from the black shoebox and removed tissue stuffed in the toes.

The taxi stand near her apartment on the rue Caulaincourt had only one car waiting. The bald driver was reading a newspaper over the steering wheel. He opened the window and asked where she was going.

Taped to the dashboard was a tiny calendar with certain days circled. Also, the photograph of a boy. It was early for a

Sunday, and Harvey asked the driver if his son would still be in bed. The driver replied that he'd most likely be up playing video games. His wife worked in a factory making in-flight meals but had weekends off. Sunday-morning traffic was always easy, he said, except in August, when everyone was going on holiday. Then he drove with one hand on the wheel and didn't speak until they were almost at the airport.

The photograph of the boy made Harvey think of Isobel, sitting at the table with her crayon, listening to her father's instruction, as people learned to read and write.

Harvey enjoyed the moments of their family life that coincided with her weekly lesson. Last month a doll shoe had been lost and was not between the cushions of the sofa nor in the transparent case of the handheld vacuum. Harvey heard Leon tell his daughter to wait until the lesson was finished before turning the apartment over. Another time Isobel's bedroom was so untidy that her father just stood there shaking his head. "It's like we've been robbed," he said, "except they brought toys."

Weeks earlier, Leon had found mouse droppings in a kitchen cupboard. Isobel spent the afternoon looking for the mouse hole, which she told Harvey would probably be a small, arched opening somewhere in the wall. A week later, their lesson was interrupted by screams of horror when Isobel discovered a box of mousetraps in the weekly groceries.

The echoes of play, and the rituals of their domestic life, made Harvey remember things about her own childhood on Long Island.

It was not difficult now for her to recall when her father was the same age as Leon. But somehow *her* father had seemed always older—or never quite so young as he must have been to himself.

As her taxi neared the terminal where her father's airplane would soon land, Harvey closed her eyes and pictured her room growing up. It came with the pale darkness of summer nights, the muffled voices from television, and the occasional rising laugh of her father, sitting alone in the next room.

Then she was able to smell the garage in winter and even brush the damp sides of a box of Christmas things kept under the counter below her father's tools. These sleeping objects, now less than shadow, all conjured unintentionally by association, were not like most memories—these Harvey felt in her body, a longing without pain.

VII

ONCE INSIDE THE airport, Harvey found an empty row of molded seats near the revolving doors and settled into the stillness of someone with nothing to do.

Her father's flight would be edging the polar regions of Canada. He might be asleep, or eating, or leafing through an in-flight magazine.

She looked at her phone and scrolled through the text messages. Then she checked her in-box, though the studio where she worked was never open on Sunday.

When an orange bus pulled up outside, revolving doors sifted people into the terminal two or three at a time. Some were in a hurry, and frantically scanned their passports at self-check-in kiosks.

Occasionally a tour group came through like a slow-moving school of fish. Someone at the front held up a paddle for the others to follow. Most of the tourists were Asian, and some were beginning the journey of old age.

When the cafés in Terminal 2F began serving lunch, Harvey bought a magazine and something to eat. When she returned to her seat, the row had been taken over by a Senegalese family repacking their cases. Harvey went outside and watched people smoke last cigarettes. Then she strolled over to Terminal 2E and found somewhere to sit near the lost-baggage kiosk. The woman on duty wore an old-fashioned hat with an Air France badge on the side. Harvey could see a little behind her desk. The woman had taken off her shoes and was talking on the phone. When other airport staff appeared at her counter, she kissed them on both cheeks but kept one hand cupped over the receiver.

By the time Harvey had finished her baguette sandwich, Terminal 2E had filled up. There was now a line outside the ladies' toilets, and an English woman complaining loudly about having to pay a euro to go in.

A boisterous queue had formed at the lost-baggage kiosk, and the woman in the Air France hat who had taken off her shoes was now handing out forms and pens.

Then the fragrance of a girl with only a handbag on her shoulder. She must be here to meet someone too, Harvey thought—and wished she had remembered to put on a little perfume herself. She pictured the bottle at home on her dresser, admiring itself in the mirror. Next to the perfume were hairpins in a saucer. There was also a photograph of Harvey with her father. They were in front of the house. It was sunny. Her father crouched so their heads were even. You could see the yellow siding and the house number in black script. Harvey couldn't recall who'd taken the photo. Maybe a neighbor, or Wanda from Social Services.

Harvey had not seen her father in almost two years. They wrote to each other a few times a week. His emails were short, but she could hear his voice speaking the words to her.

Harvey pictured her one-bedroom apartment back in Montmartre and tried to imagine how her father would react to it. As the date of his arrival had neared, she'd found herself adding little touches to the decor—moving vases of flowers around, trying to figure out where each one looked best.

She would wake at unfamiliar hours. Sometimes just lying there, rolling back over her life. Other times she got up and cleaned the sink or organized bottles in the bathroom cabinet. Cleared out a drawer. Threw away old magazines. Wiped a layer of dust from the top of the refrigerator, then stood looking at the drawings Isobel had given her.

Sometimes she lay awake until dawn, then stood at the kitchen window with something to eat, staring into her neighbors' apartments across the courtyard. In summer, with the windows open, Harvey listened to their arguments and tried to figure out whose side she was on. If only one voice was raised, she knew it was a phone conversation.

Sometimes, at night, she could hear people having sex, and sometimes an old woman on the first floor woke up screaming. Monsieur Fabrice said that when she was a girl during the war, her parents and older sister had been taken.

On New Year's Eve and Bastille Day, Harvey could always hear the thumping bass of different parties, which Monsieur Fabrice would have stopped if he hadn't already removed his hearing aids for the night (intentionally, Harvey suspected).

And each day, Sacré-Coeur's ancient bells tumbled down through the streets of Montmartre. Harvey did not hear the sound so much as feel it, the way a child in the womb must feel the tolling of its mother's heart, long before the coming separation.

VIII

AFTER GRADUATING FROM a four-year art school, Harvey had taken a job at Dairy Barn, a drive-through convenience store on Long Island near where she grew up. People pulled up to her window and told her what they wanted (usually cigarettes or coffee or beer or milk or diapers or toilet paper). She finished around eight o'clock in the evening, then went home to draw or watch movies in her bedroom until falling asleep. Sometimes her dad took her out for Mexican food or to Jones Beach for a walk along the sand.

In the months after Harvey's college graduation, one of her friends from high school got married at the Excelsior on Jericho Turnpike. People read stories onstage about the bride and groom from pieces of paper with their hands shaking.

Friends of the groom told Harvey she could get a job at the new outlet mall in Babylon. Other friends from college insisted she return to the city and look for a share in Bushwick or Greenpoint. She could work as a waitress, they said, at one of the new coffee shops on Graham or Manhattan Avenue.

Harvey listened politely but was confident in her abilities as an animator. Her final thesis—a full-length comic about an outlaw motorcycle gang whose members all had disabilities like Asperger's or obsessive-compulsive disorder—had won the Alumni Prize and gotten printed in the school magazine.

Most of her wages from Dairy Barn she used to print her portfolio and send out by courier to prospective employers.

ABOUT A YEAR after Harvey graduated, someone called from Europe—an art director for a creative media firm. During an interview through Skype, Sophie said she was crazy about Harvey's outlaw bike gang comic strip. The firm had several clients who wanted edgy comic strips on their packaging—including one of France's biggest yogurt manufacturers, who planned on targeting adolescent boys. Two weeks later, Harvey was working full-time as an assistant animator at the firm's headquarters in Paris.

Sophie had been there to meet Harvey at the airport, and found her easy to get along with. Sometimes Harvey invited Sophie back to her small apartment in Montmartre, where they took off their shoes, put their feet on the couch, and drank wine. They laughed and gossiped about work, the men who were interested in them, and the ones they thought were gay. Harvey warmed up little bites in the microwave, or cut cheese and saucisson sec.

IN THE DAYS before she left Long Island for a new life in Paris, Harvey cooked things that could be frozen and reheated. She also hid notes around the house that would make her father laugh or remember things they had done together.

Driving to JFK, the traffic was slow because of an accident. When they saw planes circling overhead, her father said they were close.

At the line for security, Harvey turned and went back. "I can't go," she said. "I can't do this."

Simon Van Booy

Her father held her and said nothing.

Then she picked up her bag and rejoined the line. He watched her inch along, then hung around the terminal until the screen said her flight had taken off.

When someone at the United desk confirmed that her plane was in the air, Harvey's father bought a cup of coffee from Dunkin' Donuts and sat watching the bags and cases move along the belts. Then he followed signs for the AirTrain.

After looping the terminals once, he got off and looked for the section where he had parked only hours before. He retraced the route he had walked with his daughter. Remembered the weight of her suitcase. Then he sat in the car outside airport parking.

He could imagine Harvey on the plane listening to her iPod or making conversation with the person next to her.

He remembered what she was wearing when they said goodbye. How he'd wiped the tears from her cheek with his hand.

He felt that something had come to an end, yet everything around him was going on as normal.

He stopped for gas near the Belt Parkway and wondered if he should have tried to enjoy things more—marveling at the finality of moments he now recognized as happiness.

Then he drove to Jones Beach and walked up and down, as if trying to find what was already his.

IX

SOPHIE MET HARVEY at the airport, and they rode in a taxi to a hotel on the rue de Rivoli. Harvey's room looked out on a Ferris wheel.

But Harvey soon found a place she liked in Montmartre. The apartment complex had a birdcage elevator with a sliding grate door. The elevator moved slowly between floors and would not come at all if the grate had not been properly closed by the previous occupant. There was red paisley carpet on the stairs, and hall lights clicked on when they sensed motion. Most residents were long past retirement and had lived in the building since their glory days in the 1970s.

The concierge, Monsieur Fabrice, was a slight, yellow-haired man in his seventies who was once connected to the fashion world of Yves Saint Laurent. He lived now on the first floor with two cats, oversize velvet cushions, and heavy-framed photographs of Richard, his late husband of four decades.

Monsieur Fabrice told Harvey where to put her garbage, not to flush the toilet between midnight and six unless absolutely necessary, and that the hillsides of Montmartre were once covered with windmills.

The day Harvey moved in, she kicked off her shoes at the front door, but then heard her father's voice and carried them dutifully to the closet. The apartment smelled of fresh paint, and it would take time to pick out furniture.

Everyone was nicer to Harvey than she had anticipated, and her new cell phone quickly filled up with numbers. She learned early on not to mistake the French aversion to change for unfriendliness.

Harvey's new workspace soon resembled her desk at home, a mess of colored markers, scraps of paper, comics, magazines, gum wrappers, empty soda cans, and various Apple devices she needed to do her job. It was one of many desks arranged in a square under an ancient skylight. Heavy rain drummed upon the glass in spring and fall—and in winter, interns balanced on ladders, melting snow with hair dryers.

Harvey loved Paris most in springtime, when sudden showers swelled the Seine, turning the water brown, and birds returned to the parks, where people ate lunch under statues dismembered by weather or furred over with moss.

In the occasional handwritten letter from home, her father shared news of his life and goings-on in the neighborhood, and would always mention some detail or moment from childhood—such as the time they went to the mansion at Old Westbury Gardens during a heat wave. Harvey had taught him to do cartwheels on the grand lawn, but the sight of him trying made her scream with laughter.

After, they went to Ben's Kosher Deli at Wheatley Plaza, and had potato pancakes with applesauce, rainbow cookies, and grape juice. Outside the restaurant, lying on the low wall of a small fountain, too hot and too full to do anything, Harvey asked her father for a penny because she wanted to make a wish.

She told him to make one too, and he wished that nothing would change.

"You weren't supposed to tell me," she scolded. "Now it won't come true!"

SHE WOULD PRESENT to him the fountains of Paris; the lush gardens; the Church of the Madeleine and Notre Dame. Maybe they would trek to Versailles and get some pictures together in a rowboat, or sharing cake at Marie Antoinette's house . . .

The last parcel Harvey received from the United States was not from her father but had a return address in Franklin, Wisconsin. The shipping to Paris had cost more than the item itself. Harvey's hands had searched among the balled-up pages of some midwestern regional weekly until she felt the smooth leather sides and rough stitching on the seams.

It wasn't the *actual* baseball from that day, but was still a baseball. The other objects that made up his Father's Day gift were already packed into the shoebox in her closet.

She had stayed awake so many nights rehearsing the moment she would give it to him, and had already picked the restaurant where he would open the box and discover the first piece. They would be sitting outside under lamps on a terrace. He would be staring at the shoebox, wondering what was inside and preparing to be overjoyed, regardless of the contents.

Sometimes, in the shallow waters of sleep, Harvey invented some vague speech or a few sentences to accompany his gift. Other times she just lay in silent thought, floating upon the surface of possibility.

X

As passengers streamed into the arrivals terminal, Harvey raised her sign.

WELCOME TO PARIS DAD!

People read it and smiled.

After making it, Harvey had worried that he might be embarrassed but decided to hold it up anyway. She was going to write JASON on the sign but thought DAD would be better. It would be something for him to look back on, to put in his letters, or to tell coworkers at the supermarket when they asked about his big trip.

Harvey's father was the only passenger actually carrying a suitcase and not wheeling it. She saw him first and was surprised at how his ponytail had thinned and gone gray. He was smaller too, in his frame, and this shocked her.

Her father sometimes used a cane to get around, but pride had packed it in his luggage, so he moved slow enough to hide his limp. When he noticed Harvey at the guardrail with the sign held up, he rushed forward, almost losing his balance.

Harvey led him to one side and they sat down.

"Did you like my sign, Dad?"

He touched it with his hand. "I'll take it back with me, if you don't mind."

"I wasn't sure if you'd be embarrassed."

"It's great," he told her. "Really great. I can't believe I'm here."

"How was your flight?"

"Awesome."

"Was the food okay?"

"Oh, yeah," he said. "I was happy just to get something."

"Did you sleep?"

"Nah," he said, wiping his eyes. "Too excited, I guess."

IN THE TAXI, the Haitian driver spoke English with Harvey's father, who was still nervous and couldn't stop talking. The driver said he had never been to New York, but his children had. He was wearing a light blue shirt and red silk tie.

When they pulled up outside her building, Harvey's father took an envelope of crisp euro notes from his jacket. "I don't know what any of these bills mean," he said to the man, "so I'm gonna have to trust you."

Harvey reached in when the change came back and handed a five-euro note to the driver.

"Merci, mademoiselle."

Harvey asked in French if he could pick them up later, but he told them he was off duty.

In the birdcage elevator, Harvey's father said he couldn't believe she was speaking another language.

"You have to meet Leon, my tutor," she said. "He reminds me of you."

When they got upstairs, Harvey gave her father the tour. He told her how grown up it all seemed. When she asked what he meant, he laughed and said, "It just looks sharp, Harvey, with the flower vases and the flat-screen—like something you'd see on TV."

When she returned from the restroom, Harvey found him standing at the kitchen window.

"You can see into other people's apartments . . ." he said. "And they can probably see into yours, right?"

"If I keep the blinds open and the lights on."

He just looked at her.

"Don't worry, Dad, I'm safe, it's safe here."

She wanted to make him something to eat, and put four croissants in the oven as he walked around the apartment. Harvey listened to the sound of his footsteps on the wooden floor. When there was no sound, she wondered what he was looking at or what he was thinking.

XI

AFTER HARVEY HAD left for Paris, Jason sometimes sat on her bed, or looked in a drawer, or peeked into the wardrobe at clothes she had chosen to leave.

The night she departed, he slept on the couch with the TV on. In the morning he made coffee and drank it standing up in her room. Then he took a pair of her shoes from the closet and dropped them by the front door.

WHEN THE CROISSANTS were ready, they ate them in the living room. Harvey asked about Vincent, her father's best friend. They went fishing twice a week now, he told her, or to the movies, or the diner where Vincent had met his wife, Bethany.

"And how's work, Dad?"

"It's good, but there's a new manager who's doing things a little different with deliveries and smartpads and all that tech stuff. Still, move with the times, right, Harvey? You taught me that." He held up a croissant. "Unbelievable."

"I know," Harvey said, "someone told me it's the water in Paris."

Her father drank his coffee and smoothed the back of his gray ponytail. "Old man now."

"You look good, Dad."

"I'll be fifty this year."

"That's not old anymore."

"Feels old."

"Fifty is the new forty."

"Mary at the store says something like that too. You know Mary, right? You met her? She said there's something her husband uses—like color dye, you know? It comes in a little bottle and you put it on with plastic gloves. She said her sister could do it for me if I wanted. She cuts people's hair out of her home since her divorce."

"Is that what you want, Dad?"

"I kind of like it gray," he said. "Makes me feel like an older Steven Seagal. You ever see his movies?"

"Only with you."

WHEN THEY WERE finished eating, Harvey put her father on the couch and undid his shoelaces. Then she pulled the blanket over him so he could sleep a little.

She cleared the dishes from their meal, then perched on the arm of the couch, looking at her father's old white socks poking through the blanket at the end. When he was asleep, she went into her room and took his Father's Day present from her closet—making sure to keep the envelope of official documents separate from the box.

A part of her wanted to open the envelope and get it over with, clear the air and not let the tension of a confession build up. Twenty years he had kept the truth from her. But now she knew, and had paperwork to prove it.

When it first came to light, she felt betrayed—but was old enough to know that emotions take time to settle. A few weeks later she told Sophie.

Then a little while later, when they were leaving a cinema on Avenue Junot, Sophie said she'd been thinking about it, and that Harvey's father might feel ashamed once he found out Harvey knew.

Harvey said that it must have seemed to him like the right thing to do at the time, and that it was too late for anything to change now. She was grown up; had her own life; and would never live at home again.

WHEN JASON OPENED his eyes, Harvey was on the arm of the couch.

"Hi, Dad," she said, giving him the box.

"What's this, Harv?"

"Happy Father's Day."

"But that's not until next week."

"I was going to give it to you in the restaurant tonight, but I can't wait."

The box fit squarely in his hands.

"Open it," Harvey said.

But when the ribbon was almost off, she began to cry.

"What's wrong, Harvey? What's up?"

"I just hope you like it. I mean, I just hope you're not freaked out."

"Oh, I'll love it. Even if it's from Victoria's Secret—though I can't promise I'll wear it . . ."

"Oh, Dad," she said, and went to blow her nose.

Harvey had completely taped the lid shut, so her father would have to rip the cardboard. She told him to make a hole in the top, then reach in and pick one thing out at a time. "There are a few pieces," she told him. "One for each day of your visit."

Simon Van Booy

When his arm stopped moving, Harvey clapped. "Do you have something?"

"I think so. It's round. I know that much."

"Don't tell me—just pull it out."

When his arm appeared from the box, he was holding a baseball. "Woah! Thanks, Harvey. It's really cool . . ."

"No, silly, don't you remember?"

Jason turned the baseball in his hands. "Remember what?"

"Well," Harvey said. "It's kinda how you became my dad."

XII

A FEW WEEKS after Jason's thirtieth birthday, Social Services wanted to schedule a visit. Jason told them he wasn't interested and hung up. The woman called back the next day and told him what a shock it must be, but that she really needed to come over and chat with him in person.

Jason didn't know what she was talking about, and was afraid they wanted to cut his disability benefit. The third time she called, he told her he was still registered disabled, then read her the number on his parking permit. When the woman tried to speak, he hung up the phone.

Wanda had worked for Social Services on Long Island since 1968 and would not be deterred. When she telephoned a couple of days later, Jason couldn't believe it.

"Why can't you just leave me alone?" he said. "I'm not bothering nobody."

He went on about how much he needed disability to supplement his income. Wanda listened. When Jason stopped talking, she mentioned how she thought they might have met at Wednesday's service—but understood how painful it would have been for him to attend the funeral, seeing as he hadn't spoken to his brother in such a long time.

JASON STAYED AWAKE all night, reading descriptions of the crash on the *Newsday* website.

He found traffic reports from the evening it happened. It said that cars were backed up for miles. Nassau County Police closed the road for an investigation. There were even a few minutes of live "on the scene" television coverage with Jodi Goldberg of FOX 5 News. Jason watched it over and over.

At first light, he got in his car and went to Dairy Barn for coffee and cigarettes. Then he drove out there.

Somewhere between Exits 45 and 46 on the westbound side of the Northern Parkway, Jason pulled off the road and stood in the wet grass. He only had to walk about thirty yards before locating the spot. He knew because the ground was churned with plastic and glass.

The car they were traveling in must have flipped and hit the tree because bark was torn off and there were gashes in the bare wood.

He touched the gashes.

Although Jason had not spoken to his brother in over ten years, he felt this was a different sort of absence—like opening your eyes upon darkness.

He remembered when they were young and walked to school along Kissena Boulevard. Jason used to hold his brother's hand. He considered how memories hold our lives in place but weigh nothing and cannot be seen or touched.

Then he went back to his car and drove along the grass to where the lives of his brother and sister-in-law had come to an end.

He took a black garbage bag from the trunk and stepped over the wet, uneven ground, stooping to collect shards of dashboard plastic, glass from a headlight, an undamaged side mirror, a floor mat, a door handle.

Soon the bag was full.

When he noticed a woman's high-heeled shoe in the grass some distance off, Jason put the bag in the trunk and went home.

WHEN WANDA CAME over the next day, she was holding a bunch of flowers. "It's probably not your thing," she said. "But I couldn't show up empty-handed."

Jason offered her something to drink, but she said she was fine. He could tell she was looking at the tattoo on his neck, trying to figure out what it was.

"Must be a shock," Wanda kept saying. "I'm so sorry."

Then she put on a pair of red-framed glasses and read silently from the folder in her hands. She had the sort of Afro hairstyle that was popular in the 1970s. Jason watched her turn the pages; watched her earrings swing when she moved her head to read or glance up at him.

Wanda informed Jason that his disability benefit payments were up to date, and she could see no reason why they would be stopped. She read the date he'd received his first payment, and told him the first name of the person who had processed the application.

Then Wanda closed the folder and asked about his brother, Steve.

Jason just turned the brass rings on his fingers one at a time.

"Looks like you're trying to crack a safe," Wanda said, pointing with her eyes. "Do those mean anything?"

One of the rings was of a snake eating its own tail. Another was some kind of demon, which the magazine advertisement said was Lucifer's first incarnation. The other rings were just skulls, but one of the skulls wore a top hat, which Jason loved because it reminded him of Slash from Guns N' Roses.

Jason said that his brother was a good guy, but they had no relationship. If Wanda hadn't called, he wouldn't even know.

"His wife also passed in the car with him," Wanda said. "Such a tragic day."

Jason thought of the woman's shoe he had seen lying in the grass. "How long was he married?" he asked.

Wanda put her glasses back on and opened the folder. "Seven years, to Melanie Morgano from Bellmore." She paused. "I was told at the service, Jason, that *your* parents passed some time ago?"

"What's the difference? Who gives a shit now?"

Wanda sighed and looked at the overflowing ashtrays, empty soda cans, take-out containers, random engine parts, and peeling iron dumbbells. One of the front windows had a long crack in the glass, and a blanket and pillow sat in a pile at one end of the couch where she imagined he fell asleep every night in front of the television.

"Did you have a good relationship with them? What was your father like?"

"My father?" Jason said fiercely. "What do you want to know about him for?"

Wanda leaned back in her seat. "What made him a good or bad parent?"

Jason shrugged as though he didn't want to talk. "What makes anyone behave like they do? You're a social worker, Wanda—you tell me."

Wanda said every case was different. "Still," she said,

"from your reaction I'm guessing it wasn't easy for you and Steve."

"My father hated everyone, especially himself."

"It's amazing you're so well adjusted, then."

"Is that a joke?"

"No, I'm being serious," Wanda said. "You invited me in. You asked if I wanted something to drink. You don't strike me as a mean person."

"Well, if you'd met my brother, Steve, you'd understand what a fuckup I turned out to be, compared to him."

Wanda shot him a hard look. "You shouldn't be so quick to judge yourself, Jason."

"Is that what you came here to tell me?"

"It's just my opinion."

Jason looked at the flowers she had brought. Imagined rolling them to bits in his hands.

"Would it be all right if I had that glass of water now?" Wanda said, touching her throat.

But Jason wasn't listening.

"I'll just help myself, then," she said, getting up. "You don't mind, do you?"

XIII

A WEEK EARLIER, Harvey was taken from her classroom to the principal's office. There was Principal Russo in her stiff wooden chair with a woman Harvey had never seen before. They both had white mugs and carried them slowly to their mouths because that's how grown-ups drink. The room was flooded with afternoon sun and smelled like coffee and white paper.

Harvey tried to remember what she had done wrong. Was playing Deadly Spitting Cobras naughty? Had she drawn something bad without knowing?

She was sitting in a red padded chair meant for grown-ups, a giant red mouth that could swallow her at any minute. When she looked up again, Principal Russo and the woman were smiling at her, and Harvey felt the rush of something good about to happen. That was it. She had done something good and was about to get her reward from the principal and this woman.

Then the principal dragged her heavy chair over to where Harvey was sitting. *Wait till I tell Mommy,* Harvey thought. She had never been so close to Principal Russo—could have reached out and actually touched her.

"We have something to tell you, Harvey," she said. "This lady's name is Wanda, and she is going to help me tell you."

Then Wanda just came out and said it.

Harvey imagined her parents in white casts, petrified except for their eyes. Sucking soup through straws. Their legs suspended by pulleys. She would bring them fruit and magazines. She would play with Duncan or with her farmyard on the bed and they would watch.

Principal Russo held Harvey's hand. Harvey saw that she was crying and felt suddenly terrified.

"They were so badly injured from the crash," Wanda continued, "that they died before even getting to the hospital. That's how bad it was, Harvey—I'm so sorry."

Harvey looked at the door to Principal Russo's office, because her real life was on the other side.

The door was blue and had always been blue. It had a square window at the height that only grown-ups could see in and out of.

"But when can I go home?" Harvey wanted to know. "It's pizza night."

"You like pizza, huh?" Wanda said.

Harvey nodded. "It's my favorite food."

"Well, that's great to know, because it's my job to look after you now. Since your mom and dad have gone up to heaven."

"They're with Jesus and the angels," said Principal Russo, swallowing as if there were something bad in her mouth.

"That's right," said Wanda. "They're safe and they're not in any pain—but they can't come back to life. Do you understand that? They cannot come back to life."

Something heavy began to shift in Harvey's body, as though part of her wanted to follow them.

"It's okay to cry," Wanda said. "This is a very tough thing to hear—a very sad day."

"That's right," Principal Russo said, her hand making circles on Harvey's back. "That's right."

FOR THE NEXT week, Harvey lived with one of the teachers from school. Some of the other kids were jealous. Miss Bateman had really long hair and looked *so* different when she shook it down at home. But her toilet didn't flush properly, and the poop just went in circles.

Her house smelled like soap, and there were plants with green leaves that made Harvey want to bite them. Miss Bateman stayed up late talking on the phone, wrapping her hair around her fingers, speaking softly enough to conceal words and giggling.

The best thing happened before bed: Miss Bateman would brush Harvey's hair. Harvey looked forward to having her hair brushed. The brush clawed a bit and pulled her head back—but Harvey didn't care about anything except having Miss Bateman brush her hair at night.

After brushing came a braid. Miss Bateman held a strand of hair. "This is the fence," she said. Then she took two more strands. "And here are two bunnies about to go jumping."

Harvey closed her eyes. "Go bouncing!" she said.

"That's right," said Miss Bateman. "Up and down the bunnies go, up and down, up and down . . ."

Miss Bateman had a cat, but it didn't like to be petted and just watched everything from under a table, licking one paw at a time, and hissing if Harvey got too close.

After a few days, the woman who had been in the office with Principal Russo came to take Harvey to a foster home.

XIV

WHEN WANDA WANTED to come over a third time, Jason figured she was up to no good and told her he was sick and couldn't get out of bed. But she called again the next day and said she really had to see him.

When Jason heard her car outside, he looked out the window. There was someone with her this time, some little kid with a doll.

After they came inside, Jason said he had only water to drink, but Wanda said they were fine. Then they sat on the couch and no one said anything. The little girl kept looking at her doll, kept touching the doll's face.

"This is my helper for the day," Wanda said.

The child pretended not to hear.

"Who is *your* helper, Harvey?" Wanda said, but still she did not look up.

Jason watched the little kid play with her doll, wondering why she was sitting on his couch with the woman from Social Services who wouldn't leave him alone.

"Honey?" Wanda said to the little girl. "Can you go get me nine pieces of toilet tissue from the bathroom?"

"Okay," the girl said, and stood mechanically. "Where's the bathroom?" she whispered to Wanda.

"Ask the man who lives here," Wanda whispered.

Slowly, the girl turned her body but kept her eyes on the floor. "Excuse me, Jason, but where's—"

"End of the hall. Light switch is outside if you can reach it, which you probably can't."

"Remember to count out nine pieces carefully . . ." Wanda reminded her.

When Harvey was out of sight, Wanda picked up the girl's doll and began arranging its limbs.

"How does the kid know my name?" Jason said.

"She knows more than that," Wanda said.

"Yeah, really? Why's that?"

"I was kinda hoping you'd figure that out by yourself."

"Figure what out?"

Wanda put the doll back where she had found it. "Harvey is your late brother's daughter."

Jason's mouth opened and closed.

"And the only family you have left to my knowledge, Jason."

She explained that Harvey's grandparents, the Morganos, were applying to adopt Harvey, and were on Long Island that very day doing the paperwork. They had flown up for the funeral from their gated community in Tampa, where they had lived since retiring. It was strictly sixty-five and older, but the board had agreed to make an exception in light of the tragic circumstances with their daughter and son-in-law. Wanda said they were still in shock.

Then Harvey returned with the pieces of toilet paper.

"I got them like you asked, Wanda."

"Count them out, sweetie."

Jason listened to the sound of the numbers, and remembered, years ago, sitting at home with his little brother watching *Sesame Street*.

The child's hair was pulled back in a braid. Her clothes were new and the dress still had a sticker on the hem that read 5X. She was wearing a green T-shirt stamped with peace signs, and her doll had fake plastic hair and a hole in its mouth for a fake bottle. It also had black eyelashes, and blinked when she moved it. On the girl's wrist were friendship bracelets. On her finger a plastic ring that once had gum inside.

When Jason went outside to smoke, he looked in through the sliding door at the woman from Social Services and at his brother's child. He wondered why all this was happening. For years he had lived alone, slept alone, eaten alone, felt alone. Most of his mail went in the trash unopened. He ignored his neighbors, and they ignored him. But despite this effort to shut himself away, despite his determination to live at a distance from the world he had come to hate, Jason found himself once again in the midst of it—tangled up in lives that had simply been going on without him.

XV

WHEN WANDA HAD come to pick Harvey up from Miss Bateman's apartment, she didn't want to leave.

Miss Bateman suggested they take a trip around the block. Walk off the tears.

When all her clothes were folded into a plastic TJ Maxx shopping bag and they were almost ready, Harvey asked if Miss Bateman would brush her hair one last time.

Wanda drove slowly because of the bad weather.

"Look at this, look at this," Wanda said as it just poured down. The windshield wipers rowed Harvey further and further toward sleep.

"The Goldenbergs are nice," Wanda said. "I think you're gonna like them."

"I like Miss Bateman."

Miss Bateman had told Harvey she would eventually get adopted by a great family who really wanted a daughter. "You are going to be *so* spoiled," she had said.

Harvey wanted to get excited, but it felt wrong, a betrayal of sorts.

Wanda looked in her rearview mirror at the girl in her backseat. Over the years, she had met many children whose lives had broken into pieces that would not fit back together. Many of them had sat in that same booster seat, harnessed by the same seat belt, drawing small scenes from their lives on the window when it fogged.

Wanda watched in the mirror as Harvey's finger traced images in the glass. She thought about the show she'd seen on PBS of our early ancestors drawing stick figures on cave walls or printing their hands on the rock in colored paint.

Some of the children who rode with her to foster care—Wanda knew from experience—would never recover. Some would end up in jail, or on drugs, or on the street, unable to live on their own or hold down a job. To think that only a few years before, they had been normal children, in normal houses, with school bags and bedtimes, fear of the dark, new shoes, presents under the tree at Christmas.

Some children were quickly adopted by relatives or friends. Others by people they had never met. It was especially hard for these children, who were expected to begin new lives while still anchored to old ones that no one wanted to talk about.

Wanda cared not only for children like Harvey, who'd been orphaned by circumstance, but also for those whose parents went to jail, or were addicted to drugs, or were abusive or negligent or a combination of those things. Over thirty years on the job had given her an instinct for who would make a good parent and who wouldn't. It wasn't always what you'd think, she told her husband. You get surprises where you least expect—for all that glitters is not gold.

After her first twenty years with Social Services, Wanda thought she had seen it all, but with each passing year came something new—and always the pinch of bureaucracy, which sometimes prevented her from placing children in the homes that best served their needs.

As retirement neared, she found herself taking more risks, "losing" data that wasn't helpful, or lying to put her own spin on things—the way she'd lied to Jason about Harvey's grandparents filling out adoption paperwork.

She told her husband everything, and he stood behind her. His name was Keith. He was from Baltimore. They had no children of their own.

"You gotta do what you gotta do," he always said. "Trust yourself."

When Harvey's case was assigned to Wanda's office and all the facts came out, no one could agree what to do. The obvious choice would have been the girl's maternal grandparents, but it turned out they had recently passed, down in Tampa, Florida—within a few months of each other.

There was a much older great-aunt who also lived in Florida, but Wanda would need to know more about her; when family members fell out of touch, it was sometimes for good reason.

Wanda had known early on about the deceased's older brother, but felt he was probably a lost cause—the obvious family link broken by a list of violent criminal charges against his name and recent investigations by the IRS into thousands of dollars of undisclosed income—possibly the result of drug deals or resale of stolen goods. Charges for burglary or criminal damage were one thing, violent assault was another.

Wanda had all but crossed Jason off the list when Harvey suddenly mentioned him on the way from Miss Bateman's apartment to the foster home. "Jason? Who's that Harvey?"

"My dad's brother."

"You ever meet him? Your uncle Jason?"

"No."

"How come you never met him?"

"Mom says he's a bad man."

"That so?"

"Tried to kill people, Mom said."

Wanda paused a moment. "Sure you want to meet someone like that?"

"Dad said he never killed people—he just made them blind."

"I see."

"Now he goes to diners and has a fake leg."

"Diners?"

"Yeah—so we know that he eats."

"Was your father in touch with him, Harvey?"

"No, but they had a dog called Birdie, and my dad said that when Birdie left, Jason cried and cried, and he'd never seen his brother cry before the dog just ran away."

"Birdie is a nice name for a dog."

"I'd cry too, if my dog ran away."

"So would I," Wanda said. "And so would my husband, Keith. He's a real animal lover."

They were getting close to the Goldenbergs', but Wanda didn't want the conversation to end, so she pulled to the side of the road and asked Harvey if she had any stories about Jason.

"Mom would be mad if she knew," Harvey said. "But Mom's in heaven, right? I don't think you can get mad in heaven, right, Wanda?"

"You don't have to tell me anything you don't want to," Wanda assured her. "Just tell me what feels right."

Harvey looked out the window, pulling together all the words she would need. "Dad said that Jason protected him at school from the bad children who stole his lunch."

"Uh-huh."

"And when Dad was sick, Jason had to get him better all by himself, but he was just a kid like me."

"How'd he get him better?"

"My dad said he pretended to read the back of cereal boxes, but he couldn't read—he was pretending, making up stories from his 'magination about why my dad was sick. They laughed about that."

"Oh," Wanda said, searching for a thread that might lead somewhere.

"Jason gave my dad his medicine from a special cup with rabbits on it. That was one cup that didn't get broken, because Jason hid it and wouldn't tell his father where it was. He liked to break stuff and put things on fire—their dad did—so it got saved. Jason used to get Dad better by letting him sip special juice made by rabbits in their home, in the dirt where they lived, in a hole. In a rabbit hole. That's where it came from."

"Hmm, I see. How special."

"Rabbits made it and gave it to him in that cup to get my dad better."

"That was nice of those rabbits," Wanda said. "Were they the same ones Miss Bateman used to braid your hair?"

"No," Harvey said. "Those ones are made up."

"And your father told you all this, Harvey?"

"And Jason used to put notes in my dad's lunch box saying he was a special boy."

"That was very kind," Wanda said. "I'm starting to like the sound of this guy."

"He looked after my dad, so he could grow up and look after me, right?"

Wanda started the car and waited for an opening in the traffic.

"Can we go to his house, Wanda?"

"I can't promise that."

"Dad said he only hurt bad people, like heroes on TV do. They only hurt bad people, right, Wanda?"

"That's right," Wanda said. "You got nothing to worry about if you have a good heart, nothing at all."

She would have to get an exception from the courts, convince her coworkers to play along, and of course find a way for the paperwork to slip through the system—legally, but undetected.

Then again, if the judge said a flat no, that was it. Nothing could be done.

The uncle might say no too. Or the uncle might say yes and not be suitable—or just be doing it for the monthly allowance.

"Could we go there now?" Harvey said. "To my uncle's house?"

"It's not our decision, little lady, so I don't want you to worry about it. But Wanda is going to do her best. For right now," she told Harvey, "the only *sure* thing is that you're going to get more love and spoiling than you can imagine."

One thing Wanda had learned in her thirty years on the job: Disappointment later on is better than no hope to begin with.

XVI

WANDA CALLED THE next day and asked what Jason thought of his niece.

"I can't take her," he said, lighting a cigarette.

"I'm not asking you to. I just wanted to know what you thought of her."

"Do I strike you as the fatherly type?"

"It doesn't matter what I think. Harvey's grandparents are doing the adoption paperwork with their lawyer right now, so it's not something you have to worry about."

Jason exhaled and pictured the Morgano grandparents bent over a table, filling in forms at some Social Security office on Hempstead Turnpike. "What are they like?"

"The Morganos?" Wanda said. "I don't personally think they can handle a six-year-old, but that's for the courts to figure out."

"But they're family, at least."

"That's right," Wanda said. "Family gotta stick together at a time like this."

Jason watched the smoke escape from his mouth through a crack in the window. "You trying to make me feel guilty or something?"

"It's the truth," Wanda said. "Whether you feel guilty about it or not."

"None of this is my fault."

"That's right, so you best stay clear of it."

"I've been trying to," Jason snapped. "But you keep fucking calling my house."

Wanda's sudden laughter surprised him.

"Behind the attitude," she said, "and the tattoos, and the record, and the foul language, and that god-awful messy house you live in—there's something about you, Jason."

Jason lit another cigarette and noticed his hands were shaking. "Yeah, what's that?"

"Like how you went outside for a smoke instead of just lighting up in front of the kid."

Jason laughed. "That don't mean nothing."

Wanda laughed too. "We'll see," she said. "Remember, I've been doing this job since you were in diapers."

XVII

WHEN WANDA CALLED three days later, she put Harvey on the phone.

"Hey," Harvey said.

"Hey, kid. Is Wanda right there?"

"Uh-huh."

"Did Wanda tell you to talk to me, or was it your idea?"

"Wanda."

"Well, I hear you're getting adopted, so it looks like you'll be okay."

There was silence on the other end of the line, then Wanda's voice came on. "You have time to talk? Harvey's just about to leave the office with her foster family, and I wondered if we could chat for ten minutes."

"A foster family?"

"Just until we get her paperwork sorted out."

"Why can't she stay permanently with the foster family here, on Long Island?"

"That's just not how it works, Jason—you of all people know that."

WHEN WANDA WAS alone in the office, she called Jason back and asked him some more about his father.

Jason told her the old man had died when he and his brother were in high school. "He'd been sick for a while,"

Jason said. "Some kind of cancer. Hadn't left his bedroom in months. The television was turned up when it happened, so I didn't hear him calling or nothing. I sat with the body until Mom and Steve came home from Shop Rite."

"So you were there," Wanda said. "That must have been a tough thing to see, Jason. You said you hated your father."

"Our whole lives, he pretty much tortured us one way or another—but it was bad when we were kids, until one Christmas the tables turned, and then he wasn't around much after that."

STUMBLING BACK IN the early hours from the Lucky Clover, Jason's father was unable to find his front door among the hundred or so in the neighborhood.

He fell asleep in someone's driveway, then woke up freezing and walked the few blocks to his own house. His wife was up making coffee because it was Christmas Day. When she asked what happened, he dragged her into the living room and threw her into the Christmas tree. Then he opened a beer and put the TV on.

Jason and his brother ran out and saw their mother with pine needles in her hair, trying to stand the tree up. Jason's father wanted them to laugh about it, but little Steve went up and snatched the bottle of beer from his hand.

"Give that back, you little asshole, it's Christmas Day!"

But Steve just poured it out on the carpet. The beer frothed and splashed on his bare feet.

Their father stood quickly, his face tightening, so Jason grabbed the empty bottle from Steve's hand and swung it at their father's head. He stumbled backwards for a few moments, touching his ear, then rushed Jason and pulled him to the carpet in a chokehold. Christmas ornaments went *pop* as Jason and his father rolled around on them. Then Jason got on top and there was blood on his father's cheek from one of the angel's wings. Mom was screaming and trying to pull Jason off. Eventually, the fight ended and their father got up and ran out of the house.

Jason vacuumed up the glass from the broken ornaments, then watched as Steve rubbed the carpet with paper towels to soak up the beer. Before opening presents, they made toast and poured two glasses of eggnog. It was sweet and so much thicker than normal milk.

Jason got blank TDK cassettes to make his own mix tapes, an Iron Maiden T-shirt, and the expensive hair wax he needed to style his hair like James Dean.

Steve got a set of Hot Wheels, a New York Jets jersey with Joe Namath's name and number, a deck of Playboy playing cards, a package of Topps baseball cards, a Slinky, and an Atari game system, which was the only thing he'd said he really wanted. Jason's mother started crying when she saw it and said she didn't know how Santa could afford electronics.

"C'mon, Mom, I saved up months to get that," Jason said. But from the corner of his eye could see Steve trying not to laugh, which made him feel good about having stolen it.

Later on Jason boiled hot dogs, then watched a Snoopy Christmas movie with his brother. Mom spent the afternoon in her bedroom, calling around different bars.

Wanda thought it was brave of Jason to stick up for his little brother. Jason said it was a much longer story.

"I like long stories," she said, but Jason didn't want to get into it.

"Was it hard for your mother to manage after your father passed away?"

"With no one around to punish her, she punished herself. It's Steve I felt sorry for, because, to be honest, I really didn't love my mother at all. She could have protected us, but chose not to."

"Were you in prison when she died, Jason?"

He could tell that Wanda wanted his version of why he'd gone to jail, but he honestly couldn't be bothered to tell her. No one had cared to listen then, and it was too late now. He had served his time—which really means putting up with what happens to you when you're inside.

Then Wanda asked him to hold on a minute while she found her cigarettes.

"Finally, the office is empty," she said. "I smoke one Newport a day, always the same time—have done for years. Be nice to have a drink with it. You still like a drink, Jason?"

XVIII

ABOUT FIVE YEARS after his release from prison, Jason started taking the Long Island Rail Road into Manhattan.

At first he was hopeful and thought he might find a job, even move into the city if things went well. But since his motorcycle accident twelve months earlier, following the breakup of a serious relationship with a woman called Rita Vega, Jason had been drinking just to get through the day.

Most Saturday nights he spent on the Lower East Side, stopping for a beer or some tequila at places he thought might give him a job. A few people told him to come back with a résumé. Another guy—an ex-marine called Rocky—said he needed someone to tend bar until four, but then lost interest when he found out Jason had a record.

One night Jason was almost hit by a yellow cab while walking across Delancey Street. He jumped back and fell down—still unsteady after four months on his prosthetic leg. Three girls in short skirts and platform heels reeled with laughter. "Oh my God, did you see that guy? Oh my God! We almost saw someone get smushed! Oh my God!"

At a liquor store on Orchard Street, Jason bought a half-bottle of whiskey, then carried it in a brown paper bag back to Ludlow Street, where there was more to look at.

An oversize fire hydrant outside a hair salon that was usually occupied by someone in grimy clothes with a cardboard sign was unoccupied when Jason passed, and so he sat down.

After a while two girls stopped in front of him to look for something in their pocketbooks. Jason raised his half-bottle of whiskey and asked if they were thirsty. The girls laughed, but then Jason noticed two men behind them, pulling fiercely on cigarettes.

One of them turned to Jason. "Think you're a fucking hero with that little tattoo on your neck?" The other one just nodded. They were both wearing black T-shirts, jeans, and polished dress shoes.

"Fucking maggot," the first man said. "You wanna fuck with me?"

One of the girls got in front of the man and pushed him back. "Why do you have to be such an asshole all the time?"

The other girl was putting away her lipstick. "Let's go," she said. "This is boring."

The other man wanted to go too. "C'mon, Michael," he said. "Forget about this asshole."

But the first man just kept staring. "You fuckin' deaf?"

Jason noticed an empty can on the sidewalk and lowered his gaze, wondering whose lips had once been on it.

By now a few people had stopped to see what was happening.

"You deaf, ya little prick?" the man went on. Then he pointed to the can on the sidewalk and stepped closer. "That your can, you fuckin' litterbug? You gonna pick it up, or am I gonna make you?"

Jason leaned over and reached for it, then in one motion exploded upward, driving the metal can into the man's face, shredding the lower part of his lip.

The man's friend was tall, so Jason had to go in low at the knees to get him on the ground, where he fought like mad—but then cried out as Jason's brass rings separated his nose.

As usual, there was blood and people screaming.

Then the first man had him from behind. Jason lowered his center of gravity and drove back as hard as he could, but with only one good leg to balance, he couldn't get enough force to send his opponent through the glass storefront of the hair salon. Even with repeated thrusts, the glass wouldn't break, so Jason turned and head-butted him over and over until the man went loose in his arms and dropped to the street, blood gushing from his nose and mouth. From a distance people were shouting at Jason to stop.

Jason grabbed his motorcycle jacket and took off. By the time he reached the end of the block, he could hear police sirens. He knew what would happen if they caught him, but felt little remorse.

"If there's one thing I can't stand," he told Wanda on the phone, "it's a bully."

FOR THE NEXT few hours Jason dragged his body through the streets of Manhattan, sobering up and realizing that his own nose was broken. One of his teeth was also loose, and his lip had pieces hanging off where the tooth had sliced into it.

Any brawler, he explained to Wanda, knows the feeling of finding an injury later on that you don't remember getting at the time.

Jason found a gash in his shin that had bled so badly, the lower leg of his jeans was completely stuck to his body.

About four o'clock in the morning, Jason decided he should

probably hop the next train back to Long Island, but couldn't find his wallet. He sat on the curb, and rifled through his pockets, wondering what would happen if the guard caught him riding without a ticket.

He walked a little more, then collapsed on some Church steps at Madison and Eighty-first Street. When a police cruiser slowed and the cops eyeballed him, Jason got up and started the lugubrious trek across town toward Penn Station. After a few blocks, he saw a sign and realized he'd been limping in the wrong direction.

He tried to focus on the street numbers but was soon distracted by the bright glow of a shopwindow just a few steps away. He shuffled up to the glass and looked inside. Things sparkled and glittered under the lights. It was a bridal boutique, and the window had been decorated in the style of a hotel suite on a honeymoon night.

Jason leaned his forehead against the cool glass. The linens on the bed were pure white, and the pillows stuffed with real feathers. Jason wondered if the woman's robe on the back of a chair was made of silk. He tried to imagine the feel of it between his fingers.

On a white carpet was a pair of high-heeled shoes with red soles. One of them lay on its side. There was a silver champagne bucket with fake ice, and a cork had been set next to a pair of flutes on a side table. Two leather passport holders read HIS and HERS.

On a cabinet were framed photos of the couple throwing leaves at each other in Central Park, unaware of the camera or that they were being watched. Another picture showed them in the cockpit of an airplane wearing headsets and pointing at the instruments.

Jason wondered where the couple was now. A warm bed maybe, ankles touching in the darkness, the soft rush of breath. They would soon wake up and go about their lives. They would look at things in the newspaper and read bits aloud between mouthfuls of toast. They would dress slowly enough to make love, then take a cab uptown to pick out plates and silverware, napkins and candlesticks, for parties where people came to laugh and share their lives. One weekend they might rent a car and drive out to New Jersey or Long Island. That was where they'd be living when their child was born. They would return late from the suburbs with catalogs from brokers and bags of apples or peaches from a farm stand.

With his bruised forehead and bloodied nose against the glass, Jason realized he would never spend a night with a woman who wore silk, nor lay back on a pillow of feathers, nor rest his bare feet on a white carpet, nor possess any photographs of himself lost forever in a single moment of happiness with another person.

There had been someone once. A woman called Rita, with whom he would make love at the beach in summer, and stay up all night smoking cigarettes and going over their lives. But she was gone now.

Then Jason thought of his father. Wondered if there had ever been a time of happiness in his life: a moment when he felt he was safe and that somebody cared for him.

JASON FELL ASLEEP on the train back to Long Island.

The guard thought he looked down on his luck and just clicked his ticket punch in the air.

When he got home, stumbling around the house in blood-stained clothes, heavy with the stink of liquor and urine, he caught a glimpse of himself in the hall mirror and thought again of his father.

Then he took a pillowcase off the bed and cleared out all the beer from his refrigerator. In the freezer were two bottles of vodka, and he put those in the pillowcase too.

After going through the house, then getting a hammer from the garage, Jason dragged the pillowcase of beer cans and liquor bottles into the backyard. Morning had come and the blue air was cool.

Jason's next-door neighbors were having breakfast when they heard glass breaking from over the fence. Enrico looked at his wife, then stood up from the table. His children, Hector and Carla, stopped eating. "I *know* it was him who smashed our mailbox last summer."

Enrico's wife put down her spoon and touched her husband's hand. "Just pray for him, Papi," she said. "Ask God to help him like he helped us."

XIX

THE NEXT TIME Wanda came over, she brought pizza. It was something she knew they both liked and hoped it might get them talking.

Harvey carried it inside and they ate on the couch. When it was finished, Wanda tossed napkins into the empty box and asked Jason if he currently had employment.

"Not enough to be ineligible for disability," he said. "Sorry to disappoint you, Wanda."

"You misunderstand," Wanda said coolly. "I think it's *good* to work—whether you tell us about it or not."

Jason admitted that he supplemented his disability benefit by selling things online.

Wanda was startled by his openness and asked exactly what was so lucrative.

"Doesn't matter," Jason told her. "You can sell anything on eBay. Make a huge profit too—if there's a buyer." He described how he spent three days a week trawling the discount stores, outlets, and thrift stores across Long Island in search of things to sell. He told her that he'd found stuff you couldn't get in other parts of the country or the world: heavy metal concert T-shirts, rare New York City souvenirs, vintage jeans that people in Japan would pay three hundred dollars to own. Some things were collectible, he told her— like Mickey Mouse and Coca-Cola—you just had to keep an eye out. Nothing too heavy, of course, because high shipping charges would slow the bidding.

Jason said he always had ten or fifteen things for sale at one time, but that eBay and PayPal took a cut, which had to be accounted for in the markup.

Wanda ventured to ask if he had anything put aside for a rainy day.

"Follow me," Jason said, getting up and leading them into the garage.

Spread out on a gray blanket were random pieces of metal that Jason said were the beginning of a custom motorcycle he was building from scratch. It was slow going, he told them—the right parts had to come up for sale online when he could afford them.

"This is my rainy day, Wanda," he said. "Once it's built, it'll be worth at least six grand—maybe seven if the paint job is decent."

Taped to the walls were posters of women in bikinis, leaning their bodies over gleaming bikes. The trash hadn't been emptied in weeks, and flies made slow circles in the stale darkness.

"You like motorcycles, kid?" Jason asked Harvey.

She thought about it, then nodded.

"Well, I think they're dangerous," Wanda told them, stepping back into the kitchen. "So the two of you are together on that one."

Harvey asked if Jason would take her for a ride when it was done.

"Oh, sure, kid," he said. "But chances are you'll be in Florida by then."

Wanda wanted to see the rest of the house and asked if Jason had a lady friend. He said he liked things his own way, so it would probably be hard for anyone to put up with that. Wanda laughed and said everyone was like that—but at least he came clean. Then she asked if Jason kept a gun in the house.

When they were back on the couch, Wanda tried to get Harvey in the conversation, but she just picked at the loose threads on her doll's shirt, nodding for yes and shrugging her shoulders for no.

Before leaving, Wanda told Jason to have a think about everything.

"Look," Jason said when Harvey was in the car and looking at them through the back window, "I don't cook, I go out when I feel like it, I got no high school diploma, I live in a shitty house in a shitty neighborhood with neighbors who can hardly speak English—so that's probably not the best for a kid. Plus, I go through a pack of cigarettes a day, and sometimes I don't even have enough to pay for that."

Wanda smiled. "All true. But just have a think. *Look inside.*"

Jason didn't know what she meant, but as she was on the threshold of the door ready to leave, he said he would.

HE TRULY THOUGHT that was the last time he would ever see them, but a few days later, Wanda telephoned.

"To be honest," he told her, "I haven't given anything much thought."

She seemed disappointed and didn't speak for a few moments.

After she hung up, Jason thought about that pizza they'd

eaten during her last visit, and looked in the garbage for the paper menu that was taped to the box. After calling in the order, he took a few hits off a joint, then poured himself a glass of Mountain Dew and quartered a jalapeño pepper. When the pizza came, he peeled a slice from under the cardboard lid and turned on the TV.

The SyFy Channel was showing *Twilight Zone* reruns from the 1960s. One of the episodes was about a plane that landed with no passengers and no pilot. It was a mystery how it got there and where everyone had gone. It made Jason think of Steve and his wife. Where had they gone?

Jason imagined their bodies getting lifted from the mess of snapped plastic and metal; two limp necks. Firefighters tossing handfuls of sawdust from buckets. Artificial lights being erected so the police can measure and take pictures.

ON SUNDAY, WANDA called to say that Harvey was going to Florida for a few days to see how she liked it. Jason told Wanda to wish her luck.

That night Jason couldn't get to sleep. He tried opening a window, but it didn't help, so he got out of bed, looked for his cigarettes, and went into the spare room.

He sat on his old drum stool, smoking. His underwear was frayed and there were scars on his body from things that had happened to him over the years. The white plastic on his prosthetic leg seemed to glow in the darkness, and he remembered the glow-in-the-dark stickers his brother had loved so much.

A single bulb lit the scattered objects. There's just too much junk for this to be another bedroom . . . he thought . . .

and the walls are dirty . . . and the windowsills all rotted out
. . . and the carpet's stained . . .

Mixed in with the items Jason had been unable to sell on
eBay were mementos from life before his motorcycle accident: a drum set, a broken guitar, shoeboxes of receipts, all
his old sneakers and boots, posters from a few gigs he'd had
on Long Island after getting out of prison.

He'd once believed he was destined for fame and money.
The more he drank, the more he felt it was possible. The
irony amused him now. After getting rich and buying a house
in Los Angeles, a Lamborghini, and an exotic pet, he had
planned to show up at Steve's house with presents and a book
of concert tickets. He would rehearse the scenes in his mind
as though they were inevitable. They'd spend Christmases
together. Wear matching sweaters. Go walking after turkey
dinners. It would be like the Guns N' Roses music video
where Axl Rose attends a summer wedding with normal
people—but dressed as a famous rock star with tattoos and a
cigarette stuck in his mouth.

Jason hadn't played drums since falling off the back of
someone's motorcycle on the Meadowbrook Parkway. The
accident happened after a concert at Jones Beach. They were
both drunk and Jason was fuming about his breakup with
Rita.

While Jason was in the hospital, his friend who was driving at the time of the crash moved to Los Angeles to con-
tinue the rock-and-roll dream, but got into heroin. He used
to write Jason from time to time, ask about his leg, boast
about the California sunshine, and brag about the girls he'd
been with. But then he started asking for money. Rents were

getting too high, and his computer had been stolen. Then the letters stopped altogether.

After the accident, Jason tried to keep up his other friendships, find work in the city, go to concerts, walk around the Lower East Side and look at all the pretty girls—but when he stopped drinking, it was difficult to be around friends he had never known sober. And the people in bars filled him with an anger he could no longer swallow.

That first year of sobriety was when Jason most wanted to see his brother again. But the failure of his life felt so close to the failure of their father's life. And every relationship he had ever attempted lay shattered at his feet like pieces of a broken mirror.

JASON REACHED FOR a drumstick and twirled it in his hands. He tried to imagine what Florida was like. He had seen it on TV. Harvey would have a good life in the warmer climate. She could ride her bicycle year-round. He imagined putting skull stickers on her seat, tying leather strings to her handlebars.

Look at that, he imagined himself saying. *It's a HARVEY-Davidson.*

He pictured the retirement community where her new parents lived. He saw them hobbling about in sweat suits, peeling oranges, driving the flat gray Floridian roadways with a perpetually blinking turn signal.

A WEEK LATER, Wanda called.

Harvey was back because there was still court paperwork to finalize.

Jason was boxing up orders when the phone rang. He had

the packing tape and scissors out. He told her a big eBay auction had ended, and he had to get to the post office because people freaked out if they didn't get their stuff in five minutes.

Wanda kept saying what a good time they'd had when she came over with pizza, and that Harvey was *still* talking about his motorcycle project and when she would get a ride . . .

Wanda said she'd like to come over again when it was convenient—maybe for the last time, she said, as it was anybody's guess when the paperwork would be finished and Harvey would be gone for good.

XX

A few hours before they arrived, Jason opened all the windows to clear any stale smoke. He washed dishes and wiped the floor with wet paper towels.

They were on time, and Jason showed them in. Harvey went to her usual seat on the couch, carrying her doll with her. When Wanda had to use the bathroom, Harvey asked if she could put the television on.

Then Wanda said she had to make an important telephone call and check some paperwork out in the car.

When she was gone, Harvey and Jason watched television without speaking. It was a show on the possibility of alien life. During the commercial breaks, Jason went to the window to check that Wanda was still outside.

"It must be a serious case," he said, "if she has to leave us alone like this."

Then a commercial came on with a woman making dinner from a can.

"Hmm, that looks tasty," Harvey said.

Jason went to the kitchen and returned with a bag of chips, which he set on the cushion next to Harvey like an open mouth. "Eat," he said. "You like TV right?"

"*SpongeBob*," Harvey said, reaching into the bag. "That's my favorite."

Jason took a handful of chips and went back to his seat. "Yeah, *SpongeBob* is pretty awesome."

"Yeah," Harvey said, reaching for another chip. "I love *SpongeBob*."

"Patrick is cool," Jason said. "I kinda feel bad for him, 'cause everything keeps going wrong."

"He's funny," Harvey said. "Do you like Mr. Krabs?"

"Yeah, he's just such a jerk it's funny."

"Yeah, he's mean," Harvey said. "Making Krabby Patties from those little men."

By the time the chips were gone, they were into a new show about people in France who were trying to kill a fat king with long hair who lived in a gold palace. When someone's head got cut off and blood gushed from the hole, Jason asked Harvey if she was old enough to watch it. Harvey said she wasn't sure.

Then she propped her doll up so he could watch the show too.

"What's your doll's name?" Jason asked.

"Duncan."

"That's a weird name."

"He told me earlier that he wants to sit with you."

"Why's that?" Jason said.

"He thinks you're his dad."

Jason shook his head. "I'm nobody's dad."

"Then you're going to have to tell him," Harvey said, and put Duncan on the seat next to Jason.

He let her do it, but didn't touch the doll or look at it.

WHEN WANDA CAME back, she said it was time to leave. Jason told Harvey to brush the chips off her dress. Then she put her coat on and stood by the door.

Jason's eyes were still on the television. Wanda had returned at the worst time. They were watching something on the SyFy Channel, and the main character of the story was about to get abducted.

"Don't forget Duncan," Wanda said, pointing. As Jason retrieved it, he noticed something drawn in Magic Marker on the doll's neck in exactly the same place he had his tattoo.

He stood at the door as Wanda backed out of the driveway. Harvey watched him through the car window, then held Duncan up to the glass, waving his plastic arm.

When they had gone, Jason took some pot from the freezer and went back to the movie. Before leaving, Wanda had said that Harvey's grandparents were about ready to pack up and go but were still waiting for a document to be approved by the courts. She told him that by Harvey's tenth birthday, the Morganos would be in their eighties.

Jason thought about it as he filled the glass pipe and then lit up. He had never known his own grandparents. His father had been the youngest of three boys, and the other two had been shredded in the early days of World War II on some beach in the Pacific.

Jason took deep drags. Let smoke roll from his mouth like a gray carpet. He saw the bodies of his uncles in their navy whites, sliding up the beach on the palm of an incoming wave. Then he saw his father—not as he had known him in life but from a photograph his mother kept on the dresser after he died. It was a black-and-white picture, and he was in his uniform, fresh out of training, a young man with sandy hair and freckles—about the age Jason was when he went to jail.

Every morning and every evening, his mother sat before it while doing her makeup.

When his parents first met, Jason's father used to tell her all kinds of stories. Make her laugh with all those wisecracks. She remembered those things. She remembered the way he was then, just before getting sent away. She was certain of when it was, because there was a dance at the school and they were *together* after.

Most of the other boys at the dance that night came home from the war in boxes or were never found. Families cried over coffins filled with yearbooks, baseball gloves, a pair of Converse sneakers worn out with play.

When the surrender came in 1945, people cheered and the streets were flooded and cars were honking. Jason's father had been in a POW camp, and it was some time before he made it back.

On their wedding night, he left the bed and went out to the fire escape, smoking cigarettes and drinking liquor from the bottle, going over in his mind all the things he had seen, all the things he had done, trying to figure it out, trying to untangle himself from it. But war only ends for those who have not been in one.

XXI

OVER THE NEXT two weeks, Wanda and Harvey visited four more times.

Wanda said she was balancing some serious juvenile cases and asked Jason if he minded being alone with Harvey while she ran errands.

Harvey was talking more now, commenting on what they were watching when Jason muted the commercials.

She kept asking to see the garage—wanted to know where each part would fit on the motorcycle and what its job was. When Jason showed her the spare room, Harvey asked to try out his drums. The room was such a mess, he had to carry her to the drum stool. Harvey touched the skins with her fingers, then tapped lightly to see what would happen. Jason found some sticks lying on the floor and told her to go crazy.

He smoked out the window and listened to her bang around. When she got tired and her arms hung down, he told her it hadn't sounded half bad. She'd been trying to work the foot pedal too, so Jason flicked his cigarette into the yard and sat with her. He positioned her fingers properly on the drumsticks, then showed her a few things. Since her legs weren't long enough to reach the pedal, he told her to focus on drumming while he did the footwork.

When Wanda came to pick Harvey up, she heard them through the door and sat down on the front step.

When Harvey was in the car and ready to go, Wanda gave Jason a gray folder she'd brought from the office. She told him that inside it showed the amount of his disability, plus the sum Harvey's grandparents would be getting each month to help pay for Harvey's food, clothes, and outings. Wanda said it was a generous benefit that included health care, and that whoever was appointed Harvey's guardian by the courts would receive it every month to help raise her until she turned eighteen.

Harvey watched from the backseat. She imagined that Jason was telling Wanda how good she was on the drums, and how she might grow up to be onstage someday—because Jason had told her that, had said she was *that* good and might be famous someday.

Harvey went over the whole afternoon with Duncan when she got back to the foster home. She squeezed his doll body, then put her cheek against his cheek, wondering what her mom and dad were doing, and if they could see her, if they could read her thoughts.

XXII

WANDA SUGGESTED AN outing for the next visit, but when the time came, Jason was clueless. He asked Harvey where she wanted to go, and she said the mall in Hicksville.

Jason bought her a pretzel from a stand outside Macy's, and they got Dots space ice cream from a vending machine. Then they sat on a bench and watched women inside the MAC store brush makeup on each other. Harvey asked if she could put makeup on Duncan.

When she needed the restroom, Jason didn't know what to do, so they lingered outside the ladies' room until Harvey was so desperate that Jason had to ask a woman taking her baby in if she would take Harvey too.

While she was in the restroom, Jason wondered what would happen if he took off.

When Harvey came out, she asked Jason what she should call him.

"Whatever you want," he said. "Jason, I guess."

When they left in the late afternoon, the parking lot was full because there was a baseball field behind the mall.

"It's Little League," Harvey said. "I love Little League. Can I go watch?"

Jason watched her run ahead. Her blond ponytail bounced against the back of her shirt. She was far away when Jason lost sight of her in a crowd.

He thought he should probably call out but figured he would spot her watching the game when he got over there. He tried to walk faster, but his leg made it hard.

When he arrived at the field, he couldn't see Harvey anywhere. There was a bunch of kids playing and Jason watched them, figuring Harvey might have found someone she knew and joined in the game. But she wasn't there, either, so he went over to the ball field to check the stands. By now he was moving as quickly as he could, which made it clear he had a prosthetic limb.

Harvey was nowhere to be seen.

Jason shouted at the children, asking if they'd seen a blond girl. Some ignored him. Others stared blankly or looked around for their parents.

The world seemed to be going on as normal, like in a nightmare. Then Jason lost his temper and stumbled out onto the baseball diamond yelling Harvey's name.

"There's a game here, buddy!" someone shouted. "Get off the field!"

"Fuck your game. My kid is missing. My kid has disappeared. Harvey!" he shouted. "Harvey!"

He kept shouting her name over and over. Then, to his surprise, a few of the parents joined in.

The game was stopped. The kid at bat just stood there.

"What does she look like?" a beefy man holding a baby wanted to know. "My wife is a Nassau County cop. I'm going to call her and get an Amber Alert."

Jason described Harvey to anyone who asked, then went back to calling her name and limping about the parking lot and ball fields.

Some people gave up on the game and went home. The Little League coach took a few kids into the mall to look for Harvey and notify security.

When the cops arrived, they said they had Harvey in the backseat. Someone had seen a little girl dodging traffic on Route 107 and called the police.

Jason was crying so hard he could hardly speak.

Harvey watched him from the backseat of the cruiser.

When they got home, Jason called Wanda's voice mail and told her to come over as soon as possible and to bring whatever paperwork they were going to need to start the process.

XXIII

It was a battle to get the courts to name Jason the legal guardian.

At the hearing, Wanda promised the judge she would visit them every day if she had to. In the end, Jason was given custody on a trial basis of three months. Wanda said it was a great victory. Harvey would have to stay in foster care until it was all sorted out, but Wanda would make sure they talked at least once a day.

Jason used the time to clean up the spare room and relist a bunch of unsold items on eBay so he could get her a closet and set of drawers from IKEA in Hicksville.

One afternoon a package came from an attorney in Garden City. Inside the envelope were official documents, a letter, and a small envelope with Jason's name scribbled on the outside.

The attorney's letter made reference to official documents which summarized his late brother's estate.

A will, signed by his brother and sister-in-law, stipulated that in the event of their simultaneous death, any remaining assets after the resolution of all claims against the estate were to be kept in a trust for their daughter and managed by the wife's parents, the Morganos, who (it was assumed when the will was written) would become the legal guardians of the aforementioned child.

However, the attorney went on to write that substantial debt, a weak housing market, sizable car payments, a business in arrears, and an interest-only mortgage product had combined to render a negative balance in the estate account after death expenses, resolution of claims, and administrative fees.

In light of the aforementioned circumstances, the letter requested that Jason kindly consider the package his first and final correspondence—unless he wished to enlist the firm at his own expense. At the bottom, the attorney had written in his own hand how sorry he was for Jason's loss.

The final item in the package was the small envelope with Jason's name written on the outside in his brother's handwriting.

Inside was a tattered piece of paper Jason had seen before.

Don't come looking for me. No visits, no phone calls, no letters, no cards, no prayers, no nothing. I blew it. Take over for me at home, live as best you can.

Do all the things I never will.

Your Brother

XXIV

AFTER A THIRD cup of espresso, Jason felt awake enough to try out the Métro.

They walked uphill to the Caulaincourt station so that Harvey could introduce her father to Murat, whose shop was on the way.

Harvey could tell that Murat was surprised by the thin ponytail and by the wrinkled tattoo on her father's neck. Murat's English was very good, and he gave Jason cake that his wife had made. There were pistachio nuts in it and a spice Harvey didn't know the name of. Then customers began lining up and Murat went back to work.

Harvey showed her father how to put his small, paper ticket in the machine, then retrieve it before going through. As the barrier opened, two young men rushed in behind Jason and went through without paying. Other people in the station saw it happen, but no one seemed to care. One of the men turned and nodded at Jason as if to thank him.

"A lot of people do that here," Harvey said. "It's part of life in Paris."

When the train rattled in, then squealed to a stop, Harvey yanked a steel lever and the doors opened. A man started to get up, but Harvey waved him back into his seat.

Next to Jason, a baby in a stroller was chewing on the plastic hand of a doll. Each time she bit down, the doll squeaked.

Then, she kicked her legs and the doll went over the side and hit the floor. When Jason picked it up, the doll squeaked and people looked at him.

THE RESTAURANT HARVEY had chosen was close to the Métro, so they only had to walk a few minutes. Harvey said it was where people came to catch up or just watch the world go by. It was a light evening sky with no clouds.

There wasn't much space between the tables, and the leather hem of her father's motorcycle jacket almost tipped a carafe of wine as he sat down.

"I love this," Jason said when the waiter seated them next to one other with a view of the sidewalk. "It's like eating on the couch but we're outside."

When Harvey took the napkin and set it on her lap, her father did the same. When the menu came, Jason said he wouldn't mind a hamburger, if they had that sort of thing in France. The waiter was polite but in a hurry.

"Of course, monsieur," he said, then asked Harvey in French if her father would like to try it with foie gras instead of cheese. Harvey ordered a glass of wine for herself and a bottle of alcohol-free beer for her father, which seemed to impress the waiter, as though he, too, had quit drinking.

While they were waiting for their food, Jason took the baseball out of his coat pocket and set it on the table.

"Remember when I ran away from the Little League game?" Harvey said.

"Yeah, and me with the cops, crying like a little girl," Jason said.

"Hey," Harvey said. "Don't dis little girls."

"Oh, Harv, I was just kidding."

Harvey threw a fake punch, "I know, Dad, I'm teasing."

Young men in jeans were lighting cigarettes at the table next to them. They nodded at Jason as if to say hello.

"The French really like you for some reason," Harvey said enthusiastically. "Maybe it's the biker thing."

"Running away from that baseball game was one thing, Harvey. But that court interview was the worst," Jason said. "Because you had that big cut on your face. Remember that?"

"No, Dad—I got that cut on the first day of school. I looked fine for the court thing."

"Harvey, I remember. You had a cut right here on your lip."

"Dad," Harvey said, "that was for school. Didn't we go to Chuck E. Cheese's after the court thing?"

Jason couldn't remember.

"Because if we went to Chuck E. Cheese's after, then that's where my little blue dog came from."

"What little blue dog?"

"My favorite little blue dog that I love."

"The one at home on your dresser?"

Harvey nodded. "Darn! I should have asked you to bring him with you."

WANDA HAD APPEARED promptly that morning, at seven o'clock, in a stiff gray suit. She was holding a bag of toasted bagels, chocolate milk, and deli coffee.

Jason was frantically undoing knots in Harvey's sneakers. He'd had a haircut the day before, and Wanda said it looked smart but that he might also want to shave. She had brought along one of her husband's ties, but Jason said he was wearing a turtleneck to cover his tattoo.

When Harvey came out still in her pajamas, Wanda frog-marched her into the bathroom. Jason sat on the couch and listened to the tub fill up. In two hours, people would judge whether he was good enough to look after a child.

When Harvey was finally ready, Wanda put her on the couch with a toasted bagel, then sat with Jason and went through everything—including what he should say if they asked about his incarceration.

When it was time to leave, Wanda had to drive because Jason was too nervous.

The county court offices took up an entire block opposite the Long Island Rail Road station. People were outside smoking and trying to get comfortable in suits that didn't fit. There were unmarked police cruisers parked on the sidewalk, and shops offering money transfers and bail bonds.

Wanda led Harvey and Jason straight in through double doors, where they had to pass under a metal detector, and Wanda had to open her pocketbook for the guard to look inside with a flashlight.

They got to Room 204-D fifteen minutes early.

"This is good," Wanda said. "Early shows organized, efficient, and enthusiastic."

She had been to plenty of these meetings and said the officials got pissed when people were late.

On the wall were posters about abuse, with phone numbers people could call for help. One of them showed three children hiding under a kitchen table, covering their ears.

THERE ARE MANY VICTIMS OF DOMESTIC VIOLENCE, it said.

The chairs they were sitting on reminded Jason of high school. There were paper cups in the trash from earlier meetings, and a lower pane of glass in the door had been cracked, maybe where someone had gotten angry or knocked it while carrying a chair.

Harvey was wearing a pink party dress with flower stitching. Jason had bought it for her at Marshalls, along with white tights and pink clogs that fell off if she walked too fast.

As they waited, Harvey made a picture with some crayons that Wanda had brought. Harvey was wearing her ring that once had gum in it, and the chair clicked as her feet swung under the table.

Then there was a knock and the door swung open. It was a woman in her forties, along with a short, stocky man who had a mustache and was about Wanda's age. The man seemed jovial and cupped Jason's elbow when they shook hands.

The woman apologized for being late and explained what was going to happen. They would chat together informally; then it would be time to speak with just Jason and Wanda, then just Harvey and Wanda. All three sessions would be recorded.

Jason said he understood and the interview began.

The first thing they asked was about school.

"There's one near my house," Jason said. "So that's easy."

"Miss Harvey is going to start second grade in the fall," Wanda added. "It was my professional opinion that Jason and Harvey should spend a few months hanging out before formal schooling began for her again."

"What do you think of starting second grade in the fall, Harvey?" the woman asked.

Harvey looked at her drawing, kept moving the crayon.

"It's big-kid school," the woman went on. "You'll get to draw lots of pretty pictures there."

"Looking forward to school, Miss Harvey?" Wanda said.

"No," Harvey said finally. "I'm not looking forward."

"You don't want to go to school?" the woman said.

"I want to stay home with Jason and watch TV."

The court officials looked at Jason.

"What sorts of things do you watch on TV?" the woman wanted to know.

"Mostly scary stuff," Harvey said.

"Me too," the man with the mustache said, putting down his legal pad. "What kind of stuff do *you* like?"

"Aliens and monsters killing people."

"Doesn't that frighten you?" the woman said. "That would frighten me."

"I change the channel if she's really scared," Jason said.

"No, he doesn't," Harvey said. "He thinks it's funny."

Wanda laughed nervously.

Harvey looked up from her drawing at Wanda. "He really doesn't."

"Well, then," the man said. "If you don't get scared of what's on TV, what do you get scared of?"

Harvey thought about it. Wanda started to say something, but the woman raised a finger to stop her.

"Nothing, I guess," Harvey said.

"Nothing scares you?" the woman said. "What if I asked you to pick one thing?"

"Well," Harvey said, thinking carefully, "I'd have to say black holes."

The woman nodded and wrote something down.

Then Harvey thought of something else. "And who will look after me if Jason dies. Maybe you, Wanda?" Harvey said, turning to look at her.

Wanda touched her shoulder. "Maybe sweetie pie."

The court officials reassured Harvey that Jason almost certainly would not die, and asked if she had bad dreams at night.

"I once dreamed that the house burned down. My toys got burned too."

The woman said it must have been bad. What a terrible dream to have.

"Their faces melted," Harvey said. "Like in a horror movie I saw."

"What horror movie was that?" Jason wanted to know.

Harvey shrugged.

"Tell us more about the dream," the man said.

"That dream was with my first mom and dad," Harvey told him. "But I'm not scared now, because if anyone tried to burn down the house, Jason would blind them."

Wanda laughed and brought up the subject of budgeting.

After talking for a little longer, the woman suggested they sit with Jason alone for a while. Harvey was taken to a room where children were supervised and could play with toys. Jason looked at her empty seat until Wanda returned and the interview continued.

The man saw him looking. "Harvey will see you as her father eventually," the man said. "If she doesn't already."

"And her mother too," the woman added. "Unless there's a strong female presence in her life, you're playing the role of both parents."

"Wanda is a good female presence," Jason said.

"But I won't always be with you, sweetie," Wanda said, patting his arm. "I have other cases, and I'm going to retire soon."

The woman wanted to know how Jason felt he might cope without being able to call on Wanda.

"Fine," Jason said. "I pretty much know what to do."

"And what's that?" the woman said flatly.

Jason looked at Wanda, who nodded for him to speak up.

"Make sure there are three good meals a day, keep the house clean, make sure there's heat and everything is safe."

Wanda had gone over this with Jason. It was a standard question, but the woman kept nodding, so Jason tried to think of more things to say.

"Spend time with her. Take her to the doctor if she gets sick, make her buckle up and shout at her if she doesn't, teach her not to steal, teach her to be a good person, don't let her use knives, make sure her window is closed at night so she can't get abducted, keep her away from stray dogs, people on drugs . . ."

"Okay," the woman said. "That's good, Jason."

"What's a typical meal like?" the man asked. "Just something you would normally make."

"She gets more than enough to eat," Jason said. "There's always leftovers."

"Like what kind of stuff?" the man said.

"Pizza, chicken fingers, french fries, Hot Pockets, toast, cereal, apple slices, pork and beans, cereal, ravioli, mini-hamburgers, ravioli, pasta, corn, mozzarella sticks, ice cream . . ."

"You're making me hungry," the man said.

"Last week Jason made his first meat loaf," Wanda told them.

This made the woman smile. "It's hard to make a good meat loaf. How did you stop it from drying out?"

"Covered it," Jason said.

The woman wrote *meat loaf* on her legal pad and circled it.

"What was *your* father like, Jason?" the man asked.

Jason thought for a moment. "Full of energy," he said.

"How do you mean?" the man wanted to know.

Wanda cleared her throat. "He was a World War II hero."

"The war messed him up," Jason said. "But we had fun in the end."

"That's excellent," said the man. "Families who laugh a lot are usually close."

Wanda then mentioned how Jason had made extra money before Harvey moved in, so he could purchase a dresser, a desk, and a mini drum set for her.

"Do you play the drums, Jason?" the man asked. "You musical?"

"I used to," Jason said. "Harvey asked me to teach her."

The man was impressed. "That's exactly the kind of thing we want to hear—music to our ears, so to speak."

AT THE BEGINNING of the trial period three months earlier, Wanda had brought Harvey's stuff in two suitcases, along with a few bags of groceries so she could cook a celebration meal.

Jason had converted the spare room, which pleased Wanda. The carpet was gone, replaced by new dark wood flooring that

Jason had bought at Home Depot and cut to size on Wanda's husband's table saw. The dresser he picked out had butterfly handles and a glass top. Wanda had found a bed frame at a yard sale near her home in Hempstead, which her husband had cleaned up and painted.

Harvey's stuff was mostly clothes and toys. Wanda laid everything out on the bed, showing Jason how to fold and keep socks and underwear in one place, shirts and leggings in another. Wanda said that Harvey was still wearing diapers at night, and she would get him a six-month supply of the nighttime Pull-Ups, courtesy of Uncle Bill.

"Who's that?" Jason said.

"We just say that when we expense things."

Wanda said she liked how the spare room was shaping up. She saw the mini drum set and told Jason how important it would be to do things with Harvey for the first time.

"She's never ridden a bicycle without training wheels," Wanda said. "So that's something else to look forward to. Make sure you take a camera."

Wanda said the next three months were very important if he was to be appointed official guardian. "Reach out to your friends," she advised him. "Have them write letters about the good things you've done and what a nice, pleasant person you are."

But three months later, a week before the court interview, Jason confessed that the only person he knew well enough to ask for a character reference was standing in front of him.

"What about the neighbors?"

"They don't speak English."

"Damn it, Jason—you could have said something earlier."

"What should we do?"

"The interview with the courts is next week . . . I'll have to get my friends to do it."

"Is that allowed?"

"If I did what the law allowed," Wanda explained, "we wouldn't even be standing here having this conversation."

FOR THE FIRST few weeks living in Jason's house, Harvey cried a lot for her parents, and kept having accidents.

One night Jason woke up and saw her shivering in his bedroom doorway. She had wet the bed a second time within a few hours and was afraid to wake him again.

Jason carried her into the bathroom and ran the hot tap. Then he washed her legs with a warm towel. "If it feels itchy, wake me up and I'll wipe you off again."

He could see she'd been crying because her eyes were red. "It's not a big deal," he told her. "Even tough guys with tats who ride motorcycles wet the bed, Harvey."

"Like you?" Harvey said.

Jason nodded.

Then he took a Pull-Up from the bag and helped her step in through the holes. Finding clean pajamas was more difficult, but there was a pair with spaceships in the laundry room, and Jason warmed them up in the dryer.

Then Harvey sat cross-legged on the floor and watched Jason strip the bed and put on fresh linens. When he was done, Harvey got in and went back to sleep.

A couple of nights later it happened again. The mattress

was wet on both sides, so Jason had to put a garbage bag over the stain, then a blanket over the bag. When he was finished, Harvey wanted him to stay and hold her hand. She asked if he knew any songs, but the only one Jason knew by heart was "Paranoid" by Black Sabbath.

"Sing it," Harvey said.

When her grip loosened, Jason knew she was asleep, and he went outside for a smoke. The night was cool and there were many stars.

THE COURT OFFICIALS wanted to know how Jason made a living, intrigued by his eBay business. Jason explained it as basically an online yard sale. When they asked about his problems with the IRS, Wanda said that Social Services was working with them directly to sort it out.

"I don't really understand this Internet business," the woman said, "but as legal guardian, it's also your job to support the child financially, and that means filing your taxes once a year."

Jason said he had applied for a job at a hardware store near the house. He said if they hired him, he could work while Harvey was in school.

The man laughed and asked if the hardware store had a name.

"Home Depot," Jason said ironically.

The man wrote it down and asked if Jason could give him the name of someone in human resources.

"You think I'm lying?" Jason said.

"We don't think that at all, Jason," the woman said.

Jason ripped a folded piece of paper from his pants pocket

and threw it on the table. Nobody moved. Then the man picked it up and handed it back to Jason without unfolding it. "I just asked because I was going to call over there and put in a good word for you."

"Oh," Jason said. "I didn't know."

"This interview is about how you look after Harvey," the woman explained, "and what's best for her."

The man nodded. "We have to be thorough because—as I'm sure you understand—we're here to act in the interests of a minor, and we answer to Judge Thomas, who quite rightly errs on the side of caution."

"Yeah, I get it," Jason said. "I'm sorry."

"Remember this," the man went on. "There is no perfect parent. We all make mistakes. You just have to do your best, keep them safe, and—you know—feed them from time to time."

"And love them," the woman added. "Above all else, you have to love them."

Wanda took out the letters of reference from Shawn Mullen of Hempstead, Rhonda Jales of Hempstead, Taquisha Suarez of Farmingdale, and Reverend Desmond Cox of East Islip. Wanda also had an Excel spreadsheet showing how Jason had spent the Social Security payments on Harvey's behalf.

When it was Harvey's turn to be interviewed, they kept her in the room for only fifteen minutes.

On the way out, Wanda called her husband to tell him how it had gone. Then she said that Uncle Bill was taking them for lunch at Chuck E. Cheese's.

"I used to go there with my dad," Harvey said.

An hour later, as Harvey was shooting plastic ducks with a

pink gun, Wanda got a call from the courts to say they were extending the trial period to six months.

Jason couldn't believe it. "We gotta go through all that shit again?"

"You think it's easy to get custody of a child?" Wanda said fiercely. "Think about it, Jason!"

Harvey's game ended and she reappeared, holding the tickets she'd won from the machine.

"Go trade them at the counter for a prize," Wanda said.

"You guys come too."

"We'll come in a minute, honey, you go on."

"They could have been real hard-asses," Wanda said as Harvey walked away. "They could have busted your ass. I've seen it happen, and it ain't pretty, let me tell you . . ."

"I was hoping today would be it," Jason said.

"That's just not how it works in New York. But whatever anyone says, you *are* her guardian, Jason. You see anyone else lining up to take care of her?"

"What about the Morganos?"

"I can't go into that right now," Wanda said, waving the subject off.

"But won't they want to see Harvey in the future?" Jason pressed. "Maybe we could all go visit them in Florida? Your husband can come too. When was it they were up here, again, Wanda?"

Wanda gave a quick little laugh. "I guess Harvey told you, then."

"You're sly, Wanda," Jason said. "But I guess you really know what you're doing with this adoption business. What else are you not telling me?"

Harvey shouted for them to come and help her choose a prize from a row of stuffed blue dogs.

"It's lucky for you the nice gentleman let that shit go," Wanda went on, "you throwing the piece of paper that way. They most certainly could have used it as an excuse *not* to renew the trial."

It hadn't once occurred to Jason they might take Harvey away.

"Mark my words," Wanda said, "Harvey could have been on her way back to the Goldenbergs' right now."

"But I'm her family," Jason insisted. "We're flesh and blood."

"What if he'd *really* pushed your buttons, Jason? What then?"

"How should I know?" Jason said, but in his mind was already dragging the man from the seat and driving his head backward toward the white brick wall. His body is light. His eyes are rolling. Jason has him by the neck and he can't breathe.

Everyone is screaming and he can feel Wanda pulling on his arms. Her voice echoes through him: "Thought you said you hated bullies, Jason? *Thought you said you hated bullies . . .*"

Now his own words are attacking him.

Harvey is still in her seat, but pee is dripping through slats in the chair.

Jason is red in the face because the cops have to pin him down with their knees.

In the back of the cruiser, he realizes what he's done and bites down so hard that his mouth fills with blood.

What will he do with her toys? With the pillow she puts her head on? Who will check on her in the early hours? Flip the mattress when she has an accident?

There will have to be a trial, of course. He may even serve time. Then Wanda telling him that Harvey has gone to a family in Buffalo and he can never see her again. He wants to know if Harvey asked for him, but Wanda refuses to say.

Once it's all done with, when time has passed and he's back at home, he'll carry her mini drum kit through the house to the garage.

Let the spare room fill up with junk again.

Carry her dresser out to the curb, then watch from the living room window as some stranger heaves it into the back of a minivan, a surprise for his youngest daughter. Doesn't matter if a drawer is busted, he just wants to get it home. There's nothing he can't fix. Amazing what people throw away.

XXV

THE MORNING AFTER her father arrived in Paris, Harvey found him standing barefoot in the kitchen, drinking a glass of water and looking at Isobel's drawings on the refrigerator.

"I still have your drawings," he said. "When you get a house, I'll give them to you."

Over breakfast, Harvey said it would likely rain the next few days, so they should pack a lunch and hop the train to Versailles—if only to see the gardens.

She told her father to pick out another item from the Father's Day box. Whatever he chose, she said, would give them something to talk about on the journey.

Harvey said she was going to make a French version of his favorite ham-and-mustard sandwiches. She also cut two slices of lemon cake to eat at Marie Antoinette's house.

Jason watched as she wrapped their lunch in foil. Then she told him again to pick something from the box, so she could pack it with the food.

The line of people at the ticket machine was so long that they missed the first train to the palace. The platform for electric RER trains was underground. Vending machines cast a warm orange glow over the swept gray concrete. Then the train marked RIVE GAUCHE arrived and they got on and found seats at the end of an upper level.

The train ran parallel to the Seine, below the main streets of Paris, which were bright and bustled with people and cars and bicycles going madly in all directions. After leaving the city behind, the train rattled past rows of crumbling houses patched with cement. When the train stopped, they noticed an old man and his wife, yards from the track, digging for carrots on a kidney-shaped plot of land.

Harvey told her father that some of the older houses had been built hundreds of years before the invention of trains, when there were only fields and sky and one muddy road that gradually widened, the closer it got to Paris.

Jason looked out at the old houses, his palms spread on the glass as though he were a boy again.

When he asked why Versailles was worth seeing, Harvey told him that in 1789 there was a revolution and the people who lived in the palace got their heads cut off because they had ignored the suffering of others.

"That's like my worst nightmare," Harvey told her father. "To get decapitated like that."

Jason shrugged. "Wouldn't bother me. When you're dead, you're dead."

Harvey put her hands on her father's neck. "But it's your head, Dad!"

"There are worse ways to go, kid."

"Like how?"

"Like, you could waste your life and then die without realizing it."

"Waste your life how?"

"By not having anyone."

Harvey laughed. "Huh?"

"Well, I mean, if you don't love nobody."

Harvey snickered "Are you getting sentimental on me?"

"I'm serious, Harvey."

"Okay, so you wouldn't mind having your head cut off as long as you're in love when the guillotine falls?"

Jason felt a sudden tightness in his throat but wanted to hear the words out loud. "I've loved three people," he said. "In my life."

Harvey looked out at the passing trees. "Is that a lot?"

"I think it's a good number," Jason said. "It's better than two."

"There's me and your brother," Harvey said. "But who is the third person?"

"That's for another day, Harv."

"Tell me now, Dad. I want to know. It was a woman, wasn't it?"

"Forget it, Harvey."

When the final stretch took them into a tunnel, Jason saw his reflection in the blackened glass. He felt from time to time, this woman he had once loved was watching him, and remembered the color of her lips, or the way her body felt.

Harvey took a bar of chocolate from her purse, and shared the pieces. The windows on one side of the train opened a few inches, and when they were out of the tunnel, Jason stuck his hand out.

"Long ago," Harvey said, "only kings and queens and their servants got to experience Versailles. Everyone else had to imagine it from what they could see through the railings."

"But we get to go in, right?"

"If it's not, like, crazy busy. But why don't you unwrap the thing from your Father's Day box?"

Jason tried to feel what it was through the wrapping. "I can't even guess," he said.

"Just open it, Dad."

When he removed the paper, Jason saw it was a two-handled Peter Rabbit cup that he knew once belonged to his brother. "How come you have this, Harvey?"

"Don't worry, Dad—it's not the one from home. I got it online."

The original cup had been among the things brought over by Wanda when Harvey first moved in.

The ceramic felt cool in his hands. Small painted rabbits bounced happily on the rim, while larger ones lower down wore human clothes, drank tea, and stood chatting over a garden fence.

The carriages near the front of the train must have been full of people, because when the train stopped, Harvey and her father followed a heavy stream of tourists down a long cobbled avenue with lanes of cars on either side.

As they neared the gates, men approached with Eiffel Tower models. Some of the men were insistent, but when Harvey spoke in French, they laughed and withdrew.

As they crossed the last cobblestone street before the heavy gold gates of the palace, a yellow postal van failed to stop and came within a yard of hitting them.

Jason followed the van up the street with his eyes until it stopped at a red light. He felt the impulse to get up there and pull the driver out, smash his face on the road, knock his teeth out—teach him a hard lesson . . .

But then he felt the pull of a hand and Jason realized he had stopped walking, and that his daughter was there by his side.

"You okay, Dad? You want to sit down for a while?"

"I'm fine," he said. "It's a great day and I'm with my daughter and everything's great. We're totally fine." He took off his motorcycle jacket and tucked it under one arm. There were visible lines of thread running up the back of the jacket, where it had been sewn up, but the cuffs had worn to strings, and the elbows and shoulders were cracked like old faces, and there were dark stains that could not be removed.

After passing through the gates, Harvey found the cobblestones hard to walk on in sandals. "People must have laid these with their bare hands," Jason said. "They're so uneven."

When they reached the entrance, people were lining up to go inside the palace and to board a miniature train that spared visitors the long walk to Marie Antoinette's house.

There was no wait to enter the grounds themselves, so Jason and Harvey crunched past everyone on a white gravel path that ran between neatly planted sections of flowers. Black birds circled cone-shaped trees. People were taking photographs at the top of a staircase, where Harvey and her father could look out at the gardens and to the green woods beyond.

Jason imagined peasants dressed in rags with jagged teeth, tearing up the plants and drinking wine from bottles, then pissing it into the fountain. He imagined the faces of people who would soon lose their heads. He wondered if they knew they were going to die and if the reason for their execution was obvious to them.

At the edge of the fountain was the bronze statue of a man with a beard leaning back on his elbows. He was being handed a bronze bunch of flowers by a bronze baby with heavy wings.

For a while, Harvey and Jason just stood looking around. Some of the other tourists had been there since early morning, and their feet dragged on the white stones as they returned from far corners of the estate. In the distance, a lake in the shape of a holy cross shimmered in the midday heat.

When they reached a flight of steps leading down to the Orangerie, Harvey said she wanted to go back and walk slowly with her father beside the pink and purple flowers. "Remember the flowers we used to plant?" she asked him.

Sunday was often spent in the yard with forks and spoons—and later trowels and spades, once they got the hang of it. Over time, Jason had learned what to plant and how to feed and water. Now roses climbed one side of the house, and daffodils unfolded in the front borders when spring came.

"Remember pushing my hands into the soil?" Harvey said.

Jason couldn't recall it.

"Kneel," she told him.

"What?"

"C'mon, Dad."

Jason looked around at all the people. "I don't want to get in trouble."

"This is France, Dad. It's hard to get in trouble here."

He sighed and got down on his knees. "You gonna make me a prince or something?"

Harvey told him to reach over the low green box-hedging and put his hands on the soil. "Hurry up," she said. "Before someone comes."

"I thought you said—"

"C'mon, Dad."

Jason hesitated, but then reached over and lay his palms on the bare soil between two rows of plants. Harvey got down next to him. "You used to put your hands over mine like this . . . " she said, showing him. " . . . And told me you were going to grow a Harvey tree."

It was hard to get up because of his leg, so his daughter helped him.

"You remember when we did that, Dad?"

"I don't, Harvey, I'm sorry."

"That's funny," she said, brushing off a few small stones. "Because I think about it all the time."

XXVI

AFTER SEVERAL MONTHS of living together, it was time for Harvey to start second grade. Jason said they were going to have a celebration dinner and took some ribs out of the freezer. They were also having barbecue pizza, french fries, tater tots, and mozzarella sticks.

In the afternoon, after watching *Return of the Jedi,* Jason said he had to change the oil in the car.

Harvey wanted to help. "We can pretend it's our space-ship," she said.

Jason didn't think it was a good idea. "If you get any oil or grease on your hands, you can't go putting your fingers in your mouth."

Harvey glared at him. "I would never do that."

Jason made her stay in the house as he drove the car onto the metal ramps. The afternoon was warm enough to wear shorts, and after he gave the signal, she came skipping outside.

Some of the neighbors were mowing their lawns, but when they shut the engines off, you could hear birds and locusts in the trees.

Harvey wasn't allowed underneath the car, even to look, so she sat cross-legged on the grass where she could see Jason working. When the oil came out, she lay on her stomach and watched it gloop into the pan. Jason brought the pan over to show her. Harvey wanted to put her finger in, and it took all of her energy to keep her hand away.

"The blacker and thicker it is," Jason explained, "the dirtier."

Harvey asked if oil was dangerous.

"When it's hot in the engine, it's dangerous," he said.

"Could it make a car crash?"

Jason set the oil pan on the ground and took a new filter from the box. Harvey followed him with her voice. "Maybe that's what happened to my mom and dad? Maybe the oil got so hot, it made them crash?"

Jason didn't answer until he was back under the car, looking up into the engine with a flashlight. "Doesn't work like that, Harvey."

"Then how did they die if it wasn't oil?"

Jason shined the flashlight in her eyes.

"Hey!" she said.

He motioned for her to come under.

"Really?" she said. "I can come?"

"Be careful," he warned her. "Crawl."

Jason put the blue oil filter in her hands and steadied it so she could screw it on. It took some time to line up the threads, but when they finally caught, Harvey shouted, "I got it! I got it!"

When the filter was on tight, Jason told her to go on in the house and wash her hands. He would back the car off the ramps. She trotted along the path toward the front door, then turned back to see if he was watching.

"I put the blue thing on by myself, right?" she called out.

"Like a real mechanic," Jason said.

When the screen door closed, Jason lit a cigarette and held it loosely between his oily fingers. When it was finished, he put it out with his foot and looked at the ground. Then Harvey opened the screen door a crack. Jason told her to stay inside until the car was down.

Harvey pushed a chair to the window and watched Jason strain to get his prosthetic leg in the driver's seat with the car up on ramps. Then the headlights came on, and in two jerks it was down and level with the driveway again.

Jason gave the signal and she ran out. Then he put the hood up and leaned in with a flashlight.

Harvey asked if she could hold the light, but instead of shining it into the engine, she put the flashlight on Jason. "I want to see your blood," she said, noticing rashy scar tissue on his forearm. "Why is your skin messed up here?"

Jason pulled his arm back. "Look, Harvey—this is where the new oil goes in." He handed her a gray funnel and showed her where to position it over the opening. Harvey said it was just like a trumpet and went to blow, but Jason slapped her hand away before it touched her mouth. She felt a tremor in her bottom lip but tried to concentrate.

"Sorry," Jason said. "I guess it kind of does look like a trumpet."

For a few moments, Harvey couldn't speak, or look at him.

"Oil was once trees and bushes that got pressed in the ground so long that they turned into liquid. You wanna pour it in?"

Harvey shrugged. "What if I mess up?"

Jason placed the container in her hands, then helped her tip the contents slowly. When she was halfway done, a burst of excited laughter escaped from her mouth and oil splashed over Jason's wrist.

"Shit, Harvey, hold it steady now."

She felt her confidence coming apart, and the container began to shake.

"Harvey!" Jason snapped, but then remembered what Wanda had said about how important it was for them to do things together for the first time. He steadied her hands until they stopped shaking. "You're doing great, Harvey—just keep pouring. Pour out all those plants from dinosaur times."

Harvey said she couldn't believe that oil was old dinosaur food. Jason couldn't either, but had seen it on TV.

"Why are there no dinosaurs now, Jason?"

"They're extinct."

"What's that?"

"It means they're dead and can never come back."

"Like my mom and dad," Harvey said. "They're *eggs tint* too."

When the container was almost empty, Jason asked if she was ready for the next quart.

"It needs another one?"

Harvey mopped her brow with a frayed sleeve. "Did the dinosaurs know they were going to die?"

"Doubt it."

"How come we don't know when we're going to die?"

Jason didn't answer, but as Harvey was pouring in the second quart, he said, "You just have to live each day with the best you got."

"You've got me," Harvey said.

"That's right."

Then her eyes lit up. "And I've got Duncan."

. . .

WHEN THEY WERE finished, Harvey wanted to wash the car. Jason said no but then went inside and came back with a bucket of warm water and soap. Harvey skipped behind, clapping her hands.

"First day of school tomorrow," Jason said. "Excited?"

"No."

Jason put the key in the ignition and the radio came on. When he turned the dial, there was static; then Spanish music tinkled out through the speakers.

"Can we listen to this?" Harvey said.

Jason raised the volume so they could hear it with the windows closed.

"Reminds me of my mom," Harvey said.

"She was Italian, right, Harvey?"

"No," Harvey said, sponging the door. "She was Spanish. Grandma and Grandpa Morgano came from Ecuador."

Dirt ran down the side of the car in suds. When they met at the bucket to dip their sponges, Jason asked whom she'd visited in Florida with Wanda if her grandparents were dead.

"Mom's great-aunt," Harvey said.

"What was she like?"

"Nice," Harvey said, dipping her sponge, then slopping it against the front panel. "But Wanda said she's sick."

Jason wiped his rag over the spokes of the front wheel. "Sick with what?"

"I don't know," Harvey said. "I can't remember."

Then she remembered. "Lung cancer! Lung cancer!"

Jason was wiping the tire with a circular motion. "That's pretty bad, Harvey."

Harvey dipped her sponge. The water was a dirty gray. "Does lung cancer mean you're gonna die?"

"Depends on how bad it is," Jason said, scrubbing the headlights. "Why are bugs so hard to get off? They're so little."

"Let me try," Harvey said.

When the body and all four wheels were covered in a soapy film, Jason lifted Harvey up to sponge the roof.

"Why don't we all die at the same time?" Harvey wanted to know. "How come we die apart, usually?"

"You're asking the wrong guy."

"Why aren't you the right guy?"

"It's just an expression. It means I don't know."

By the time they had finished wiping all over, the soap had dried in the pattern of their streaks. Jason lit a cigarette.

"It's still dirty," Harvey said. "After all our work, we've made it dirtier."

Jason laughed and it made him cough.

"Looks like we just spread the dirt around," Harvey went on, throwing her sponge into the bucket. Then she sat in the driveway with her legs crossed and her bottom lip pushed out.

When Jason went to get the hose, Harvey followed. "Are *you* going to get lung cancer, Jason?"

"Not planning on it."

"Wanda said Mom's great-aunt got it from smoking, and that a person should never try it because it's addicting."

Harvey watched Jason's hands move quickly on the faucet. Water rushed through the rubber pipe. They could hear it rushing through the pipe to make a spray. When they got back to the car, Jason told Harvey to get the sponge. But she turned around and went into the house.

Jason waited a few minutes for her to come out, then continued on by himself. The water from the hose made his hands cold, but he was careful not to drop the sponge on the driveway, where little stones could stick to it, then scratch the paintwork. This was something he would have explained to Harvey. But she had gone into the house and he didn't know why.

On the back of the car were two fading bumper stickers. One said:

JESUS LOVES YOU!

BUT EVERYONE ELSE THINKS YOU'RE AN ASSHOLE

The other was a Nirvana sticker that showed the medical cross section of a pregnant woman's stomach.

When it was almost done, Jason gave the wheels another going-over. One of his tires was almost bald, and the rubber sidewall was cracking. Looking at the worn-out treads made Jason tired, so he sat with his back against the wheel and closed his eyes. Music was still playing from inside the car. He wondered if it might be draining too much of the battery, but he couldn't get up. It was a slow song—the sort that comes on just before a bar closes, and people look around for someone to fight or go home with.

When he opened his eyes again, he noticed gutters along the edge of his house that were sagging with dirt and stagnant water. One section had already separated and was almost completely off.

Jason bought the house after he got out of prison, using money his mother had left when she died. His brother had deposited Jason's share into a bank account and mailed a statement to the prison.

The property was cheap, because you could hear the freeway, and the neighborhood was considered a high-crime area—though more families were moving in, and you hardly saw cops anymore. The house had been empty for a long time, and was probably used as a place to take drugs. People had almost certainly died in it.

The carpet was rotten when Jason moved in, so he ripped it up and for a while just lived with the concrete slab. He found two hundred dollars stashed in a lamp, and shells from a handgun in the sink trap. He put in new pipes and drywall and spent the last of his inheritance getting central heat and air. Everything else, he fixed over time with the money saved from not drinking.

Jason hadn't noticed how bad the gutters looked until now—or that the siding was coming off on the far corner of the house. In another place, it was actually bent back, exposing the wood frame and insulation.

When a tear in the screen door caught Jason's eye, he noticed a face looking out through the mesh. It was a small face. And from a distance it could have belonged to a girl or a boy. When he raised his arm to wave, the face disappeared. Jason sat there wondering if it had been there to begin with—and if it wasn't Harvey's face, then whose? Ghosts, he realized, are not the people who've died but the people who won't.

His shirt was wet where he sat against the wheel. He felt for his cigarettes, but they weren't in his pocket.

He imagined driving Harvey to school in the morning. Her first day of second grade. She had probably wanted to wash the car so it would look nice beside all the other cars. He pictured them lined up in the school parking lot. Then, with an effort, Jason got up and stepped over to the trunk. He bent down and peeled off the JESUS LOVES YOU sticker. Then he sat on the rear bumper, feeling the car dip with his weight.

He tried to imagine what Harvey's classroom would look like, but saw only the classrooms from when he was a child, and heard the sound of a bell, and shoes tapping through the corridors. It had been his job to carry crates of milk from the nurse's office to each grade, because he was disruptive in class, and had to be given a physical task that would keep him busy.

His brother, Steve, was in a classroom with the youngest kids. They used to paint with their feet. Clap along to songs. Raise their hands and then forget what they wanted to say. Jason used to stand on a milk crate and watch through a window in the door.

Giving the milk out meant slipping Steve an extra carton or an extra straw. The first time Steve got embarrassed and tried to give it back, but Jason told him to shut up and hide it. If anyone suspected anything, Jason's plan was to say that one was leaking and he'd tossed it. He even kept an empty carton hidden in his bag in case anyone wanted proof. The only thing that could give him away was the date stamped on the top—it would have to match the date on the one that had gone missing.

But no one ever said anything about stolen milk, and

Jason figured out there were extras because of kids who were sick. There were so many extras during flu season that Jason started bringing them home, so his mother would always have something for her coffee and Steve didn't have to run water from the faucet on his Lucky Charms.

Jason had trouble at school because he had to stay awake at night for the same reason he couldn't run away. And he wanted to run away, to leave everyone and everything behind—the way you escape from a nightmare.

Since Harvey had moved in, there were times like that: times when he felt he couldn't go on, when he looked at the telephone, or started to dial Wanda's number, or imagined leaving the house and never coming back.

Once he sat in the garage and told himself that after completing the motorcycle, he would ride out into the night with only the clothes on his back.

It was when little problems mounted up that Jason felt the worst. The toilet isn't flushing. The AC is broken. Harvey won't stop coughing. No more diapers.

But in the end Jason realized that it was also the little things, like pizza night, playing drums, and watching cartoons, that made life worth living.

As he sat there, weighing out the moments of their first summer together, his eyes settled on the neighbors' mailbox, mottled where he'd struck it with an empty beer bottle several years ago. Someone had pushed out the dent with a hammer, but you could still see the damage.

The husband worked on a construction site and came home with dust on his pants. The mother cleaned houses.

Jason knew because she had a sticker on the side of her minivan.

HEAVENLY SHINE CLEANING SERVICES
(516) XXX-XXXX
24/7
SE HABLA ESPAÑOL

On her days off, the woman snipped things in the garden wearing her husband's old coat. Sometimes she sat on the front porch in bare feet and talked on the phone in Spanish.

They had two children who, on warm days, ran around the garden in pajamas, jumping over a plastic house that was too small for them.

Sometimes the son waited on the porch for his father to pull up, then carried his hard hat or put it on himself.

The neighbors had flowers lining the driveway and rosebushes at the side where the sun fell heaviest. There were hanging baskets too, which Jason had seen getting watered by the children on footstools with glass jars.

Twice a year, a blue or pink balloon was tied to the ruined mailbox. Minivans with chrome wheels pulled up one by one. Soon the backyard was full of people. Salsa music. A piñata. A spread of things to eat. Children running with their shoes off. Older girls in bright dresses standing with their mothers. Men in shorts and sandals, holding bottles of beer, laughing occasionally about work, and moving their feet to the music.

Sometimes the parties went on until dark. Then the music was turned off. Voices filled the driveway as sleeping children were buckled into seats.

Jason used to watch from the spare room. Used to sit there watching until everyone disappeared and there was only darkness.

XXVII

HE FINISHED DRYING the car with old T-shirts, then dragged the hose over the dead yellow grass of his yard. When he got inside, Harvey had all her Polly Pocket dolls on the floor. The dolls were at school, Harvey said. It was their first day, and they were eating raisins in the cafeteria and braiding each other's hair. Harvey asked Jason if he could braid hair—asked if he knew about the rabbits jumping.

"Want to get McDonald's for dinner?" he said.

Harvey was trying to force a rubber shoe on a doll foot. "What about ribs and barbecue pizza?"

"Washing the car wiped me out. How about Taco Bell? You're half Spanish, after all."

Jason washed his hands and looked at the ribs defrosting in the sink. Then he sat in front of the TV and noticed all the oil on his pants.

"Holy Christ!" he cried.

Harvey looked up from her dolls.

"There's shit on my pants!"

"It's on your face too," Harvey said. "But I was afraid to tell you."

After a long shower, Jason sat on the bed drying his hair with a towel, listening to Harvey play with the dolls in the living room. She was talking to them and they were talking to each other. He wondered if she knew it was all pretend, or if part of her believed what she was making up.

Tomorrow would be her first day of school. She had picked out what she was going to wear three weeks ago. Her T-shirt still had the tag on. Jason wondered if she'd outgrown it already.

After loading his soiled pants and shirt into the washer, Jason opened the refrigerator and stood there looking in. Harvey put her dolls down. "Thought you were too tired to cook?"

"I am," he said, spooning macaroni and cheese from a plastic container.

Harvey got to her feet. "We're having leftovers for our celebration dinner?"

"We'll celebrate tomorrow," he said. "Ribs take a while to bake, anyway."

Harvey stood watching him sprinkle ground beef on the macaroni. Then he cut a jalapeño pepper for himself. "Find something good on TV while I heat this up," he said.

"I thought we were getting McDonald's or Taco Bell because I'm half Spanish?"

Jason stopped what he was doing and looked at the plates. "Well, I've made this now. Just go put the TV on. We'll get McDonald's later this week."

He poured Harvey a glass of milk and opened a can of Mountain Dew for himself. When they were sitting, Harvey scarfed her food down and asked if there was any more.

Jason looked at her. "Thought you weren't hungry?" he said, then scraped the rest of his food onto her plate.

"How come you get soda?" she said.

"Because I don't like milk."

Harvey looked at her glass. "Me neither."

Then they didn't talk because there was a show about how camels survive in the desert.

"That's like our yard," Harvey said, pointing to the endless yellow plain on the screen. "Can we get a camel?"

When they had finished eating, Jason went out for a cigarette, then came back in and told Harvey to get her shoes from the cupboard.

"Where are we going?"

"Out."

"What time is it?"

"Almost five."

"But I have school tomorrow. It's my first day."

"Then hurry up."

When they were in the car, Jason turned around to make sure she was buckled. They drove down Hands Creek Boulevard. It was warm, and they passed a few people on motorcycles.

"That'll be you someday," Harvey said. "After your bike is builded."

When they pulled into a strip mall, Harvey recognized where they were. "Why are we going to Home Depot? Did you get the job?"

"No, I did not."

"Then why are we here?"

After passing through the automatic doors, Jason took Harvey's hand and they followed signs to the garden center.

"What are we doing here?"

"Getting stuff we need," Jason said. "You'll see."

The garden department extended into an area with a clear plastic roof. There were flocks of small trees, bags of mulch, water fountains on pallets, and trays of flowers on trolleys.

Jason stopped a man in an orange apron and asked which flowers were the best for a new garden. His name, Bernie, was written in Magic Marker on his apron.

Bernie led them to a trolley of plants he said were a mix of perennials and annuals. The man explained that perennials would come back to life every year, while the bloom of an annual lasted only the summer, as the plant itself would not survive the first frost.

Harvey thought perennials sounded better.

"If they die before the end of summer," Bernie said, "just bring them back."

They were also going to need topsoil and a bag of mulch, which Bernie said was essential for protecting new plants.

When they got home, Jason and Harvey walked around the house to find the sunniest spot. They decided the best place was right in front.

"And if we put them here," Harvey said, "anyone who comes to visit will say, 'Oh, look, what pretty flowers.'"

Once they had marked the spot for each plant with handfuls of yellow grass, Harvey asked how they were going to dig, because the earth was hard and dry.

Jason had a look in the garage, but most of his tools were useless as gardening implements. In the end, he took a carving knife from the kitchen drawer and found that repeated striking was quite effective. As he was chopping up the ground, the neighbors went past in their minivan. Harvey waved.

Jason looked up from his stabbing. "What the hell are you doing?"

"Just waving."

"Well, quit it. We don't talk to them."

Once the ground was churned up, Harvey said they should add water to make it soft. Jason filled a bucket, then lit a cigarette and watched Harvey pour.

When the earth was grainy and they could move their hands around in it, Harvey squeezed the soil between her fingers. "I used to work in the garden with my mom," she said. "In winter we made piles of leaves and I jumped in them."

"That's nice."

"Can I do that with you?"

They dug holes for the flowers with dessert spoons, then laid each plant in the ground root-first. Once everything was done and the mulch was spread, they sat on the front step.

Jason said it didn't look much different. That they should have gotten more flowers.

"I think they're cute," Harvey said. "I like them."

After putting her pajamas on, Harvey opened the front door to say good night to the flowers. Then, in bed, she imagined them growing into bright trees with branches she could pull herself into and swing from. Jason could watch and tell her what a good climber she was.

THE NEXT MORNING Jason got up early to make French toast as a surprise for Harvey's first day. As he was splitting the frozen segments with a knife, he heard a loud bang. Harvey had fallen off the bed and cut her lip on the side of an open drawer.

He couldn't remember where Wanda had put the first-aid kit, so he went back to the kitchen and grabbed a frozen piece of French toast which he told Harvey to press on the swollen part. Then he rummaged around in the garage and found a Band-Aid, but the sticky part was old, so he used small patches of duct tape to hold it on.

Her lip was soon very swollen. When Harvey saw herself in the mirror, she cried and said she couldn't go to school because everyone would make fun of her.

"I told you not to jump on the bed, Harvey!" Jason shouted. "I told you a hundred times not to do that."

Her face darkened over the half-cooked French toast on her plate.

"Eat," Jason commanded. "Or I'm really gonna lose it."

"I can't," she sobbed, touching the fat part of her lip. "I'm not hungry."

Jason stood there and made her eat half a piece before she could leave the table and go cry in her room.

SCHOOL WAS TEN minutes away.

Harvey looked out the window as they passed all the places that were now familiar.

Jason stared at her in his rearview mirror. The old Band-Aid was leaking blood and Harvey was licking it.

When they were a block or so from school, Harvey threw up. Jason stopped the car and turned to see her panting as though out of breath. Her arms and legs were covered.

"Shit shit shit!" he screamed. When he punched the steering wheel, Harvey threw up again. It was now on the back of his seat and pooling on the floor.

Someone behind in an SUV laid on the horn. Jason jumped out of the car with his fists raised. "Why don't you go fuck yourself!" Spittle sprayed out with the words. He expected it to be some meathead with blow-up muscles and a crew cut, ready to jump out and fight with him—but it was a small, shocked woman with children in the backseat.

Jason got back in the car and pulled away, turning onto the first side road he could find. Then he got out again and stood in the empty street. His hands were shaking and he needed a cigarette. He swung open the back door and undid Harvey's seat belt, which was coated with pale yellow chunks. The seat, her clothes, and her shoes were covered with sick, and the acrid smell filled his nose and mouth.

Harvey's face was red and her lip was still bleeding. "I don't want to go to school!" she screamed, throwing her arms around as if trying to hit something. Sick flew everywhere.

Jason shut the door and leaned against it. He could hear Harvey inside, but the sound was muted, as though she were underwater, or far away, or in a dream.

Then he clenched his hand into a fist and drove it into his palm as hard as he could several times.

Most of the houses on either side of them were redbrick with white garage doors. A dog barked, then a back door slammed, and the street was silent again. The ground was damp from a night of rain.

The longer he just stood there, not doing anything, the less he felt rage pushing him to act. Then something from long ago came back to him. Sneaking away from school to fix a sandwich for his brother, with things he could steal from a nearby supermarket. An older boy had taken Steve's lunch, and Jason had found him sitting alone at recess, licking salt packets he'd picked up off the cafeteria floor.

After watching his brother eat the sandwich, and cleaning the blade of the flick-knife he'd used to cut the bread into pieces, Jason said he was going to find the boy responsible, then pummel him until he threw up the stolen food. But Steve didn't want him to go and put a hand on his big brother's shoulder, asking that he stay for the final minutes of recess.

Most nights Jason kept himself awake until their father was in from the Lucky Clover and passed out on the couch or in his bed.

He felt that he was awake again now. But instead of his brother slumbering in the bed next to him, it was a girl screaming in the backseat of a car, with sick on her clothes.

She didn't care what Jason had done—the way he punched the steering wheel and screamed at that woman in the SUV—or even that he had been a thief and spent time in prison after blinding someone in a fight.

Of all those things, Jason felt suddenly that he had been forgiven, that Steve had forgiven him and was there now, in the trees or in the sky, watching, somewhere close, somewhere without a name.

XXVIII

When Jason threw open the back door, Harvey stopped crying.

"Look at us, Harvey," he said, trying to smile. "We're like clowns!"

He released her from the seat and helped get her clothes off. At first she was embarrassed, but Jason said it was the only way, and draped his motorcycle jacket over her before cleaning up the backseat. Harvey watched him load the sick-heavy clothes and the car seat into a black trash bag he found in the trunk. The bag was already heavy because it contained bits of plastic and metal that Jason had picked up when he drove out to the Northern Parkway to see the place where his brother had died.

He wiped down the vinyl seat using water from a gallon jug, then picked soft bits out of the carpet with his hands. When it was done, Jason carried the trash bag over to a Dumpster sitting in the driveway of a house under construction. With a few swings, he managed to get the bag in. Then he noticed construction workers sitting in a truck eating breakfast. They must have seen everything. Jason took a few steps toward the vehicle and put his thumbs in the air. The driver wound down his window and said it was okay.

As Jason was walking away, one of the men in the back of the truck leaned forward. "I think that's my friend's neighbor," he said. "Really crazy guy."

. . .

THE CAR WAS very hot by the time Jason got back in, and there was little relief from the smell.

"Does this mean I can sit in the front from now on?" Harvey said.

"No," Jason said, adjusting the seat belt on her shoulder. "This is just for today. And if you see a police car, get down."

Old Navy hadn't opened yet, so they sat in the car with the AC running.

"Did you ever throw up in a car before, Jason?" Harvey wanted to know.

Jason nodded. "Yeah, a lot—even once while I was driving."

"Did it go on the windshield?"

"No, it mostly went on the steering wheel."

"I think you would crash if you threw up when you were driving," Harvey said. "Do you think my mom and dad threw up when they were going to die?"

"I don't think anyone really believes they're going to die," Jason said. "Until it's in your face, you know?"

Harvey tried to imagine death in her face. Felt its breath upon her. More heat than fear.

When Jason noticed someone inside Old Navy unlocking the doors, he went around to Harvey's side and gathered her up in his jacket. "What's this?" she said, pointing to a dark stain on the arm where the leather was pockmarked.

"That," Jason said, trying to think of something, "is probably oil."

"Oil!" Harvey screamed. "You said oil was poisoning!"

"That's olive oil, Harvey, not engine oil."

"Why do you have olive—"

"Let's just go in, can we?"

As he lifted her out, Harvey was worried that people might see she was naked under the jacket.

"Just think about your dream outfit," Jason told her. "Because today's the day."

He carried her across the parking lot, then straight through the shop, where hundreds of pairs of blue and pink jeans were suspended on wires.

A teenage worker came over and introduced himself as Tyrone. Jason told him that Harvey's clothes had gotten ruined and it was the first day of school.

"That's too bad," Tyrone said. He asked Harvey what school, but she didn't know.

After they picked out new T-shirts, pants, leggings, and socks with colored dots on them, Tyrone unlocked a fitting room. "Just holler if you need something."

Most everything fit, but Harvey was disappointed that she hadn't found anything with a dog on it.

"I don't know about dogs," Tyrone said when they asked him. "But we got pandas . . ."

When the fitting room door opened, Harvey stepped out in blue sparkly trousers and a shirt with cartwheeling pandas that said PANDA MONIUM. Jason told Tyrone that Harvey was going to wear everything right away, and asked if he could rip off the labels and scan them. Tyrone looked at Harvey in her new clothes. "You Daddy's girl now, right?"

AT MCDONALD'S, JASON asked the woman if they had any fresh Band-Aids for his little girl, and she went to find a manager. After cleaning up Harvey's lip in the restroom, Jason ordered two milkshakes, and carried them to the edge of an empty play area.

"Wish I didn't have to go to school," Harvey said. "Wish I could just stay with you."

"After all this?" Jason said. "If you don't go today, Harvey, you'll never go."

When they finally got to school, Jason wanted to carry Harvey in through the main doors on his shoulders, but she was too embarrassed.

As it turned out, the first day of school was just a morning of orientation for the second-graders, with only an hour left to go.

A gang of parents had gathered in the lobby to wait. They watched Jason sign in. The receptionist explained where the second-grade classroom was. Jason wanted to tell the woman why they were late, but Harvey's face begged him not to say anything.

When they passed the other parents on their way to the classroom, Jason looked straight ahead. The school was in an affluent neighborhood outside Jason's official district, but Wanda's husband was a superintendent and had pulled some strings.

The classroom assistant said she'd been expecting them and helped Harvey get settled in a chair.

Jason watched through a small window in the door. Then he returned to the car and smoked three cigarettes, one after the other.

A few minutes before noon, Jason went back inside the school and stood near the classroom door, but at a distance from the other mothers and fathers. When Harvey appeared, there was blue paint on her hands and on her new panda shirt.

Some of the other children didn't want to leave, so the parents talked about going to Friendly's for lunch. Harvey asked if they could go too.

When they got home, at least a hundred more flowers had been planted in the front yard. Harvey got out of the car and ran to look at them. She thought Jason had done it while she was in class. But Jason said he'd just been waiting outside.

"Maybe fairies? Or angels?" Harvey said.

"Or Wanda."

"But it could be angels, right?"

After making peanut butter sandwiches, they sat on the front step near the flowers. Jason opened a soda to share, but Harvey said she wanted milk, so he had to go back inside.

"Looks like a real garden now," Harvey said when Jason returned. Then she took the glass but it slipped out of her hand. The bottom step turned white. Jason got up and went into the house. Harvey stood holding her sandwich but not eating.

"Are you mad?" she said when he appeared with a roll of paper towels.

"Yeah," Jason said, looking at her. "But I'm tired of it, Harvey. I'm tired of being mad."

XXIX

AFTER THEY ATE sandwiches on the steps at Versailles and shared a bottle of water, Harvey said they should go exploring. Above their heads, birds flew in arcs toward the palace, disappearing into tufts of nest beneath the windows.

Morning tours of the interior were concluding, and people were coming out into the gardens with paper maps and cameras. In some places it was difficult to walk a straight path without being caught in the background of someone else's memories.

When Harvey had to take a work call on her cell phone, Jason listened to his daughter speak French. In a few years, he thought, she would be thirty years old, though never completely a woman in his eyes—more a child pretending to be a woman and convincing everyone in the world except her father. With each passing year, she needed him less. And one day, probably soon, she would find some stranger to share all the feelings she had once shared with him. This eventual, unspoken loss was something Jason thought about after his best friend, Vincent, got married a few years ago.

One night they were all in front of the television. The Mets had lost and *The Simpsons* was on. Whenever Vincent found something funny and laughed, his wife laughed too, and they turned to face each other. And when Vincent's glass was empty, his wife noticed it was empty and said, "Another pop, Vince?" or "How 'bout something to eat Vin'?"

That night Jason sat on his front stoop in the darkness and thought about the woman who had once loved him, who had once tried to help him. The sound of her name in his mouth brought it all back, as though no time had passed since their separation.

When Harvey was a senior in high school, she had asked her father one night at dinner why he never dated anyone. "I want you to be happy, Dad," she said. "I think you should find someone."

"Think about it this way," Jason had tried to explain. "I'm a single parent with no money, a dead-end job, a fake leg, bad teeth, and a criminal record. Plus I'm a recovering alcoholic. What loser could ever love a person like that?"

Harvey stood up so quickly her chair fell backward. Then she went outside and Jason could hear her crying on the patio. When he realized why she was so upset, it was like a flood through his body.

WHEN HARVEY HAD finished on the phone, Jason asked if she would take a photo of him, maybe with the palace in the background.

"Oh my God, Dad—are you actually going to smile for once? Stand here," she said, and positioned him beneath a statue. Then she took a few steps back. "C'mon, Dad," she pleaded. "Just a little one . . ."

"I am smiling," he said. "This is how I smile."

"I don't have one picture of you happy—not one picture where you're smiling."

"I smile on the inside, kiddo. You know that."

"You're just weird, Dad. But I love you anyway."

"I love you too, Harv."

She remembered the first time they had said it to each other.

She was in her bedroom crying over something. He was outside her door, pacing the hall in his socks. Was it that first day of second grade? She couldn't be sure, all she knew was that it started in the afternoon, after going out to get the mail.

Jason was stuffing the soiled car seat cover into the washer. She remembers the faint aroma of vomit, and the discoloration on dark fabric as it dropped silently into the machine.

"Your favorite magazine is here."

"Okay."

"Don't you want it?"

"Just leave it on the couch."

Harvey watched Jason pour detergent in, then looked at the magazine in her hand. On the cover was a tattooed woman in a bikini and cowboy boots, sitting on a motorcycle. Harvey held up the magazine. "Can I open it?"

"Just put it on the couch, like I said."

After dinner, Harvey asked if she could sit with him and flick through the magazine. "I want to be a mechanic when I grow up, remember? Might help me to see engines."

Jason was clearing the plates. "What do you want for lunch tomorrow?"

Harvey didn't know.

"Hot dogs and potato salad?"

"If you don't look at the magazine, how are you going to finish your motorcycle?"

"I ain't going to finish it," Jason said. "That bike is a pipe dream."

He carried the remaining dishes into the kitchen, then returned with a fresh pack of Camel cigarettes.

"What's a pipe dream?"

"Something that'll never happen."

"Why is building your motorcycle a pipe dream?"

"Because I ain't got the money," he said, taking a cigarette from the pack. "I'm going out to the patio."

Then Harvey thought of something. "If you stopped smoking, you could use the money to build your motorcycle. Then it wouldn't be a pipe dream anymore!"

She considered getting down from the table and shouting *Eureka*—the way she'd seen SpongeBob do once when he had a good idea.

Jason laughed mockingly. "Good one," he said, then opened the patio door just enough to let himself out.

When he came back in, Harvey heard him banging the ashtray against the side of the trash can. Then the faucet. Then the freezer drawer opening. She knew it was ice cream because the lid on the container made a *pluk* sound.

"I want to stay here with you tomorrow," she said when Jason appeared with two bowls. "I can help you build your motorcycle instead of going to school."

"Gotta go to school, kid."

"But I don't need school. I already changed the oil. I could work at Jiffy Lube."

"How you gonna make any friends? A little girl gotta have friends."

"I'm not little anymore," Harvey tried to explain, searching the room with her eyes for something to prove it. "And I don't want to go back to second grade."

Jason opened a newspaper and flicked through the pages. "I thought you had a good time."

"No, I didn't."

"What about your new outfit with the pandas? And when I picked you up, you didn't want to come home, remember? You wanted Friendly's."

Harvey looked at the rough black hair on Jason's cheeks. There was a vein in his neck that always stuck out and made him look like he was shouting, even when he was eating ice cream and reading *Newsday*.

"Where are *your* friends?" she asked him. "Where are the friends *you* made in second grade?"

"When you're done with that ice cream, go and get ready for bed. It's been a long day, and we're both tired."

"What's on TV tonight?"

"Nothing until you've got your pajamas on."

"What then?"

"Maybe a movie."

Harvey mashed the rest of her ice cream into a paste. "There's always movies," she said. "They're always on."

"When you've finished eating, go wash up and get your pajamas on."

Harvey stopped mashing and dropped the spoon into her dish. "But it's still light out!"

"You have school tomorrow, and if you wanna watch TV, do as I say."

She snorted. "Then I don't wanna watch TV."

"Go get ready for bed."

"But I'm still eating."

"When you've finished."

"I'm not going to school tomorrow."

"Yes, you are."

"You don't have a best friend, and I don't need one either."

Jason closed the newspaper and snatched Harvey's dish from under her chin.

"Hey!" she cried. "I wasn't finished!"

"There's nothin' in it," Jason said, sticking his finger into a pink pool at the center of the bowl. "It's just juice."

"I like the juice."

"Go clean up for bed."

"I'm not dirty."

Jason stopped, halfway to the kitchen, and turned to the wall. "You threw up in the car," he said in a low voice. "You threw up all over yourself."

Harvey just sat there with her arms folded.

"Then you can go to bed right now," he growled, "with no fucking movie and no bedtime book. I'm going out for a smoke."

Harvey slid off her chair and followed him to the patio door.

"Don't be in this room when I get back."

"Mom said you were mean!"

"I don't give a shit what your mom said."

"And my dad never cursed like you. He didn't smoke either."

Jason took the cigarette out of his mouth. "Well, then, it's lucky I'm not your dad, ain't it?"

When he came back in, Harvey was sitting on the floor crying. He tried to speak, but she ran to her room and threw herself on the bed. It felt like she was in the air for a long time.

She wanted to do it again, then remembered she was upset and felt afraid. She wondered if Wanda would come and take her away for being naughty, and remembered her smug face at the table, talking back to Jason in a way she had impulsively thought was grown up and would impress him.

A minute later there was a knock, and she heard Jason say through the door he was sorry.

"Go away!" Harvey yelled. "I hate you."

But he didn't go away.

"Go away," she said again.

But he just stood there, shuffling his feet. She could hear him outside her door, shuffling his feet, unable to say the words, but she knew.

XXX

THERE WERE PEOPLE out rowing on the lake, though some were just going in circles and laughing. Harvey said she wanted to be on the water too, so they handed over some identification, and an attendant walked them along a floating dock to a white boat.

"Wow, you're good at rowing, Dad," Harvey said as Jason pulled them past the other boaters.

Jason shook his head. "Who the hell makes a boat where you can't see where you're going?"

"Uh sailors, Dad, for like, hundreds of years," she said with a laugh. "Just look over your shoulder. It's easy when you get used to it."

When they were in the middle of the lake, Jason brought the oars up onto the sides of the boat. Harvey reached into the bag for some lemon cake. There was a baseball hat stuffed into a side pocket, and Jason asked for it. Yellow writing on the front said TRIUMPH MOTORCYCLES.

After eating the rest of their food, Harvey wanted to row. Jason hovered over her, but Harvey said she could do it by herself.

Rowing was harder than she'd thought, and one of the oars kept skimming the surface of the water. When she turned to ask her father how she was doing, she noticed he was soaking wet.

"Oh my God, I'm so sorry!"

"Keep practicing, Harvey."

By now, many of the other boaters had gone in; it was hot and there was little shade. When Jason had the oars again, Harvey took off one shoe and let her foot trail in the water. They were at the far end of the lake, where there were no attendants to say she couldn't.

Jason stared at her from under his cap. "Want to talk about the Peter Rabbit cup you got me?"

Harvey's eyes fell to her father's hands on the oars. The wood was dark where water had soaked in, and she remembered the painting of an old man and a child in a rowboat, something she'd seen on a school trip to a museum. The girl had on a flowing, dirty dress and the man had a pipe in his mouth. In the boat was a net of fish. Harvey had wondered if any of the fish were still alive, and if the girl in the picture felt sorry for them. She wanted to know if the girl could swim, and thought how the dress would pull her down. Harvey's teacher saw her looking and came over. "He loves that little girl so much," the teacher said. "You can just tell."

The sun was so strong by midafternoon that Harvey felt somehow at a distance from her life. She hoped her father would drop the subject of the Peter Rabbit cup until later, when they were home in the shade with something cold to drink. But he kept asking.

"It was the only cup in the set that didn't get broken, all thanks to you," she said weakly.

After a few more strokes, they reached a bank. Jason took a rope at the front of the boat and attached it to a ring in the grass. "Let's sit out of the heat for a while under those trees," he said.

"Can we do that, Dad?"

"That's why they put the ring and rope there," he said.

"But I don't think those rings have been used for a long time," Harvey pointed out, fingering the rusty circle. "I don't know if we're supposed to tie these boats up."

"They don't care as long as we're paying for the time."

The grass was a hard dark green and grew unevenly around the trunk of a gnarled tree. It felt good to lay down in the shade.

"How did you know the Peter Rabbit cup came from a set?" her father wanted to know. He had taken the cup from the lunch bag and was holding it.

Without sitting up, Harvey said her first dad had told her stories about his childhood, and one of the stories was about the Peter Rabbit cup.

"It would have been better if he'd told you nothing," Jason said.

Harvey lifted her head to look at him. "If I'd known it would upset you," she said, "I wouldn't have put it in your Father's Day box."

"It's just ancient history, that's all I'm saying."

"But it's *your* ancient history, Dad. And it's my story now too."

Jason sensed that she was trying to fit together all the different pieces of her life, and it reminded him that above all else, he was there to look after her.

"Wanda told me that you'd see things differently with each new stage of your life. She was right about that, I guess."

A breeze rolled over the lake making ripples.

"She was right about everything," Harvey said. "Wanda's amazing."

"We should send her a postcard from Paris. She's retired now, you know?"

"I told Wanda everything I could about you," Harvey admitted. "That's why she brought me to see you in the first place—because I told her you were special."

"She called me first," Jason said. "Then she came to visit. Then she brought you."

"I remember," Harvey said. "We were in the car. It was a station wagon, and there were all these paper towels on the seat next to me."

Harvey thought of Miss Bateman. Her late-night whispering phone calls. How young she must have been then.

"It was raining, and the windows were fogged up. I was drawing a picture and it looked like a motorcycle. And then I thought of you, and I told Wanda everything my dad told me, but I also made a few things up. I knew it was dishonest, but I wanted her to feel what I felt, so I made things up. Is that okay, that I lied to Wanda?"

"What did you tell Wanda about the Peter Rabbit cup?"

"My dad said that your father came home one night, took all the birth china out of the living room cabinet, and smashed it under his boots. But then he realized there was a piece missing."

"That's right," Jason said softly. "Because I'd taken it the night before—just by chance."

Harvey moved closer to her father across the grass so she could hear. In the distance, a young family was splashing about. Their laughter mixing with the sound of water.

"What else did you tell Wanda?"

"Something about how you nursed my father back to

health by making him take medicine from the Peter Rabbit cup. Is that true, Dad?"

"Yes. But it's not why the cup was missing."

"I wanted so much for Wanda to like you, so I just made things up."

Harvey handed her father a tissue to wipe the sweat on his face.

"But you'd never met me."

"I just knew," Harvey said, rearranging her skirt. "Weird, right?"

A FTER SWEEPING OUT all the pieces with his arm and stomping on them in his work boots, Jason's father had some-how managed to sneak Steve out of bed without his older son waking up.

But then Jason opened his eyes and saw his brother's covers pulled back.

His father had never done anything to Steve before, but he was older now, had soft hairs over his lip; and was playing baseball and traveling to games on a bus with other boys.

Jason looked through the crack in the door and saw his brother sitting on the carpet in his underwear. Steve was too young for his muscles to have any definition, and the tops of his arms and his back were covered in goose bumps.

Their father kept saying he would sit there until admitting where the missing Peter Rabbit cup was. What remained of the set lay broken on the carpet between them, like the ruins of a once great city.

When their father reached down and picked up a piece of the broken china as though he meant to throw it, Jason stepped out from behind the door and stood beside his brother. Before his father could say anything, Jason blurted out that Steve had done nothing—that *he* had borrowed the Peter Rabbit cup because he wanted to draw it for art class at school. When Jason looked down at his brother, his thighs were wet because he'd been crying.

Their mother was awake now too, and watching from her bedroom doorway, watching everything in her robe. She had saved up two years for that christening china; had wanted something she could pass down through the family. When their father noticed his wife behind him, he gestured toward the broken pieces, as though unveiling a work of art.

"Look what they made me do," he said. "Your best china."

It was the middle of the night.

Then Steve just got up and ran into his room. Their father bolted after him, but Jason blocked his path.

It was like bricks being dropped on his body from a height, but not once did he cry out or make a noise. Steve was listening and would not have been able to forget.

The next morning their mother wouldn't let Jason go to school in case the teachers said something. She was mad at them for not giving their father the Peter Rabbit cup. Over breakfast, she told Steve and Jason that it was unfair to gang up against their father. When Steve started bawling into his Lucky Charms, their mother just stood there. "You can cry all you want to, Steven, but that's *his* food you're eating, and this is *his* roof we all live under. Next time think about how you behave, and things like this won't happen." Then she knelt so her head was level with their eyes. "He's a good man deep down," she said. "I wish you could see that."

THEY ROWED BACK across the lake toward the palace in silence.

Harvey kicked off her shoes again and trailed both feet in the brown-tinted water. When the assistant came to moor the boat, he was in good spirits because it was almost closing. The other attendants were smoking cigarettes and gesturing to some Italian students trying to paddle back with their hands.

Everyone was moving toward the exit, and the sun cast long shadows over the statues and the fountains where people had been posing for photographs.

As they reached the edge of the gardens, near where they had entered, Harvey's eye was drawn by motion to one of the borders. A bird was mincing on the gravel, trying to take flight on a single wing. The other wing was spread out on the gravel, covered in dust. The bird's chest heaved with each effort. It knew that Harvey and her father were there but did not look at them.

"What should we do?" Harvey said. "I think its wing is broken."

DURING THEIR SECOND full summer together, Harvey got addicted to a show on National Geographic Juniors. It showed kids curing animals or rescuing them or saving their lives by learning how they ate and made homes. There was a seal cub that washed up in Florida, her parents the victims of a boat propeller. No one had known what to do until the

Simon Van Booy

National Geographic Juniors arrived in a Jeep with their logo on the side, and hoisted the seal into a bathtub on the back of a truck.

Jason and Harvey watched the show every week, as the seal grew up and became more accustomed to her new surroundings. The National Geographic Juniors team named the seal Salad. Eventually though, Salad would have to go back in the sea. Everyone knew that. But for now she was safe living on a bed of wet towels at the aquatic center.

After the first show, Harvey told Jason she wanted to be a National Geographic Junior.

"I thought you wanted to work at Jiffy Lube?" Jason said.

A week later, he was passing Harvey's bedroom when he heard voices.

"I'm sorry to tell you this, Gordon—but you've got fleas, and you won't be able to sleep with the others tonight . . ."

Later, instead of just brushing her teeth and going into bed, Harvey insisted on taking Jason on a tour of the hospital in her bedroom, describing each animal's condition, and explaining why he or she had been arranged in a particular box with blankets made from folded squares of toilet tissue.

"I like the camel," Jason said, patting its head. "Hey, Gordon."

"Please don't disturb him," Harvey said. "Gordon is very ill."

"I thought he had fleas . . ."

"No, he has cancer from smoking."

WHEN SHE GOT into bed, Jason watched her pull the sheets up. But instead of saying good night and turning over, she just lay with her eyes open.

"You've never really tucked me in before," she said.

"Tucked you in?"

"Mom and Dad used to tuck me in."

"You mean tuck the sides of the sheets?"

"That's how it starts," she said. "I'll show you . . ."

Jason found the edge of the blanket and forced it under the mattress.

"Now pat the covers down," Harvey said. "And make sure the kid inside is sort of trapped."

When it was done, Jason watched Harvey get comfortable under the tight sheets.

"Now," Harvey said, "lean down and pretend to give the child a hug. That's the last bit."

"Pretend to give you a hug?"

"Or a real one, it's up to you."

WHEN THEY SPOTTED an official palace gardener digging in the soil beside a wheelbarrow, Jason went over and beckoned him to follow. When he saw Harvey and the bird on the gravel, he shook his head, and Jason could tell there was nothing to be done.

When Harvey spoke to the gardener in French, he pointed up at the small mounds of dirt beneath the window ledges. He explained the problem to Harvey, and she translated it for her father: "The nests are too high," she said. "And even if he could reach them, the other birds would reject the injured one."

They all looked at the bird, which was sucking up pieces of gravel and spitting them out.

"It is the nature," the gardener said in English, smoothing the front of his apron.

Then Harvey spoke to him in French again.

"Oui, Madame," the gardener replied, putting on his gloves.

"I asked him to move it away from the sun," she told her father.

"Maybe give him a worm too," Jason said. "That's what I'd want."

The bird seemed to know it had been in an accident and was dying. It had stopped trying to move, and on the surface of its round black eye were tiny, identical versions of Harvey and her father standing side by side.

"I know it's silly," Harvey said, "but I feel like crying. I want to cry."

"It's not silly," Jason said, putting his arm around her.

When they were past the gift shop, Harvey pointed out the lines of people trudging back to the subway and said they should find a taxi, because she didn't feel like getting on a train and fighting for a seat.

Outside the gates, a line of cabs stood waiting. When the driver saw them, he started the engine.

"Hot," he said as they got in. "Too hot."

A few minutes into the journey, Jason looked around for the lunch bag and realized he'd left it on the grass back at the palace.

Harvey was annoyed. "Don't tell me the Peter Rabbit cup was in there! That was one of your presents . . ."

Jason said he was sorry, but after a while Harvey realized that it didn't matter, that someone would find it, and the story of their afternoon on the lake at Versailles would be as much a mystery to the new owner as the story of the person who had made the cup in an English factory decades ago, on a morning or an afternoon, in summer or in winter, painting the rabbits with a small brush before stopping to eat something—perhaps even going outside where there were real rabbits, and a war had not long ago been fought and won.

XXXI

WHEN THEY WERE halfway back to Paris, Harvey's cell phone vibrated. Her tutor, Leon, wanted to know if she could bring her father over for dinner. One of his students had canceled and the evening was open.

Leon's apartment was on a busy, narrow street near a well-known bakery, and when they got there, people were lining up for their evening baguettes.

Harvey rang the buzzer. After a click, she pushed on a wooden door that led into a courtyard of recycling bins, children's toys, and plants in pots. At the bottom of a staircase was a purple tricycle, which Jason had difficulty stepping over.

Leon's daughter, Isobel, met them at the door. She flung her arms around Harvey, then looked up at Jason. "Alloo," she said, and ran away.

Leon was wearing an apron, and there was classical music on the radio. "It's so wonderful you could come," he said. "It's a joy for me that you are both here."

Harvey led her father into the sitting room while Leon made drinks. In the oven was a mound of paella crowned with giant crayfish. Leon said that the electricity kept going off and he was having a hard time getting anything prepared.

Isobel perched on a wooden chair opposite Jason with her knees pulled up. She was in her socks and had pumped floral room spray onto her shirt.

"Don't ask what's for dinner," Isobel said, puffing her cheeks out as though she were about to get sick.

Jason chuckled. "That bad, huh?"

They could hear Leon hitting the side of a pot, then something drop into a pan of hot oil.

When they gathered at the table, Isobel watched her father serve the paella and made retching sounds whenever his tongs touched the crayfish. Leon said something to her in French, and she stared silently at the single slice of microwave pizza on her plate.

Over dinner, Jason told stories about Harvey growing up. Whenever he finished speaking, Isobel would make a rolling motion with her hand and say, "Keep going, please . . ."

Then everything went dark, and the classical music coming from the radio ceased. Leon apologized and said he would have to reset the fuse box in the cellar.

"But there are spiders down there," Isobel said. "What if you don't come back?"

"We can't eat in the dark," her father told her.

"Blind people do," Isobel said gleefully. "Every day of their lives."

THE MOMENT THE lights went off, Harvey screamed and dropped her spoon. Jason said it was a power cut because everyone on Long Island was running their air conditioners.

Harvey wanted to know what a power cut was, and if they would have to live in the dark for the rest of their lives.

When Jason went to find a flashlight, Harvey panicked. "Help!" she cried. "Where are you? Help! Don't leave me alone!"

For a moment there was no sound or movement. Then she felt Jason's hand on the top of her head. "Wherever *I* go," he said very quietly, "*we* go."

"Okay, but why are you whispering?"

"I don't know. I guess because it's dark."

They couldn't see anything. Even the streetlights were out. Harvey said it was as though the world had closed its eyes.

They got up and felt their way around the house. Harvey knew when they were in the garage by the smell of oil and the cool, stale air. In her mind she could see Jason's bike on the ground, assembled now into what he called a "rolling frame."

Finally, Jason found the toolbox with the flashlight inside, but when he clicked the button, nothing happened. Harvey asked if she could try.

There were no candles in the house either, and the batteries in the TV remote control were not the right size for the flashlight.

Jason said the couch would be the safest place for them to stay until the power came back on, and that Harvey would have to sleep there too, which she was happy about. Harvey wanted to know what would happen if the power stayed off for a week. Jason said he could build a fire in the backyard and they could grill whatever was in the freezer.

"What if we get attacked?" Harvey said. "By robbers?"

"That ain't going to happen," Jason said. "I wouldn't let that happen."

"Do I still have to put my shoes away when I get home from school?"

"No, Harvey—while the power is off, you can leave them by the door. Which is what you do most of the time, anyway."

They spent the next hour fetching things they would need to get them through the night. The first trip was to Harvey's bedroom, where she identified (by squeeze) Duncan, Lester, Jig, Mr. & Mrs., Simple Bear, Blue Bear, Tuesday, Foxy, and Megatronus.

After that, Jason felt in the cupboards for cookies, donuts, cans of soda, bars of chocolate, and chips. Then they sat together as if watching television, except that it was dark and couldn't even see each other.

Jason doled out some of the snacks and they slurped soda from the can. Then it started to feel late, even though Jason said it was only eight o'clock.

Harvey asked what would happen if she needed to pee. Jason said he'd carry her.

"Okay," she said. "Because I need to go."

Jason thought it was best if she got on his back so that his arms were free.

"It's so weird," he said, "to be creeping through our own house like we've never been here before."

Harvey wanted Jason to sit in the bathroom with her, but Jason said he'd come in only to help wipe when she was done. She had a habit of rushing, and he told her to sit for a while so they wouldn't have to come back in ten minutes. Then he got down with his back against the door. It reminded him of their first outing at the mall, when she needed to go and he didn't know what to do.

Even though Harvey was almost in third grade, Jason felt she was still too young to go in public restrooms alone. A few times other men made comments, saying he couldn't bring a girl into the men's room—perhaps not realizing he was a single father. The first time it happened, Jason told the man to mind his own goddamn business, but Harvey told Jason off when they got outside, said he shouldn't be so rude even when the other person was wrong. The next time it happened, Jason just nodded at the guy, then did a hundred push-ups in the garage with his teeth clenched the moment they got home.

"Hey, Harvey," he said, tapping on the door. "Remember our first trip to the mall? How I made you go in the restroom with that random woman?"

Harvey laughed.

Then Jason asked why she'd taken off at the Little League game.

"I don't know," Harvey said. "Guess I wanted you to come and find me."

"How would I have known where to look?"

Harvey said she didn't know, but it seemed like the right thing to do at the time.

"What if you'd gotten hit by a car?"

"Then at least I would be with Mom and Dad."

"You shouldn't say that."

"But they're in heaven."

"It doesn't work like that."

"But aren't they in heaven with the angels?"

"Yeah, sure, *they* are in heaven, but *you* are on Long Island sitting on the can during a power cut."

"But I'll go to heaven one day," Harvey said. "Then I'll see them again."

Jason's eyes moved around for something to see, but the darkness was impenetrable.

"Anyway," Harvey went on. "You're older, so you'll probably be in heaven before me and can say hi." Jason could hear her getting off the toilet. "You'll say hi to them from me, right?"

"I ain't going to heaven, Harvey. People like me don't get in."

Jason wondered if his comment would make her cry. But then her voice came through the door. "I'm sure my dad has told God all about you. You know he had a jewelry business at the mall?"

"Yeah. So what?"

"He sold golden crosses, and some of them had Jesus on, so you're definitely going to heaven."

When the door opened, she felt in the air for Jason's hand. "You're the sort of person they want up there," she said.

When they got back to the couch, Harvey lay on top of her blanket, and went to sleep.

Jason was on the floor with his eyes open, listening to insects scratch in the trees. Then he reached out and fingered the hem of the couch, then moved his head toward the television, the patio door, the kitchen . . . familiar places he knew were there but had to be imagined.

In the darkness there was a door to the garage behind which his tools hung on nails above the workbench. Next to it was the rolling frame Harvey liked to sit on and pretend she was riding across America to the famous bike show Jason had told her about in South Dakota.

He continued lying there, very still, looking at things he

could no longer see—but which, he knew, somehow held their lives together.

As a teenager, Jason had no safe place—only safe things, like his flick-knife, the toys he stole for Steve, and the wax that allowed him to style his hair like James Dean. He used to cut his arms deliberately in the bathroom at school. It was an emblem—a visible sign of the suffering that pulled him apart every day. Cutting was a pain he could control, a release from mental anguish, and what a thrill at the sudden line of blood a moment after the knife crossed.

Only two people knew about that. The first was Rita Vega, the woman he had once been in love with. He thought of her now in the darkness as he listened to the rise and fall of Harvey's breathing. He even said her name several times without moving his lips—and heard her voice say *Jason*.

She would be in darkness now too, he thought.

He imagined that Rita was down there on the floor with him. The smell of shampoo in her hair. The cushions moving as she tried to get comfortable. Every day some part of her rose to the surface of his life.

Another person he'd told things to, and who knew about the cutting, was someone he met during his incarceration. A young prison minister who sat Jason down and asked if he could name five good things about the world. Jason had been able to think of only one: that his little brother had managed to avoid getting beaten, and was probably going to graduate high school and have an awesome life.

Encouraged, the minister asked him to go on, to tell him more. It was simple, Jason said. The good of his brother's life outweighed the terror, so Steve wasn't afraid of everything.

The minister leaned forward and put his hands close to Jason. "And are you afraid?" he said. "Do you live in fear?"

"Of course," Jason told him, grabbing more of the candy the minister had used to entice him into the meeting. "Why else do you think I messed that guy up in the bar? Aren't we all afraid, Father?"

The minister couldn't believe it. "Yes," he said. "It's remarkable that you can verbalize it. But tell me, if you know this, Jason—why do you still act out? Why did you hit your cellmate in the face with your lunch tray last week?"

"Why do you believe in God?" Jason said, reaching for another handful of jelly beans. "There's no proof of it."

"Because I *feel* it . . ." the minister said.

"Well, I feel rage," Jason said. "So that's what I believe. That's my religion."

Jason could tell the minister liked him. That he was intrigued with what he was saying.

"If only you would let God in," the minister said, "you might start to feel otherwise."

"That's *your* savior," Jason said. "The only god I know is the one who left his son to die on the cross with his mother watching."

STEVE'S IMAGINED FUTURE happiness was the reason Jason never wanted to see him again. To get involved in his life once out on parole would almost certainly have led to his younger brother's ruin.

The one time he came close to failing was when Steve graduated from high school. A week before, Jason bought a dress shirt and some slacks from a discount store. Each day he came up with a new excuse as to why he should show up at the ceremony. But deep down he knew they were all lies, and the deceit reminded him of his father.

Then graduation day came, and after half a bottle of bourbon, Jason dressed himself in the fancy clothes and set out by bus for his old high school. But then he got close and saw families parking their cars and moving in groups toward the football field. He stood and watched the procession of rented suits and silk dresses, uncomfortable shoes and gelled hair.

Everyone would know he'd been in prison. Everyone would remember how he'd broken a janitor's nose freshman year, and that their mother had killed herself in the bathroom without her clothes on.

Worse yet, he knew that a single comment could set him off.

Jason could see the police with their fat bellies and shaved heads. Could already feel them dragging his cuffed body across the lawn. Steve would be there, begging them, pulling on their arms, on the verge of anger himself.

In some ways he just couldn't understand what was happening. Their father had been dead for several years, yet the danger of violence seemed greater than ever.

He turned and ran back the way he had come, crossing block after block, following streets the bus had taken only moments before, dodging cars at intersections, jumping up and down curbs in his thrift-store dress shoes.

When he could go no farther, he dragged his body through an open gate and collapsed in the wood chips of an empty playground, his fancy shirt saturated with sweat, and a tear in the seat of his pants.

When his breath returned and the sweat on his body had

dried, Jason got up and brushed off his clothes. Then he sat on a swing and imagined the ceremony taking place across town. Steve getting helped into his gown by the teacher he was living with. He might even have a girlfriend. What if she were graduating too? Her parents would make a big deal of it for both of them—give a dinner in their honor, include Steve as one of their own.

Jason could already envision his brother's diploma, framed on the wall of a split-level home with two cars in the driveway. A wife who spent Sunday in the garden, and folded his clothes at night; who planned surprise birthday parties, and made albums of the places they went, the things they saw.

Jason gripped the chains that suspended the plastic seat, then pushed off—letting his body swing through the air, as though he weighed nothing at all and could have gone on forever, with only his mind for company.

He imagined the applause, the podium where each graduate would be officially recognized. Then his brother in a satin gown, shaking hands with the principal, who leans in to give words of encouragement before finally presenting the diploma. Like the others, Steve is supposed to walk off the stage, but instead, stands for a moment, lingers in the midst of their shared victory—perhaps even unraveling the scroll and raising it to a surge of applause.

In Jason's mind, it's like the end of a movie, with music and wide shots as people in the crowd leap to their feet, whistle with two fingers, and toss the flat, rented graduation hats high in the air, screaming and holding on to each other's bodies. Then the camera freezes on a single moment; fades to black, but you can still hear voices as the mottled lockers and empty classrooms, uneaten sandwiches and scribbled yearbooks, nicknames and first kisses, begin their retreat to that flickering, unattainable country of childhood.

XXXII

WHEN THEY WOKE up next morning, the electricity was back on and their dinners lay half-eaten from the night before.

After wiping Harvey's mouth and hands with a cool cloth, Jason reset the air conditioner and cleared the table for breakfast. Harvey watched him spread a wave of butter over her toast and asked if there was going to be another power cut.

With time to go before school, Harvey carried a glass of milk to the front step. The flowers from last summer were in full bloom, and she wondered if they would ever be taller than the house. When her glass was empty she went back inside. Jason was vacuuming crumbs off the couch. Then he went out to the patio and smoked a cigarette.

Harvey was curious to see how Long Island would look after a night without power, but nothing had changed, and the faces of other drivers showed no sign of having gone to bed blind.

When Jason got back from dropping her off, he spent several hours writing descriptions on his computer and listing items for sale on his eBay site. When he added up the approximate value of everything, he was still a little short for the month, so he sat on the front steps with a mug of coffee, and searched in his mind for anything he could sell at a quick profit.

After a second cup on the couch, he decided to look in the

attic. It was another warm day, and the moment he stepped off the ladder could feel his shirt begin to stick. Near the opening, Jason discovered a pair of silver-handled salad servers, some Mickey Mouse comics from the 1950s, a Donald Duck telephone, ten Brooklyn Dodgers baseball cards that smelled like mothballs, and a brass candlestick. There was also a vintage Snoopy doll still in the box with the original price sticker. Jason had bought most of the items at a Catholic thrift store in Commack, at a time when he was flush with profitable inventory.

Wondering what other treasures lay undiscovered, he went in deeper, opening boxes, and making small tears to see inside plastic bags. In a far corner of the attic, near some exposed insulation, was a plastic container of semi-valuable items that Wanda had stuffed into boxes before his brother's house was repossessed following the accident. There were watches, a pearl necklace, pocketbooks, letters, books, and photographs in manila envelopes with dates written on the outside. Jason sat on a rafter, and raised each picture to his face the way a jeweler looks at rare stones.

His eyes stinging with sweat, he came downstairs with his eBay finds and a dozen photographs, which he looked at again in the light, over an egg salad sandwich and glass of orange soda.

He tried to imagine the sounds and the voices when each picture was taken. How unlikely their fate would have seemed to them.

IN THE CAR on the way home from school, Jason told Harvey she had a surprise waiting—but all she cared about was a boy who had borrowed her pencil and then lost it. When they got home, she kicked her shoes off at the door and went to watch TV.

"Harvey!" Jason called after her. "Put your shoes away."

As she slid over to the hall cupboard in her socks, Jason waited for her to notice. But she just slid back to the couch, scooping up the remote on her way.

"I was in the attic today," he said. "I found some pictures of you and your parents."

Harvey was flicking through the channels. It was so hot outside, she said. And were there ice pops in the freezer? Was that the surprise he'd told her about in the car? Or was it McDonald's?

OVER DINNER, JASON decided he couldn't wait any longer for her to notice, and told her that he'd framed and hung some old photos, at a height where Harvey could see them. *That* was her surprise.

"Oh," she said, shoveling refried beans onto a tortilla. "So it's not a toy or anything?"

"I got some nice frames at Marshalls. I'm surprised you didn't notice, Harvey. They're all around the house."

Harvey looked at the tortilla in her hand. "It's parent-teacher night next week."

"Oh, cool," Jason said, imagining himself in her little orange chair, listening to the teacher go on about drawings and macaroni art.

"Didn't you get a letter or something, Harvey? Usually, they send a letter or something, don't they?"

"It's in my backpack."

"When did you get it?"

"You don't have to go. I can just tell them you're working."

"But I'm not working."

"But we can tell them that."

"Don't you want me to go?"

JASON WENT OVER their conversation as he washed dishes.

Harvey was watching television. Jason could hear the voices of cartoon children, laughing and finding things out.

After making coffee, he sat on the couch, but his presence did not distract Harvey from the flickering screen.

When the cartoon was over, Jason got up. "Come and look at the pictures," he said. "I spent the whole frickin' day putting them up, Harv."

Harvey melted reluctantly off the couch, then followed Jason into the hall. When she stopped in front of the first picture, all she could do was grimace. "You can't even see my face," she said, touching the image of herself in a green snowsuit. "Are you sure it's me?"

"I had it blown up, Harvey. It looks like you're building a snowman in the yard of your old house. Don't you remember that?"

Harvey thought for a moment. "I broke a mug of hot chocolate and got in trouble," she said. "Snow is soft, but the mug still broke."

Standing before the largest image—a grainy candid photograph of her parents leaving church on their wedding day—Harvey asked Jason if he knew who the people in the picture were, because she couldn't tell.

He tried to disguise his anger with a laugh, but the words

came out quickly. "That's your dad and your mom, Harvey. Can't you see that?"

"Yeah, but I wasn't born then," she said. "So we were strangers."

The last one, at the end of the hall near Jason's bedroom, was a baby picture. "Look how little you were," Jason said. "Look how tiny."

But Harvey just looked past Jason toward the sound of the TV. "I think *SpongeBob* is on. Wanna watch it with me?"

When SpongeBob had finished, Harvey got up and went to her room.

After an hour flicking through the channels, Jason heard banging on the drum set and listened at her door. Then he went to the freezer, took a joint from a Ziploc bag, and sucked down a few hits on the patio.

She was trying to beat out the rhythm he'd taught her last week, but kept stopping to rest her arms.

Jason poured grape juice into a tall glass inscribed with the logo of the Hard Rock Café New York, then carried it to Harvey's door and knocked. "Want some juice?"

As she was gulping it down, Jason told her not to use the drumsticks until she got the rhythm going with her foot. "Try it," he said. "One, two, three, four . . . one, two, three, four . . . one, two . . ." He took the glass away, then counted and watched her foot flap on the steel pedal.

"Now bang the drum on the count of three, like this," he said, doing it in the air. "When you have that down, use the other drumstick to hit this one." He pointed. "But don't do the third one until— Harvey, are you listening?"

"Just let me do it my way."

Jason had told her all this before, but she kept forgetting. He wondered if memory needed to grow and strengthen, like the other muscles.

But then suddenly, Harvey was doing it on all three drums. Jason made guitar noises that he thought went along with the beat.

When Harvey lost the rhythm and stopped drumming, Jason clapped and told her to take a bow. Harvey said she didn't care, but was blushing. Jason could feel the buoyancy of the marijuana inside him, thoughts unraveling too quickly to remember.

He told Harvey he'd be right back, then returned with a portable CD player and some cookies. Harvey stopped drumming and watched him plug it into the wall.

"I'm going to put on some Nirvana," he said. "Try and play along as best you can."

For a while he watched her arms flail as she tried in vain to keep rhythm. But after listening to the same song a few times, she got some good beats going, and Jason sang along as the words came back to him.

When Harvey got tired, she put her drumsticks in the empty juice glass and just sat there until the song ended. Night had fallen, and cool air was pouring in through an open window.

"That man in the song is like me," she pointed out. "He said he tried to have a father, but instead he got a dad."

"Yeah," Jason said. "I guess so."

"Maybe he got adopted too?" Harvey went on. "Wanda said once you get adopted, that's it."

"What do you mean, that's it?"

"Like, you have parents once you get adopted. You're no longer like Annie."

"Annie?"

"You know, that kids' movie I hate."

"Oh yeah. Daddy Warbucks, right? I hate that movie too."

THE FOLLOWING AFTERNOON, while Harvey was in school, Jason dug out some old tapes of British punk bands, then played them for her in the car on the way home. "This is the original grunge," he told her. "These guys didn't give a shit."

Harvey said it sounded like people having a fight. When they got back, Jason showed her pictures of 1980s punks in old music magazines. "That could be you someday," he said, pointing to a woman with an orange Mohawk and a spike through her nose.

"But I want to work at Jiffy Lube," Harvey said. "Or rescue animals on TV."

After she'd brushed her teeth and put on pajamas, Jason told Harvey there was a shortage of girl drummers in the music world, and she definitely had something.

Late that night, Jason woke up and saw Harvey standing in his bedroom doorway. His window blinds were open, and the falling moon made her look porcelain.

"You okay, Harv?"

"I had to pee, and I wanted to see if you were up."

"I was sleeping. Did you have an accident?"

"No. I just wanted to see if you were awake."

"How long have you been standing there? Did you have a bad dream?"

"No, I had to pee."

"Want me to tuck you in again?"

"No, it's okay. Just don't forget that parent-teacher night is coming up."

"I thought you didn't want me to go."

After she went back to bed, Jason tried to fall asleep, but a car brushed the wall with its headlights, and he sat up and looked at the alarm clock. For a few moments, he wondered if he'd dreamed the whole thing, then got up and went to make sure Harvey was back in her bed.

As he passed the hall closet going back to his room, Jason remembered what Harvey had told him as she stood in the doorway about parent-teacher night.

He flicked on the closet light, then found her backpack and sifted through its contents—empty chip bags, bits of wool, a rubber ball, a torn comic, shoelaces, Pokémon cards—until seeing the note sent home from school. Parent-teacher night for Harvey's grade was to take place in her classroom in a few days' time. Harvey's time slot was seven P.M. As Jason returned the letter, he noticed a colorful piece of card stuffed into a side pocket.

He took it out and looked for a long time at what Harvey had drawn, and at what she had written. Then he went to the bathroom and stared at his face in the mirror, saying the word that had stood out to him most, saying it over and over, as if hearing it for the first time.

XXXIII

THE NEXT DAY, after dropping Harvey at school, Jason drove out to the cemetery where his brother and sister-in-law were buried. He found the headstone using a map outside the custodian's office. Then he stood in the grass wondering how deep the bodies went. In one pocket he'd brought a drumstick he got years ago at a Satanic Hell Slaughter concert, after drunkenly wrestling it from someone who'd drunkenly wrestled it from someone else. In his other pocket was Harvey's second-grade class picture, which he'd placed in a freezer bag to keep the rain off. He set both items on the grass, where the stone disappeared into the earth. Then he stood back and read their full names.

"You probably don't even know I'm here," he said. "But here I am."

He sat in the grass for a while, then lay back so there was nothing but sky.

Closing his eyes, Jason imagined he was stuffed in the casket with them—trying to move his arms, a nest of hair at each cheek—unaware if, on the surface of the earth, it was day or night, summer or winter. He wondered if—even for a split second—the dead knew they were dead, or if any shred of memory remained.

After he was officially granted guardianship of Harvey, Wanda said that if he kept smoking, he might not live to see her graduate from high school. Over time, Jason had considered her warning, and the more concerning consequences of what would happen if he died within the next twenty years . . . What if Harvey took up with the first asshole who told her she was pretty? Who would be there to save her when things turned nasty? Who would care enough to knock the guy's teeth into the back of his head? If saving Harvey meant another stint in jail, so be it. If it meant fighting to the death in a parking lot, so be it. But if he was prepared to die for her, shouldn't he be prepared to live for her too?

Jason sat up and looked at the grave where Steve's grown-up body was buried, imagining his own name there alongside his brother's. Then Harvey's name chiseled underneath. It would happen one day for sure, though what tortured him the most was not the certainty of his death but the possibility that Harvey would be alone; that they might never find each other again, once this life had ended.

WHEN HE GOT back from the cemetery, Jason threw his cigarettes in the trash, then took the leftover marijuana from the freezer and flushed it down the toilet.

He would miss getting high in the evenings—but had known for a long time that he would lose custody of Harvey if the police found out, or if the courts demanded a urine sample, which Wanda said they could do at any time.

On the way to pick Harvey up from school, Jason stopped at the drugstore for some sleeping pills, thinking he'd pop one, or maybe a half-one, if he got anxious from the nicotine withdrawal, which was already clawing at him.

He wandered the aisles looking for nicotine gum but all he

could find was cough medicine and dental floss. An employee stacking small boxes of lipstick stopped what she was doing and asked if Jason needed help. There was a tattoo on her wrist of a bird in a cage.

"Trying to quit then, huh?" she asked.

"Something like that."

"How long's it been since you had one?"

"About an hour."

The woman laughed, then led Jason to a locked case behind the registers. She took out a few different no-smoking kits and explained the differences between gum and the patch. When Jason picked out what he wanted, she rang him up and put his purchases in a plastic bag.

"Come back and let me know how it goes," she said.

"I've been smoking for a long time," Jason said. "So it's not gonna go well."

"You have to really want it."

"It's still gonna be tough."

"Well, you look pretty tough to me," the woman said, then turned because a man with some severe hip disability was trying to get through the door with his walking sticks.

"At least you're not like that," she said with a laugh. "Can you imagine?"

AFTER BUNDLING INTO the backseat with her school bag, Harvey buckled in and told Jason she was starting a dog club with her friends.

"But we don't have a dog," Jason said.

"No—*we're* the dogs. I'm a greyhound called Bryan that got rescued. You can be a dog too if you want." Then she noticed that Jason was chewing something. "What's in your mouth?"

"Gum."

"Can I have some?"

"No."

"That's so selfish," she said. "You never think about me."

XXXIV

WHEN HARVEY WAS asleep, Jason lay in bed going over what he might ask at the parent-teacher conference. He still had the black turtleneck he'd worn for his court interview, and that would cover the tattoo on his neck.

Other parents would probably be there, waiting for their time slots, so his plan was to get in and get out. Over the past year, Harvey had pleaded with him to organize play-dates with girls from school on an ever-changing roster of best friends. Eventually, he gave in and contacted their parents over email. He would drop Harvey at the curb, then watch her go up the front steps and ring the bell. When the other parent waved, Jason took off, then returned a few hours later, honking the horn, which meant it was time for Harvey to come out. He had never met any of the other parents in person.

THE FOLLOWING AFTERNOON after school, Harvey sat on Jason's bed eating pizza, watching him pick out clothes. When he found the black turtleneck, it was in a ball at the bottom of his closet with moth holes in the front. His only other option was a black button-down shirt with the tie Wanda had brought over. Jason had no black pants to match the shirt, so he put on some dark blue sweatpants, which from a distance Harvey said looked dressy.

Jason had never left Harvey alone in the house, but she assured him that she knew which channels on the TV she wasn't allowed to watch, and promised not to eat anything in case she choked.

When it was almost time to leave for the school, Harvey got up to pee and found Jason standing at the mirror sticking Band-Aids over the tattoo on his neck.

"What are you doing that for?"

"What do you need, Harv?" He said in a voice that meant he was about to get irritated.

"Can I have some root beer?"

"You shouldn't drink fizzy drinks so late. Remember what the doctor said."

"What about chocolate milk?"

"Sure, but get it before I take off."

"Okay, but I need to pee."

Jason stepped out of the way, then closed his eyes until Harvey got off the toilet seat.

When he was about to leave, Jason noticed Harvey's Converse All-Stars sitting by the door. "Jesus, how many times I got to tell you to put your shoes away?" She sprang off the couch, but Jason waved her back. "Actually, just stay there until I get back," he said, fingering the Band-Aids. "Does this look stupid?"

"A little."

"Then what do I do?"

Harvey shrugged. "Keep them on, I guess."

"What if someone asks what happened?"

Harvey took a slug of chocolate milk. "Just tell them you accidentally cut your head off."

. . .

WHEN JASON RETURNED home a few hours later, Harvey was asleep on the couch with the television on. When he nudged her shoulder, she stirred.

"I only had to pee once," she mumbled. "And I didn't eat anything, in case I choked."

"Good girl."

"Did you meet my teacher?"

"Yeah."

"Did she say I was good?"

Jason carried Harvey into the bedroom and set her down on the mattress. "Arms up," he said, and she put her arms up so he could get her pajamas on.

"What about my teeth?"

"It's too late now. Just brush twice in the morning."

When she was under the covers, Jason stood there looking at her. "You're a great kid," he said.

Harvey opened her eyes. Her fingers on the edge of the blanket. "And you're a great man."

AFTER MAKING COFFEE, Jason took his mug out to the front step and sat down. It was late, and his neighbors' houses were already dark. He reached for his cigarettes but then remembered and let his hand fall. The coffee was so hot he could only take sips.

The teacher had shown him Harvey's schoolbooks. "Look how neat her numbers are," she said. "Especially the eights."

Jason looked at the numbers, written slowly in pencil. There were math problems too, and green checks the teacher had made where Harvey got things right.

Jason asked where Harvey sat. The teacher pointed to a wooden desk. Stacked on top was a metal-framed chair—like all the others, except that it was where Harvey sat, and where she waited all day to come home.

"Harvey is so helpful," the teacher went on. "If there's a hat or a shoe on the floor, she picks it up and puts it away rather than just stepping over it."

"Yeah, that's good."

"I think it's very mature," the teacher said. "Probably something she learned at home?"

Harvey's main lesson books had pictures of sheep and short sentences about wool. "She really responded to this subject," the teacher told him. "Did you grow up on a farm, maybe?"

She also mentioned that Harvey was the only girl the boys included in their games. "And I have to tell you," she said, "Harvey talks about her father all the time in class—oh my goodness."

"What does she say about him?"

"Well . . ." the teacher said, "We all know about the motorcycle you're building in the garage, and that your tacos and meat loaf are amazing—but your chicken is a little dry, I'm afraid."

XXXV

IN THE TAXI home from Leon and Isobel's apartment, Harvey watched the flickering outline of her face on the glass. She remembered how she'd felt the moment the lights went out over dinner, when they were only four voices.

Low voices came now from the car radio. They had lulled her father to sleep. Passing streetlight washed over his hands and his face. The shoes he'd bought for the trip were dusty from their day of walking at Versailles. His feet rested at a slight inward angle, which made Harvey realize that he was once just a child like Isobel.

When they got home to her apartment on rue Caulaincourt, Harvey made up his bed on the couch and slipped Duncan in as a surprise. Then she took off her makeup and set the dishwasher.

In the middle of the night, Jason was woken up by a noise outside. For a moment he didn't know where he was. Then he saw Duncan on the floor next to his shoes and it all came back.

The time flashed in pale green on the DVD player, and he counted six hours back, then reached for the TV remote. It was hard to see which button to press in the dark, but he held down the big green one, and after a few seconds the flatscreen lit up with people speaking French in a news studio.

Jason flicked through the channels, but it was all foreign-language shows. In the end, he settled for a program about train journeys in Switzerland. He got Duncan and brushed him off, as a red train snaked through snowy mountains. The tattoo Harvey had drawn on Duncan's neck had faded, but his eyes still opened when you sat him up, and closed when you laid him down.

After the program, Jason went back to sleep but woke again at first light to the sound of rain. He put on his clothes, folded away the bedsheets, and sat waiting for the day to begin.

When he couldn't sit anymore, he went into the kitchen and stood by the window. Most of the neighbors' shades were still pulled down. In the sky, an airliner moved in and out of gray clouds. Rooftops glistened.

Then Jason stood outside his daughter's room. The door was open a few inches, the way she liked it at home. He peered in at the shape of her body under the bedclothes.

When she used to fall asleep in the car, he would lift her out of the seat, then carry her on one shoulder. Her favorite pillowcase was brown with owls on it. Harvey would close her eyes and rub her cheek on the fabric. In winter, Jason gave her a hot-water bottle. She used to remove Duncan's clothes and bounce him on it.

An hour later, when Harvey opened her eyes and pulled on her robe, she found her father sitting at the table with breakfast laid out.

"Oh my God, this is amazing."

Jason selected a chocolate croissant for himself, then held out the plate for Harvey to take one. "Sleep well, Harv?"

There was a box of macaroons and some éclairs with colored icing. Jason passed Harvey a paper cup of coffee.

"But I have a coffeemaker," she said.

"Yeah, but I didn't know how to work it. Deli coffee is good here."

"I can't believe you went to the patisserie."

"I had to point at everything," Jason said. "Because she doesn't speak English."

"She doesn't speak French either," Harvey said. "It's the owner's wife, she's Russian."

"I wanted to tell her that I work around food too—but nothing so beautiful as what she got in her shop."

"Well, I'm glad you didn't go to the new boulanger on Caulaincourt," Harvey said, dipping her croissant in the coffee. "Because it's a total rip-off."

During breakfast they talked about Leon and Isobel, chuckling over what Isobel had said about blind people eating in the dark. When Harvey asked how her father had slept, he told her all about the red mountain trains of Switzerland.

Harvey said it was early enough to see Notre Dame before the lines started forming, if they got ready quickly.

"And don't forget, you have to pick something else from your Father's Day box."

When they had finished eating, Jason carried the breakfast plates into the kitchen and put them in the sink, as though they were back at home.

Then he watched his daughter make coffee in her machine, and drank a cup in front of the television. It was mostly news programs and soccer, so Jason settled on something called *Hélène et les Garçons,* which seemed easy to follow because there were kids in it.

When they passed the patisserie on the way to the Métro,

the Russian woman who had served Jason was in the window setting out cakes.

A train was arriving when they got to the platform, and most of the cars were empty because it was after rush hour. They almost missed their stop because Jason didn't realize you have to open the doors yourself.

They approached the cathedral from the north, passing the Hôtel de Ville, which Jason thought at first was Notre Dame. Harvey told him it wasn't even a hotel.

When stone walls and dark towers rose into view, Harvey told Jason that when Notre Dame was built, Paris was just straw-roofed houses and people pulling wagons through mud.

When they arrived at the entrance, people were already waiting to go in, so Jason said he'd be happy just to walk around the outside. Then a thunder of bells announcing the hour changed his mind and he told Harvey that he wanted to hear them from inside.

The line moved quickly. When they were almost through the main doors, a young couple sneaked in behind them. Jason felt anger rising in his stomach. He was about to say something when he realized that the girl, who was about Harvey's age, was just copying her boyfriend. It would be something they looked back upon, he thought, when they were old and their lives had almost passed.

Once inside, the line broke up and people took separate paths. Iron stands of lit candles illuminated carved faces, and signs everywhere asked visitors not to talk as they shuffled with cameras and backpacks beneath a glowing patchwork of stained-glass windows.

Jason dropped some coins into a metal box marked MERCI,

then took two candles from a wooden crate and gave one to Harvey. Behind the silent choir of lights was the wooden statue of a man holding hands with a young child in despair. The man was wearing a hat that looked like an acorn. There was an ax on his belt. The child's face was twisted with crying, and one of his feet lifted off the ground as he pulled on the sleeve of the woodcutter.

Jason said that Notre Dame was like being inside someone's body, moving around under the ribs, and breathing in the musty air of old lungs. Then he remembered the bells, and they found a quiet pew from which to listen. But when the hour came and went, Jason and Harvey realized that you could only hear them from outside the cathedral.

"That's so weird," Jason said. "I don't get it."

Harvey said she felt safe inside the church.

A hundred feet above their heads, a banner was strung across the ceiling. A distant figure in a small boat was rowing through a storm. Jason asked Harvey what the words meant.

"It says, 'Come,'" she told him, "'for He has been calling you.'"

"Who's *He*? God?"

"Or Jesus," Harvey said.

Jason looked at the banner again and nudged his daughter. "If that was Vincent in the picture—there'd be a fishing pole hanging off the side."

WHEN THEY WERE at the exit, Harvey turned quickly and went back inside the church. She stopped at one of the iron candle stands, took a few coins from her purse, and dropped them in the metal box. Then she lit a single candle and set it on the highest tier.

When they were outside, Jason asked whom it was for, but she wouldn't say.

The streets leading away from the cathedral toward the Latin Quarter were crowded. In some places it was hard to walk, as people had bunched up, waiting for a sign to cross rue du Petit Pont.

After twenty minutes of walking, they stopped at a Quick hamburger restaurant on the corner of Boulevard San Michel. Jason said they should sit side by side in the window. The restaurant was busy with tourists, but the staff spoke English and Spanish, and the lines moved quickly. Harvey warned her father that the fries didn't come salted, so he should pick up a few packets with the straws and napkins.

"Why don't you get us a place to sit?" she said. "I'll get the burgers."

Jason handed her a twenty-euro note and looked around for empty seats. He imagined finding a table at the same time as a gang of French thugs. But then when he got to the front window, there were plenty of empty seats, and the thugs he'd imagined were a pair of teenage boys laughing at something on their cell phones.

Harvey appeared a few minutes later with their burgers and a Sprite for Jason. They chewed in silence, watching people go by outside. Then Jason asked Harvey what she would do if two people cut the line in front of her.

She thought about it for a moment. "I wouldn't do anything," she said. "Because it doesn't matter."

"But if you got there first . . ." Jason said. "They have no right to push in, right? It's not fair."

"I guess so. But it's just a line for fast food. It's not like we're starving and they're giving out the last few pieces of bread on earth."

"What would you do then?" he said.

"Then I'd probably fight," Harvey said. "Unless they had a baby to feed or kids. Then I'd just let them have it."

Jason laughed, and the aggression that had begun to manifest outside Notre Dame quickly broke apart. "You always know the right thing to do, Harvey," he said. "I wish I was more like you."

WHEN THEY GOT to the Luxembourg Garden after lunch, people were sitting on green metal chairs with ice cream cones. Jason asked Harvey if she wanted a cone, then dragged together a pair of chairs for them to sit on.

On a patch of grass near an overflowing trash can, a man about Jason's age in torn clothes was pretending to do martial arts. Jason watched as he waited in line at the ice cream stand, as the man raised his fist to an invisible enemy, then threw his leg out to one side with a cry. When he started jumping in the air and punching at the same time, people turned and laughed. Next to the man was a metal shopping cart with a rolled-up sleeping bag, portable radio, several pairs of shoes, a tennis racket, and a stack of flattened boxes and old blankets.

Harvey had been watching the man too, and when Jason got back with the ice creams, she asked him what it's like to beat someone up.

"It feels like the right thing to do," he said. "Until you actually do it."

"I wonder if I'll ever get into a fight," Harvey said.

"People don't fight like they used to," Jason said. "When I was growing up, it seemed like everyone was fighting. Your generation is different. Kids today fight with themselves more than with other kids."

When they finished eating, Jason saw that the line at the ice cream stand was gone, so he bought another cone and took it over to the man doing martial arts.

Down by the fountain, children were sailing wooden boats on a pond.

Harvey and her father watched. Then Jason went to the shed where you could rent them, and returned holding a blue boat with NO. 15 printed on the sail. He handed Harvey the cane that came with it. "You can push off first," he said.

Part of the fun was seeing if you could get to the other side of the small lake before the boat did. Harvey challenged her father to a race, but he kept holding her arms, so it wasn't fair.

After half an hour, Harvey returned the boat, and they found an empty bench under some lush, wide-leafed trees.

"All we do in Paris is eat and sit down," Jason said.

"Well, tomorrow we're going to my office, Dad. I want to introduce you to my boss, Sophie, and show you what I've been working on. It's like being at art school, but the deadlines are tighter, and the client is in charge of how the finished product looks. Which is a bit sad, as they usually have bad taste."

"But you get paid," Jason said. "That's important."

In the background, they could hear the roll of children's laughter. School had ended for the day, and the Luxembourg playgrounds were filling up.

Jason asked if it was a good time to open the present he had brought from his Father's Day box. The item he had picked out was very small, and he thought it might be a token from Chuck E. Cheese's—to signify all the birthday parties, the games they'd lost and won, and the tickets exchanged for things now forgotten. Jason remembered Harvey's school friends lined up at the long colored tables, chewing hot dogs with their mouths open. Parents waiting in small groups with their coats on.

Harvey said there was one more place she wanted to take him, and he could open his present there. Around the bench, the uncut grass was wet from rain that morning. Jason could smell it and could smell the trees.

The Avenue de la Grand Armée was only a few Métro stops from the Latin Quarter. Harvey explained that this was where Parisians came to browse for new scooters and motorcycles. She kept saying she wanted to buy him a mug from his favorite motorcycle shop, or a key chain, or sweatshirt, or a hat.

The first store they went into sold Royal Enfield bikes, which Jason said were modeled on famous editions from England in the 1950s, but that the engines were too small to really do anything with. The shop was small too, and most of the bikes were kept outside on the sidewalk with films of plastic over the seats.

"Remember the skull I painted on the gas tank for your birthday, Dad?"

When Vincent and his wife would come over on Saturday nights to watch movies and eat pizza, Jason sometimes took the gas tank down from the shelf to show it off. Harvey had painted a skull with her name above it.

The next shop they went into sold Italian bikes that were mostly red and black, with wide back tires and shallow treads.

"These are fast bikes," Jason told her. "Dangerous bikes—which means you can always get parts for them, because so many get wrecked by inexperienced riders."

Harvey told him to pick something out. "I'm working now, Dad," she said. "So if you see a jacket or some awesome boots, or if there's a bike you just love, let me buy it for you."

"That's wild," Jason said. "You win the lottery or something Harv?"

In another shop, the salesman asked Jason if he wanted to sit on their latest café racer, but he politely said no.

"Go on, Dad," Harvey insisted, then noticed the bike was in a narrow space, and it would have been impossible for him to get his leg over.

When they were back on the street, Jason bought two apples from a fruit stand, and they ate them walking.

"When I think of all the bits I welded together," he said, "it's amazing my bikes even ran."

"Why don't you get one of these new bikes, Dad?" Harvey said. "I'll buy it for you. Come on."

Jason laughed and smoothed the back of his ponytail.

"You should wear your hair down sometimes, Dad," Harvey told him.

"I've gotten too lazy in my old age to fuss with it."

Putting his hair in a ponytail was something new. One

night, drying it in the mirror after a bath, Jason couldn't believe how much it had thinned—more medieval than metal, he thought. And in a ponytail, no one could tell he was slowly going bald.

Near the Métro, Harvey said they should find somewhere for Jason to open his Father's Day gift, so they kept walking until there was an empty bench.

The gift wasn't a token from Chuck E. Cheese's but a poker-chip key chain. Jason sniffed it. The original one had reeked of oil.

"So you finally figured it out, huh, Harvey?"

He could see from her tears that she had.

When it all happened, she had been so angry—so disappointed in him.

She felt he'd let her down. But now she understood.

Now she understood what had happened.

XXXVI

FOR HARVEY'S NINTH birthday, Jason got tickets for *The Lion King* on Broadway. Harvey had seen the commercials on TV and said it was her dream. The plan was to go into the city by train, then have McDonald's after the show.

Jason was going to pick her up from school at recess, then drive to the Long Island Rail Road station. Her fourth-grade teacher, Miss Hills, said she wished that more parents were into theater. Jason had never been to a live show with people acting, and he wondered if it would be anything like TV. He called the box office several times to make sure their seats would be near the front so Harvey could see everything.

The night before the show, Harvey complained of feeling tired and went to bed early. When Jason checked on her later, he noticed she was burning up. He opened the window to let cool air fill the room.

He set his alarm for earlier than usual, so he'd have time to cook a big breakfast: sausages, eggs, bacon, baked beans, toast, and pancakes, all Harvey's favorite things.

It was still dark when he got up, and the first thing he did was make coffee. Then he heated some oil in the pan and dropped the sausages in one by one.

When everything was cooked, he made up a birthday tray with chocolate milk, SpongeBob napkins, birthday cards (from him, Wanda, and Duncan), and a small bear he got on sale at Party City.

Harvey was already awake when Jason pushed open the door with his foot.

"I don't feel good," she said.

Then she smelled what was on the tray and ran to the bathroom. But there wasn't anything in her stomach, so it was just muscles pinching and the dry growl from her throat.

Jason carried Harvey back to bed and propped her up with the pillows. Then he filled a glass with cold water, but she wouldn't drink anything, so he just sat with her.

Before he took the tray back to the kitchen, Harvey asked if she could have the bear. "Sorry I ruined breakfast, Dad."

While Jason was in the kitchen covering the food, he remembered a thermometer in the first-aid kit Wanda had left in the laundry closet. He carried the box into Harvey's room, read the instructions, then told Harvey to keep it under her tongue without moving. After a few minutes, the thermometer beeped and Jason took it out. It read 104.6.

"What shall we name him?" Harvey said weakly, touching the bear's nose.

Jason was still looking at the number on the thermometer. He imagined her eyes lolling back as the fever spread to her brain, then rushing her out to the car, tearing through traffic, her limp body rolling around on the backseat. He saw the hospital staff in their baggy green pants and rubber shoes, imagined yelling at them as machines and wires were attached to keep her alive.

He took up Harvey's hand and stroked it. Her face was red

from vomiting, and the bedclothes were hot because she was sweating.

When he tried Wanda, her phone rang a few times, then went to voice mail. It was too early to call Social Services, so Jason went online and typed in Harvey's symptoms. But there were too many things to choose from, and when he typed her temperature into Google, a message flashed on the screen:

IF YOU HAVE A FEVER OVER 103.5 F
PLEASE SEEK PROMPT MEDICAL ATTENTION

When Jason checked on Harvey again, she asked if they were still going to *The Lion King* and McDonald's.

Jason had saved up for the tickets. He had played over their trip to the city so many times in his mind that he'd witnessed a thousand shows, and was prepared for any crisis—except the one that was actually happening.

When he took her temperature again, it was even higher. He rushed into the kitchen and filled a bowl with ice, but when he got to Harvey's bedside she was throwing up again, though it was just the sound and her tongue coming out.

Shit, fucking holy shit, Jason said. And underneath panic, the sting of his loneliness. The truth that he had no one to turn to.

When she couldn't keep her eyes open, Jason went into the hall and grabbed his jacket and motorcycle boots. He combed his hair quickly in the mirror and told Harvey to sit tight.

"Don't leave me," she said, starting to cry. "Please, Dad!"

"I ain't leaving you, kid. I'm going for help."

The air outside felt good and he gulped it down. He jogged quickly up the neighbors' driveway, then bounded onto the porch, knocking his head on a hanging basket. When he couldn't find a doorbell, he banged with the side of his fist.

A moment later, a shape appeared behind the glass. Jason heard the security chain being attached, then a teenage boy appeared through the crack.

"Where's your mom?" Jason said.

"Mama!" the boy shouted.

Jason wondered why he was still in his pajamas and not in school.

"Who is it?" came a woman's voice from somewhere in the house. Jason could hear the sound of dishes being stacked.

"The guy from next door!"

The sounds abruptly ceased, and over the boy's head Jason saw his mother rushing down the hall in her slippers. She closed the door to release the chain and stood in front of her son. "Can I help you, mister?"

"I'm your neighbor," Jason said, pointing in the direction of his house.

"*Sí, sí.* You have a little girl living with you?"

"Well, she's real sick."

"Oh no, I'm sorry to hear that."

"She's burning up."

"Did you take her temperature?"

"It's a hundred and five point something."

"That's very high. What you have given her?"

"Nothing. She won't eat or drink."

The woman nodded and looked down at her bare feet, but Jason could tell she was thinking.

"Go home," she told him. "I'll get some medicine and be right over."

HARVEY WAS IN the bathroom when Jason got back. The door was open, and Jason saw her feet dangling a few inches off the floor.

"You pooping?" he called out. Harvey leaned forward but was too weak to answer.

Jason lifted her off the seat and looked into the bowl. "That's diarrhea," he said. "You've got diarrhea."

"I can't wipe," she mumbled. "Get it off, Dad."

The smell clung to the air, and there were traces of it on her fingers from where she'd tried to clean herself.

Jason spooled off several squares of toilet paper, which he held under warm running water. The diarrhea had dripped down her legs and into the seat of her pajamas.

"You're gonna have to step out of your pj's," Jason said, turning the shower on. "I'm gonna run a little warm water on your legs so you don't itch, okay?" Then he lifted her into the shower. Her legs were shaking with cold.

When Harvey was clean and back in bed, someone knocked on the front door.

"Is that doctors?" Harvey said.

"No it's the people from next door."

"The ones I'm not allowed to wave at?"

"Yeah, them," Jason said.

Mrs. Gonzales had brought little bottles in a white plastic bag, along with a small container of Gatorade. "Is it okay if my son sits out here and watches TV?" she said. "He's off school today."

Harvey had pulled the sheets up to her neck when Mrs. Gonzales entered her room. "It's okay, sweetie," Mrs. Gonzales said, putting the bag of bottles on the dresser. "You'll feel better soon."

"It's my birthday," Harvey said. "I got sick on my birthday."

"Oh, you poor thing. You so brave." Mrs. Gonzales put the back of her palm on Harvey's forehead and made a sad face. "You're burning up, baby girl."

Harvey held up her bear. "Look what my dad got me."

"Your own little friend. That's so nice of Daddy." Mrs. Gonzales took one of the bottles from the white bag and measured some purple liquid into a plastic shot glass. "I'm going to give her this," she said. "It's what I give my own kids. She allergic to any medicines?"

"No. I don't think so."

"You'd know by now if she was, but I brought some Benadryl just in case."

After Harvey had swallowed the medicine and was getting comfortable, Mrs. Gonzales's son, Hector, appeared in the doorway and said he needed the restroom.

Jason pointed. "Second door on the right."

"I'm going to sit with Harvey awhile, if you don't mind," Mrs. Gonzales said. "Make sure she keeps the medicine down."

"What can I do?" Jason said.

"Maybe make sure Hector is okay?"

Hector had finished in the bathroom and was just standing around. The television was on and there were Spanish voices, but he wasn't interested. Jason handed him a glass of root beer, then asked if he liked motorcycles.

"Yeah, sure," Hector said. "They're pretty cool."

"Want to see one getting built?"

TAPED UP ON the brick walls of the garage were posters of panheads, choppers, bobbers, and Fat Boys. Women in bikinis and platform heels leaned over immaculate, gleaming machines.

Jason asked Hector to point out his favorite bike. The boy pointed to a photo of a blond woman bending over the front forks of a custom Harley chopper in a bra and thong panties made from beads and brown suede, Native American–style.

"That bike's a killer," Jason said. "No rear suspension, no front brake."

"I think it's cool," Hector said.

Jason took the poster down and rolled it up. "Here," he said, handing it to Hector. "Something to dream about."

Then Jason pulled the dust cloth off his bike and they stood beside it. Chrome pipes sparkled in the garage light.

"It's *so* awesome," Hector said. "I can't believe you built this."

"It's taken almost ten years," Jason said. "Sit on it, if you want."

Hector put his leg over the bike, then moved around in the seat.

"Hold on to the handlebars, Hector. Get a feel for it."

Hector reached over the teardrop gas tank and put his hands around the grips.

"Looking good, Hector. You were born to ride."

A poker-chip key chain dangled below the gas tank, and Hector asked what it was for.

"It's attached to the ignition key," Jason said. "Turn it."

Hector cautiously followed the silver chain until his fingers rested on the key. Jason told him to go ahead and turn, but when he did, nothing happened.

"Still needs a battery and some electrical," Jason said. "One day soon, though, it'll be finished."

"My dad could help you," Hector told him. "He's a really good electrician."

Jason pictured the man he'd seen glaring at him from the minivan whenever they passed his house. "I don't think your dad likes me much."

Hector nodded. "It's because he thinks you broke our mailbox with a beer bottle."

Jason bent down and rearranged a few of his tools. "It was nice of your mom to come over and help. I was really freaking out this morning."

"Oh, she's nice to everybody," Hector exclaimed, still holding the handlebars. "Did you like the flowers we planted when your daughter first came to live with you? There was a bunch left over from the ones at church, and Mom asked if she could have them. She even got my dad to help."

XXXVII

By the next morning, the medicine was doing its work, and Harvey's fever had fallen below a hundred. Mrs. Gonzales had written down a list of danger signs that Jason should watch for, which he taped to the refrigerator door.

In the late afternoon, after her husband was home, Mrs. Gonzales returned to see how Harvey was feeling, and to stay with her while Jason went to the drugstore for supplies.

By the weekend, Harvey was picking at fruit cups, fish sticks, and french fries. She spent the daylight hours on the couch in her pajamas, watching TV, and the early evening on her father's bed, listening to him read the third Harry Potter book.

Duncan was there too, and had made friends with the bear from Harvey's breakfast tray.

The following week she was back in school, and life went on as before, with excursions on Saturday to playgrounds, or the beach, or Marshalls for new shoes or a winter coat. On Sundays, Jason did laundry in the morning while Harvey put her toys away or did homework. In the afternoon, if there was nothing special on TV, she kept Jason company in the garage, glancing up from her dolls now and then at her father on the ground in dirty jeans as he hammered or wrenched something into place.

One evening when they were on the couch with nothing

to do, Jason showed Harvey a video about a disabled man in Florida who'd built a swing arm mechanism into his Kawasaki sport bike.

"It comes out at red lights," Jason said as the video played. "See, Harv, look at that—it stops the bike from tipping over."

"Are you going to get that, Dad? So you can ride?"

"I'm going to make one myself," Jason said. "I just have to figure out how it works, then get the parts."

"So you can take me to school on the back when it's done?"

Jason nodded. "Oh, sure."

"Wait till you see their faces, Dad!" Harvey said. "When I pull up to school on the back of a motorcycle!"

Jason explained that most bikers with disabilities ride trikes, but Harvey couldn't picture such a thing, so Jason went to find a picture in one of his old magazines. When he returned, Harvey was watching a cartoon.

"Look what I found in the garage, Harvey, it's one of my old scrapbooks from back in the day."

"But I'm watching this show right now . . ."

"C'mon, Harvey—I gotta show you this."

Jason fixed her another glass of juice, then muted the television. "My brother and I used to make these scrapbooks when we were kids. This one even has my mom in it."

Jason sat down and peeled open the book. "That's your grandmother, Harv."

The photos were very small, with a child's handwriting beneath a few of them.

"We had a real basic camera," Jason said. "Jesus, look at that! It's Steve with the dog we found!"

"Birdie?"

"That's right. We called him Birdie because he was always chasing pigeons."

"Is this my dad as a little boy?"

"That's him."

"He has a nice face."

"He was a sweet kid. Saw the best in everybody—even me."

Jason turned the page.

"Look, Harv, here's me building my first bike in the driveway. It's so weird to see it after all this time."

"You've got long hair!"

"That's right. I had long hair then. Maybe I'll grow it out again. It was curly though. Once I dyed it blond, and everyone started calling me Goldilocks, so I dyed it back."

"Can I dye my hair?"

"No. It'll get screwed up. Now, look at *that* bike!"

"Why would I screw it up?"

"I bought this one as a rolling frame, then built it from the ground up, learning as I went along."

Jason's first machine had been featured in the Readers' Rides section of *Back Street Choppers*. It was orange with chrome springs in the front and a small nickel headlamp. Jason had cut the picture from the magazine and pasted it in the scrapbook. "That bike really stood out, with those extended forks."

Harvey's finger pressed down on a chrome pipe. "What does this long thing do?"

When Jason explained its function, Harvey's finger slid to another part of the engine.

"And that's part of the ignition, Harvey. Some bikes have an electric start," Jason told her. "Others have to be kicked."

Harvey thought that was funny and wanted to know if you could kick it anywhere.

Jason had bought the frame and wheels for only a few dollars when he was a freshman in high school. There was also a box of parts that came with the sale, but most turned out to be for a different machine. He worked on his bike in the driveway and kept the rain off with a blue cover.

When his father was dying of cancer, he sometimes went outside and pulled the tarp off. Once Jason caught him out there, leaning on his cane and rolling his eyes over the half-built machine.

"C'mere, boy," he said, pointing at something in the engine. "That bit ain't right. See there . . ."

Jason listened as his father listed all the things he was doing wrong. The old man's once giant hands were now small and birdlike. He hadn't been able to drink for months and was too weak to put up a fight. It was the first time Jason and Steve had seen their father sober for longer than a few hours, and he'd begun telling them things about his life. Made them agree never to join the military, and to listen to their mother—do what she wanted.

A week later, Jason's father was out in the driveway again, this time on his knees, doing something with a wrench and cursing when it wouldn't latch. When Jason got home that night, his mother was loading bedsheets into the washer.

"Your father said to tell you he fixed your chain," she said. "And that you did a good job with the gears."

Jason just stood there. "He didn't say that. You're making it up."

A week later, Jason's father died. The television was on, and his eyes stayed open even after they laid his body down.

For the next two nights, Jason worked to get his bike running. He had told his mother he wasn't going to the funeral, but then followed the hearse on his motorcycle and watched from a distance as strangers in military uniforms lowered the casket. When they lifted their rifles to fire, birds flew out of the trees.

ON ANOTHER PAGE of the scrapbook was a teenage girl on a 1937 Indian Chief.

"There's my mom again," Jason told Harvey. "When she was seventeen."

The bike belonged to Jason's father before the war. His mother was in high school when they met. In the summer they used to pack towels and drive to Long Beach. Sometimes the bike broke down, but someone always stopped to help.

In another picture, Jason's mother was standing on a boardwalk in a hula-girl outfit. In the background couples danced. Jason said it was most likely Robert Moses, maybe the Rockaways.

"I'd wear that," Harvey said, pointing at the grass skirt and coconut top. "Do you still have it?"

Jason said it was long gone and that Steve must have rescued the scrapbook before their mother's house got sold.

There were two very old photographs loose in the book near the end. Both were dated 1910. Jason didn't know who the people were, but Harvey said the man in the bow tie could have been Jason's great-grandfather because he was the only person in the picture not smiling.

On the final inside page of the scrapbook was a color photograph that had been torn up, then taped back together. It was of a woman on a couch in a basement. She was quite young and had on a white T-shirt and tight blue jeans. She was laughing at whoever was taking the photograph, laughing so hard that her eyes were closed. Her hair was long and straight and very dark.

Harvey pointed to it. "Who's that?"

"No one," Jason said, closing the book and getting up.

"She's pretty," Harvey said, but Jason was already halfway back to the garage.

XXXVIII

JASON MET RITA Vega at an Irish pub in Hicksville.

She was playing pool with a few girlfriends. When it was time for more drinks, she came to the bar with her money out. The bartender was stacking glasses in the back, so she made small talk with the man at the bar who had a tattoo on his neck. Her hair was long and very dark.

By the end of the night, she'd written her number for Jason in lipstick on a cocktail napkin.

They saw each other once the following week, then a few days after that. She learned to ride on the back of Jason's motorcycle by locking her arms around him and leaning in to curves. Sometimes they went to Jones Beach. Their favorite time was twilight. They took walks on the sand, with Jason stooping to pick up shells because Rita collected them. Once he found a giant clam with so much seaweed it looked like hair.

"That's so weird!" Rita said.

"You think everything's weird!" Jason said, and tried to chase her with it, but was laughing too hard to run.

In late summer, they would collect driftwood from the dunes and build a fire. Rita brought things to eat, like hot dogs or meatball sandwiches. When it was dark and they were the only ones left, Jason would spread out a blanket. When they got underneath, Rita let him take her clothes off, then touch her, then slowly get on top.

All Jason could hear was the sea, then Rita saying his name over and over as though she were calling him, but he was there.

She had been born in Costa Rica and came to Long Island as a little girl, where she was raised Catholic in a Spanish neighborhood. Jason sometimes heard her praying at night in a low whisper. She had a tattoo on her arm of her grandparents' names, and often painted her nails black or sometimes dark green.

Back then Jason was working in a furniture warehouse, packing plywood parts and hardware into cardboard boxes for people to assemble at home. It paid just over minimum wage but included benefits and a product discount. The manager didn't mind that Jason had been in prison—said he believed in second chances.

Rita was working as a waitress at an Italian restaurant where the food was served family style. Jason sometimes stopped by the restaurant when Rita was working—ordering appetizers and beer until Rita's boss said that family style wasn't designed for one person and Jason could meet her in the parking lot when her shift ended.

Family, Rita said, was to her the most important thing in the world, so when she found out Jason had a younger brother, she wanted to meet him, get them talking again— but Jason was against it.

Rita liked scary movies, drive-through restaurants, and free refills. Sometimes they just sat in the car and talked about nothing.

If anyone hit on Rita in a bar while Jason was in the restroom, he would come out, put his arm around the guy, and say,

"How about me instead, baby?" Which made Rita laugh and gave the guy a chance to laugh too.

Rita didn't mind that Jason had a criminal record. And when he talked about how things were for him growing up, she held his hand. He had never cried so much in front of anyone. Rita said it meant he was learning to trust.

She planned to attend community college after she'd saved enough money and her English was better. She wanted Jason to get his high school diploma and open a custom motorcycle shop—said he was wasting his life in a factory job.

Jason listened to her. Thought about it. Had to admit he'd be happy working with bikes.

"It's us now," she would say, and always went with him to Dairy Barn when they ran out of milk or beer.

One day Rita said she'd show him Costa Rica. He could meet her grandmother and grandfather. Swim in a turquoise sea. Pick fruit to eat. Take walks along the road in wet weather, because rain makes the jungle sing, she said.

After six months together, Jason told Rita she should move in with him, because she was always there anyway and her landlord was an asshole.

Jason wanted to meet her mother and father, but Rita said they were quite religious and didn't even know about her tattoo, or that she went to bars.

Jason was in a band then, and Rita came to his rehearsals.

One night when he got home late from work, Rita jumped up off the couch and said she was ready to quit drinking and smoking, and maybe Jason would be too.

He laughed, thought it was a joke, lit a cigarette right

there. But Rita didn't laugh, or punch his arm, or grab his hair and kiss him.

The next night they argued about it. Jason lost his temper.

"What's gotten into you all of a sudden? Is it this God shit?" he said, and stormed out.

A few days later, they were watching a movie on TV when Jason lit a joint. Rita asked if he would smoke on the patio, but he told her it was his house and he had a right to smoke in it. She started crying and locked herself in the bedroom. Jason shouted at her through the door then tried to kick it down.

A week after that, Jason came home very drunk. He was already angry about something and Rita said she'd had enough. When Jason went to the refrigerator to get another beer, Rita blocked it with her body and tried to kiss him. Jason reached behind her and pulled on the handle with such force that Rita flew forward and hit the edge of a cupboard. When she ran to the bathroom holding her chin, Jason just stood there.

"What'd I do?" he kept shouting. "What'd I do?" Then he looked down and saw spots of blood on the tiles. "What'd I do?"

In the morning they both cried about it. Jason said he'd change, try and drink less, not get so angry. But another night, instead of picking Rita up after her shift, Jason rode his motorcycle over to a bar his father used to like because they stayed open past closing. The jukebox was loud, and the music made him feel invincible. By the end of the night, he couldn't even walk, so the bartender let him sleep on an old couch out back near the ice machine. In the morning, Jason had breakfast in a diner on Jericho Turnpike and went straight to work.

When he got home that night, Rita's stuff was all gone. He sat on the bed taking shots of whiskey. Then he smoked a pack of Camels, waiting for something to happen, but nothing happened, and he fell asleep in his clothes.

In the morning he reached his arm across the bed and realized that Rita was gone. That he had lost her.

He went to all her favorite bars and restaurants. No one had seen her. Jason's disappointment hardened into rage, and he began riding faster and more dangerously on his motorcycle, drinking in the parking lot before work, and talking viciously to the people who cared about him.

When the factory floor manager called Jason into the office for a chat, Jason threw a chair at him, then walked out.

Things got worse. One by one, the bartenders at his favorite spots told him not to come in anymore. He kept getting in fights, hurling insults at people he didn't know.

One afternoon he ripped his telephone out of the wall and tossed it into the yard. One of the neighbors' children was learning to ride a bike, and saw it land in the grass.

Three months later, a letter arrived.

Jason recognized Rita's handwriting and cracked open a fifth of whiskey. When the bottle ran dry, he washed away the bitter taste with a twelve-pack of beer, making a list in his head of the things she had done to spite him. The more he drank, the more imaginative he became, until the string of her offenses was so long that it choked the sentences inside the envelope before he'd even opened it and read them.

When he dropped his beer on the floor, some terrible fury tore through his body, and he ripped up the unopened letter, then burned the pieces until they were nothing.

In the morning he ran his fingers through the ashes of what remained, then cursed and cursed as he stumbled through the house looking for something to break the dryness of his mouth.

When another letter came a month later, Jason was already drunk, and he convinced himself that opening it would be like tearing open an old wound. Nothing could come of reading it but misery, he told himself. She had only been *pretending* to love him, after all. He remembered her getting upset when he lit a cigarette in his own house. He remembered the day she blocked the fridge. How could he have a woman like that in his life? What was she hoping to prove with these letters? And what more was she capable of? This letter was thicker than the last one, so Jason burned it whole on the grill, with a fork in one hand and a bottle of tequila in the other, humming a song by Guns N' Roses.

Jason thought he was over her, until a year later, he went to a concert at Jones Beach with a few of his friends. They got there early with coolers and camped on the sand. After a few drinks, Jason went off by himself. He stood looking out to sea, at the endless water, remembering how Rita had held his hand. The shape of her body under the blanket. The softness of it. Her laughter at being touched, the sound of his name in her mouth.

He had told her things about his life. About what had happened to him in prison. Even his father fixing the chain on his motorcycle a week before he died.

He had told her about Steve, the success his brother was having and how much he missed him.

Halfway through the concert, Jason got so drunk that security had to carry him out. He screamed at them from the parking lot, then tried to get back inside. They watched him writhe outside the gate, watched the veins in his neck push out.

Jason wanted to ride home and set fire to the couch, or rip the sink off the wall, but couldn't find his bike keys.

While he was on the ground looking for them, he saw something move. It turned out to be a seagull, but next to where it landed was a pay phone. There was a quarter in the pocket where Jason kept his cigarettes, and he felt for the shape of it.

When he put the coin in and dialed Rita's number, there was a click and the coin disappeared. He waited, then pushed down on the metal tongue; nothing happened. His coin did not come back. Two security guards were still watching through the fence with their arms folded. Jason took the phone receiver in both hands and brought it down with such violence that the earpiece split in two.

"That's your fuckin' heads!" he screamed, hoping they would come out into the parking lot and fight with him. Then he felt very thirsty and wondered where he could get a drink. As he was searching for another coin, one of his friends appeared.

"Jason, man, I've been looking for you everywhere, asshole."

"Can't find my keys," Jason told him. "Musta lost 'em. Got no money, neither, can't find my wallet."

"I've got your frickin' keys right here in my pocket. You're way too fucked up to do anything. I'll drive. I always wanted to take your chopper for a spin."

"Help me use the phone," Jason said. "I gotta call some-body."

But his friend just stood there staring at the broken receiver. It occurred to Jason that Rita had moved, and he remembered her number had been disconnected for some time.

When Jason's friend pulled on his arm to get up, he said he didn't want to leave the parking lot until he'd had it out with the guards. But his friend convinced him the cops were coming. "C'mon Jason, let's hit some bars," he said. "Let's go party."

Jason thought about it and said he wanted to be dropped outside Rita's old apartment. He didn't care if she was there or not. He'd finally get to have it out with her landlord.

Then, on the Meadowbrook Parkway, his foot got caught in the back wheel of his own bike, and he flew off at sixty miles per hour, flopping along the tarmac like a rag doll.

XXXIX

WHEN HARVEY WAS feeling better, Jason took her bowling to make up for missing *The Lion King* and McDonald's.

It was the middle of the day, and the parking lot was empty. Harvey had been wanting to go bowling for months, ever since she'd stayed up late to watch it live from Las Vegas on ESPN.

The woman at the counter was reading *Newsday*. "Whaddya need?" she said.

"Uh, we'd like to bowl," Jason said ironically.

The woman looked up from the newspaper. Her eyes were very small and her cheeks had red veins in them. "Cash only."

Harvey was so excited, she kept pulling on Jason's arms.

The woman asked for one of their shoes apiece, then carried them over to a cupboard. She returned with two pairs of tattered bowling shoes in red and cream. There was a vending machine with disposable socks, she said, and a long rack of balls on the back wall had six-pounders for kids.

"You want your names on the monitor?"

"No, thanks," Jason said.

"Yes!" Harvey interrupted. "Yes, yes, we do."

When Jason asked the woman to put him on as DAD, she warmed up and said each letter aloud as she typed it into a computer. "And what about you, hon?"

"Strawberry Shortcake, please," Harvey said.

"That's too long. How about Shortcake?"

"Or Strawberry?" Harvey said.

The woman nodded. "Lane twenty-six. DAD and STRAW-BERRY. Have fun."

They took their bowling shoes over to a bench and laced them up.

Their lane was at the far end, near the lockers. There were blue molded-plastic chairs and a hook where they could hang their coats. Harvey was carrying their two remaining regular shoes, and when they sat down, put them next to each other. "There," she said. "Now they can make friends, and you can't tell me to put them away."

"It's birthday bowling today," Jason said. "You can do anything you want."

"Even curse?"

Jason looked up from what he was doing. "Sure. What is it you want to say?"

"Shit, stupid, bitch, shitting, hell, jerk, bitch, stupid, shit, jerk."

Jason smiled. "Feels good don't it?"

There were names stenciled on most of the bowling balls. The one Jason chose said SAM MORRIS III.

Harvey went first. The ball was heavier than she'd thought. Jason told her to get a six pounder, but she wouldn't.

When she got to the foul line, she stopped dead and plonked her ball into the lane with both hands.

Jason looked at her. "Watch the pins."

"Dad!" she kept saying. "Just let me do it *my way.*"

Their lane was near the café, and Jason could read the menu from his seat. "Want to get the share platter?"

Harvey shrugged. "I'm not hungry."

"It's your birthday."

But Harvey said she wasn't hungry yet.

A man inside the café was putting frozen french fries into little bags, then weighing each bag on a scale.

When her ball kept lodging in the side gutter, Jason said she could take his turns to practice, but Harvey just went on releasing each ball with both hands at the line, like a watermelon.

"You have to swing your arm back," Jason said. "That gives it momentum."

Harvey sighed and fell into a seat. "It's too hard," she said. "And there's grease in the holes!"

"Grease?"

"Yes, Dad!" Harvey exclaimed, holding up her fingers. "Grease!"

There were disco lights and a disco ball on the ceiling, but no music because it was only lunchtime.

Jason had hoped to bring Harvey birthday bowling on the motorcycle, but he hadn't found parts for the swing arm yet, so all Harvey could do was sit on it in the garage. She had asked if, when it was finally done, she could get a black leather jacket, and a helmet with Strawberry Shortcake on the side? Jason said he'd seen SpongeBob helmets but that anything could be airbrushed at the chop shops in Queens, so maybe they could find a way.

Whenever Jason's ball rolled into the gutter or struck a single pin, Harvey threw her head back with laughter. "This is your face when you miss," she said, gritting her teeth in mock rage. "It's so weird!" When she opened her mouth to laugh, Jason noticed that some of her teeth were dark and crooked.

There was music playing on the loudspeaker now, and a few of the disco lights threw blues and reds into their lane.

When a group of bowlers came in, Harvey said they had to be a team because of the matching sweat suits. They stood watching Harvey and Jason bowl for a few moments, then unzipped their bowling bags and started stretching out. Harvey pretended to stretch too, but couldn't stop laughing.

"When was the last time you went to the dentist?" Jason asked her.

"None of your beeswax, Dad."

"Did Wanda take you?"

She seemed to be thinking about it but then got distracted. "My shoe is ripped."

Jason felt anger balling up inside him. He was going to tell her she'd better answer because her teeth looked pretty bad, and you have to look people in the eye when they talk to you . . . but as he opened his mouth to release the words, the impulse to attack dissolved, and he remembered they were birthday bowling, and that she was probably worried about her teeth, but didn't know what to do and was afraid to tell anyone.

Sitting there with his fingers in the slots of a bowling ball, waiting for his name to appear on the monitor, Jason realized that something had changed. That *he* had changed and was no longer at the mercy of sudden, violent impulses.

On their second game, Harvey hit the pins a few times. The music was louder too, and she was dancing. Jason ordered apple turnovers from the café, and they ripped bits off between turns. Whenever Jason got a strike, the monitor over his head flashed:

STRIKE DAD!

Harvey made fists and drummed on Jason's back. "Strike Dad!" she cried. "Strike Dad! Strike Dad!"

During the fourth and final game, Jason and Harvey found they were throwing more balls in the gutter. They'd been bowling for over two hours, and their arms had nothing left. The place had filled up and the café was overflowing with high school kids in backpacks sucking down soda.

THAT NIGHT, WHILE Harvey was getting ready for bed, Jason said he wanted to brush her teeth.

"No way." She scowled. "I don't ask to brush *your* teeth."

The next day Jason went to get advice. From Mrs. Gonzales, who couldn't believe he'd never taken her to a dentist. "What about the eye doctor?" she asked. "You should take her there too. Hector needed lenses very early."

Wanda had mentioned it a few times, but Jason figured that Harvey's baby teeth were going to fall out anyway, so he'd never seen the point in getting them checked.

The dentist recommended by Mrs. Gonzales was on the second floor of an office building in Westbury, not far from where they'd bowled a week earlier in Mineola. The waiting room was full of moms telling their kids to shut up. There was only one seat free, and Jason told Harvey to sit in it.

There was a pile of magazines on a low table, and a messy basket of children's books with cardboard pages that had been chewed on.

When they arrived, the receptionist asked Jason to fill out some paperwork. Jason pored over questions about Harvey's medical history—trying to remember if Steve had anything wrong with his mouth, because Mrs. Gonzales said stuff like this runs in families.

In the box for health insurance information, Jason wrote CASH, then felt in the pocket of his motorcycle jacket for the roll of bills he'd been saving to buy the swing-arm kit.

Jason was the only man in the waiting room. He had taken off his skull rings and was wearing the smart black button-down shirt and blue sweatpants.

When they were finally told to go in, Harvey had to get her teeth cleaned and her mouth X-rayed, so it took a while before they could meet the dentist.

When Dr. Sarah appeared holding transparent sheets, she asked Jason how long it had been since Harvey's teeth had been examined. Jason didn't know and explained that Harvey had lived with him for only the past few years.

Dr. Sarah made a note. She told Jason that from now on, Harvey should come in at least every six months.

"Does she floss?"

"No," Jason told her. "We brush instead."

The dentist said that Harvey was naturally missing a tooth, and felt she would need orthodontics right away. She also had two cavities in the upper teeth, which could be filled immediately.

Harvey gripped her father's hand as Dr. Sarah administered the first of two shots. Jason could feel her body shaking as the needle broke the gum.

When the dentist went to get something, Harvey sat up and tried to get out of the chair. But Jason held her down. After a while, Harvey said she couldn't feel her lip, and the doctor returned wearing a surgical mask.

Jason took her hand again. "Look at me," he said. "Just look at my eyes."

By the time Dr. Sarah had finished filling Harvey's cavities, there was no one else in the waiting room, and the receptionist had her coat on.

"How much?" Jason asked.

"Normally, we just bill whatever your insurance doesn't cover."

"But I don't have insurance. I've brought cash."

"Oh," the receptionist said. "Let me go talk to Dr. Sarah."

She returned a few minutes later with Dr. Sarah, who had changed into her everyday clothes.

"No insurance, Dad?" Dr. Sarah said.

Jason held up the role of bills.

"May I ask how much you budgeted?"

"Four hundred cash."

The receptionist looked at Dr. Sarah. "What do you want to do? Should we call Dr. Romanov?"

"No," Dr. Sarah said. "I'll explain it to him when he comes in tomorrow." The receptionist took Jason's money and wrote out a receipt for four hundred dollars.

"Try and get some dental insurance," Dr. Sarah told him. "Orthodontics aren't usually covered, but it still helps with scheduled visits."

"Orthodontics is braces, right? Retainers and all that?"

"Right," Dr. Sarah said. "But call that number I gave you earlier, and they'll explain the process, payment plans, and so on. Dr. Foster is the best orthodontist in the area. And don't wait, Dad—for Harvey's sake, make an appointment immediately. Tomorrow, if possible."

On the way home, they stopped at McDonald's for milkshakes, and Jason sweet-talked the cashier into putting an extra toy in the bag.

When it was time for bed, Harvey's mouth was still sore from the shots. Jason stayed and read Harry Potter. Then he stroked her arm and her eyes closed.

THE NEXT DAY, while Harvey was at school, Jason called Dr. Foster's office and wrote down everything they said. None of it seemed real. Jason kept looking at the numbers, couldn't believe it was going to cost more than their car was worth.

He decided to call Wanda and find out if Social Services would cover it. If not, there were other ways. He could rob a gas station—wrap one of his tools in a plastic bag and march right in there at closing. But then the car might be caught on a security camera, or the attendant might have a real gun and shoot him dead. He tried to imagine Harvey's face when the police came and said that her father had been killed. That he'd been shot in a robbery. That her dad was the robber.

THEIR FIRST VISIT to the orthodontist was only a consultation. The doctor wore a striped bow tie. In his wait-

ing room hung framed diplomas from the Harvard School of
Dental Medicine.

Harvey told Dr. Foster that he looked like a wizard from
Harry Potter.

"Is it the bow tie or the white hair?" Dr. Foster said.

Before leaving, Dr. Foster explained to Jason what was going to happen and what all the final costs were likely to be.

"My daughter is in good hands with you, right?" Jason
said. "Because this is a lot of money for us."

The next day Jason called Wanda again and went over
what he'd learned. If he wanted help from the state, she said,
he'd have to fill out some forms and go to certain dentists.
Dr. Foster's name didn't appear in the directory of approved
providers.

For the next two weeks, Jason drove around as many thrift
stores as he could, looking for things he could put on eBay to
sell quickly. He also asked Mr. Gonzales to try and get him
hired on a construction site, but it turned out to be impossible
with his prosthetic leg.

That weekend Harvey said she wanted to go bowling
again or to Chuck E. Cheese's, but Jason told her it was too
expensive.

"Other kids go."

"I can't right now, Harv, I ain't got it."

"So we're poor?"

"We got food, a TV, a refrigerator, a car, air-conditioning,
TV . . ."

Harvey asked to leave the table, then carried her plate to
the kitchen in silence and went to her room.

"And you've got your own bedroom!" Jason called after

her. "Your own private part of the house. I could rent that, y'know! Make a lot of money!"

Their weekly visits to Pizza Hut and Taco Bell ceased. Jason limited their grocery shopping to sale items. But Harvey just didn't get it.

"If you're hungry enough, you'll eat anything," Jason told her as he loaded the cart with blackened half-price bananas. "Any kind of animal, Harvey—even insects."

"Gross."

"Even human flesh," Jason went on. "I saw a movie where a father and son were trying to get away from redneck cannibals who wanted to eat their flesh. That could be us."

In the weeks that followed, when Harvey mentioned what other kids had for dinner or did on the weekend with their parents, Jason just bit his lip and said, "Uh-huh. Okay, Harv, whatever."

After three weeks, between his savings and eBay profits, Jason had close to a thousand dollars—more than enough for the down payment. He told Wanda he wasn't taking Harvey to no charity dentist—she was going to the Harvard guy and that was final. Wanda admired his determination and sent him a personal check for fifty dollars. Mrs. Gonzales's church group also gave a hundred. Every penny counts, Jason told Harvey as they searched the couch for loose change.

One night when Harvey was in bed, Jason sat in the garage staring at the motorcycle it had taken him almost a decade to build. It could easily have been in a custom motorcycle showroom with balloons tied to the handlebars. The tires were jet black, without even a single inch of distance on them. Harvey had helped hang leather strips from the ends of the grips and polish the nickel-plated headlight. When they started the engine for the first time, the roar made their ears ring for hours.

He remembered Harvey saying that she couldn't wait to see the faces of everyone at school when she showed up on the back of her dad's bike. "No one believes me when I tell them you've been building a motorcycle in the garage. They think I'm lying."

"See what they say when we roar up to the gates!" Jason promised. "I'll even rev it up a bit—or just skip school altogether, and we'll ride all the way to Montauk and then back like it's nothing."

MONTHS LATER, AFTER endless consultations and instructions from Dr. Foster, it was time for the retainer to be fitted in Harvey's mouth. When they got home that afternoon, Harvey couldn't stop looking at herself in the mirror.

"Oh my God," she kept saying. "Oh my God!"

"You'll get used to it," Jason said.

"It hurts and I look stupid."

"This is for the future, Harv, so that when you're older, your teeth are straight and look good."

Harvey stamped her foot. "I can't keep this in my mouth!" she yelled. "I look stupid. Why did you let them do this to me?"

"You needed it," Jason said. "Dr. Sarah said so, and Dr. Foster too. Try and see it as medicine."

"But I'm not sick," Harvey screamed. "My teeth were fine, and now they're ruined! I'm a freak!"

Jason closed the hatch on the coffee machine and listened to her bang around in the bathroom. "You think those doctors have those fancy offices from getting it wrong?" he called out to her. "They make a lot of money helping to put kids' teeth right. They get rich from being right."

Suddenly, she was standing right in front of him. "No, Dad, they make a lot of money from suckers like you! This is a nightmare and I can't wake up!"

Jason thought of the Metallica video where a man comes back from war without any arms or legs and says the same thing to the doctor: *This is a nightmare and I can't wake up.*

Then Harvey said in a low voice, "My *real* father never would have let this happen."

Jason slammed down his coffee cup and waited for the impulse to pass. Then he said calmly, "Steve would have done exactly the same thing, Harvey, it's money well spent."

When the coffee was ready, Jason poured it, then went to get milk, but Harvey was blocking the refrigerator.

"I look stupid!" she hissed. "Like a cheese grater."

Jason reached around her to open the door, but then let his hand fall and backed away.

Harvey was livid. "You've ruined my life!"

"I think you should go to your room and calm down."

But Harvey wouldn't. "I'm not a child anymore—I'm a *tween*. But then you wouldn't know what a tween is, would you? You just don't get it. And you never will."

When she had gone, Jason leaned on the counter and shook his head. A cheese grater, he thought. What next?

When dinner was ready, Jason realized she might be embarrassed to eat in front of him, so he left a bowl of chili, some buttered cornbread, a glass of Sprite, and a napkin outside her bedroom door.

A few hours later, when he woke up from a nap, Harvey was already in her pajamas and fast asleep. The bowl, plate, and glass were in the sink, and the paper towel she'd used as a napkin balanced on top of a full trash can.

He thought that was the end of all the drama, but as he was making breakfast the next morning, Harvey burst in from the garage, and Jason dropped the toast that was in his hand.

"Your bike's been stolen!" she cried. "I just went out to get my skateboard, and your motorcycle's gone! We have to call the police!"

Jason picked up his toast and brushed it off. Then he reached deep in his pocket for the poker-chip key chain that had once hung from the ignition key. Harvey didn't understand.

"How come you have that?"

But Jason just nodded. Could still smell the oil and the rubber from new tires. He had built that motorcycle with his bare hands.

XL

THE NEXT MORNING it was raining, so they shared an umbrella up the rue Caulaincourt toward the Métro station.

It was rush hour, and the train was full of people carrying briefcases and bags. When they got off at Madeleine, however, the streets were empty because it was early and the shops were still closed.

For breakfast, Harvey wanted to take her father to a café on rue Saint-Honoré, near the grand fashion boutiques.

The enormous stone pillars of the nearby Madeleine Church, blackened by decades of traffic, seemed ancient and made Jason want to come back when he was alone to sit somewhere, and think about how quickly he felt life was passing now.

When they reached a quiet corner with some shelter from the rain, Harvey asked her father to stand still and close his eyes. Then she described a solemn line of horses and rickety wagons moving across the cobbles, full of people on their way to the guillotine.

When they continued on toward the café, Harvey asked Jason what he thought people in the future would say about what people living now had done wrong.

"I'll be long gone by then," he said. "And you'll be an old woman in a spaceship with grandkids on your lap in aluminum foil diapers."

"You're so weird, Dad."

"If you think about it, Harvey—you might be the only person left alive who remembers that a guy called Jason once lived on Long Island."

When they reached the café, the waiter wasn't there to seat them, so they sat along a narrow bar, watching workmen line up at the front for hot croissants. On a shelf in the background, a television was showing a video of bakers loading baguette dough into ovens on wooden paddles. The screen was dusty and the television set too high up for anyone to watch comfortably.

When the waiter finally appeared, he seemed to recognize Harvey, but not well enough to ask who Jason was. There were faint patches of flour on his pants where he'd been leaning against a counter. He apologized for being absent and asked what they would like to eat.

When the croissants arrived, they were on two small plates with butter, jam, and the café name written in gold script on brown napkins. Below the name was a sketch of a little girl holding flowers behind her back.

"I can't wipe my mouth with this," Jason said. "It's way too pretty. Reminds me of you."

"It's just a napkin," Harvey said. "Wait until you see my office."

Her building wasn't far from the café.

When they got close, the rain stopped and Jason folded up the umbrella. At the entrance, Harvey typed in a code, and they stepped through a small wooden door into a cobblestone courtyard where a few cars and motorcycles were parked.

"This is like in Harry Potter," Jason said. "What was that place? Diagram Alley, right?"

Harvey grinned and told him that the art department had its own entrance, which was easier than having to go through the main gate every morning, with all the security on rue du Chevalier-de-Saint-George.

The building had once been a music school, she explained, then during World War II, the students were sent away and the building was used by the Nazis, who draped flags on the outside and piled sandbags by the doors.

Harvey's desk was in a large, open area, near other designers who looked up from their work to say *allo* when they saw her appear with her father.

Then a woman came over and kissed Jason on both cheeks. "We love your daughter," Sophie told him. "Please don't take her back to America."

Harvey's desk was a mess of papers, crayons, cans of felt-tip pens, pictures cut out from magazines, cartoons, and a miniature camel she'd brought from home. On a cork bulletin board were drawings with dates written over them in heavy black pen. Harvey said these were her assignments. In a frame beside her giant Apple monitor was a photograph of her father. "Look," she said. "Here's that guy Jason who lived long ago on Long Island." The picture had been taken at Jones Beach a few summers before.

"That's a lovely photo," Sophie said. "But you're not smiling."

Taped to an electric pencil sharpener, Harvey had a small picture of her first mom and dad. Jason pointed to it. "It's cool you have that," he said.

Over the years, Harvey had grown comfortable asking Jason more about what they were like. Jason had never met her mother—so they both had to imagine what she was like from the photos, and from the things of hers that Wanda had brought over.

After Sophie found Jason a seat, someone made coffee and put out cookies. Harvey checked her messages, then clicked Jason through different art files on her desktop, explaining what her main role was at the company.

When it was time to leave, Jason asked to use the restroom. All the espresso had made him dizzy, and after splashing some cold water on his face and neck, he caught himself staring at his reflection in the mirror, wondering how the people in Harvey's office saw him, and if his daughter was ashamed of the thinning hair and the shriveled tattoo on his neck. He remembered their conversation that morning in the rain, as they walked to the café, about how one day he'd be gone, how she would be the only person left to remember him.

HARVEY TOLD EVERYONE in the office she was taking her father to Galeries Lafayette to check out the toy department. Sophie walked them to a taxi stand, then kissed Jason again several times on both cheeks.

Harvey could tell her father was a little embarrassed. "I thought the French didn't like Americans," he said, blushing.

Sophie laughed, "No, that is not true—or maybe just the Republican Party."

It was a short ride, and they got out behind the Paris Opéra. Harvey said that she spent a lot of time at Galeries Lafayette, just strolling around the different departments, looking for new colors and designs to inspire her. They entered through menswear, then, stepping off the first escalator, came upon small mountains of powder and dried teas. A group of Chinese tourists were taking photographs of themselves in front of a four-foot bottle of brandy.

Once they'd seen all the spices, they strolled past refrigerated cases full of cheeses and meats. Harvey wanted to buy some famous Jamaican Blue Mountain coffee for Jason, but there were too many people waiting, and the young male attendant was surrounded by teenage girls who kept pointing to different coffee beans and giggling. One of the girls kept covering her mouth, the way Jason remembered Harvey used to, after her retainer was fitted.

Passing through the jams and mustards, Harvey noticed a security guard trailing them. When she turned angrily in his direction, the guard sidestepped into some Spanish hams. Harvey wanted to confront him, but Jason thought it was funny.

"His instincts are pretty good, Harvey—I do have a criminal record, after all."

"But you just beat the crap out of bad people," Harvey said. "You never *stole* anything, did you?"

At the rear of the food department was a folding table stacked with sale items: chocolate kittens with cracked paws or missing ears, dented cans of Portuguese sardines, sweets left over from Christmas, broken Hanukkah candles.

"I guess this is the reject pile," Harvey said.

Jason picked up a box of chocolates that had melted into one uneven mass and looked at his daughter. "This is the section where the French Jason would work."

"C'mon, Dad," Harvey said. "That's not funny."

When they ascended to footwear, Harvey asked if Jason wanted to try anything on, but he already had new shoes, so they went up another escalator and found themselves in the fabled toy department.

The colorful shelves were crammed with cars, helicopters, buses, board games, soldiers, dragons, horses, knights, fairies, soft animals from every jungle and forest, river and sea. In another section were rows of pistols, ninja stars, bazookas, and boxing gloves. Two boys dueled with plastic swords for the attention of their blond nanny, who was busy texting.

When they passed into the girls' section, Jason noticed an entire shelf of Polly Pocket dolls. There was a Polly Pocket beauty salon, a pizzeria, even a stable of ponies. A sign at the top of the shelf said POLLYVILLE.

"Look, Dad, they've got play sets now!" Harvey said. "That's so cool."

Jason couldn't believe they had Polly Pocket dolls in Paris. "I used to buy you these all the time, Harvey—used to save up and buy them for you from Stop and Shop."

"Yeah, I still have a box of them somewhere. In my room, I think."

"Remember when we took them camping in the backyard? And made tents out of leaves?"

"Wow, that was so long ago," Harvey said. "More than half my life."

"It wasn't long for me," Jason said. "Or it doesn't feel like it was."

Harvey sifted wistfully through the play sets. "God, I was so young then."

Simon Van Booy

"You like something Harvey?" her father asked. "Can I get you something?"

"No thanks, Dad."

"C'mon, Harv. Please? When was the last time I bought you a new toy?"

"Well," Harvey said, reaching for a doll, "I don't have this one! Will you please get this one for me? Please, Dad? Please? I'll do extra chores! I'll do my homework! I'll even put my shoes away . . . please, Daddy?"

The cashier, a Muslim woman wearing a head scarf, must have sensed it was important and took a lot of care with the doll, wrapping it in paper and tying the package with a ribbon.

When they got outside, Harvey wouldn't let on where she was taking her father for lunch, but on Boulevard Haussmann she handed him a small item in tissue paper.

"Last thing from my Father's Day box?" Jason said, turning it over in his hands.

"Almost," Harvey said. "There is something else, but it's an envelope."

As they strolled beneath the statues of long-dead French writers, they talked about the future. Harvey said she wanted to live in Tokyo for a while, then get married, maybe buy a house in Montauk, where a new art scene was happening. Jason said that after he retired from the supermarket, he wanted to ride a Harley-Davidson trike across the country and get pictures of all the people he would meet along the way.

When they arrived at the Hard Rock Café Paris, Jason couldn't believe it. He wanted a picture of them next to the sign out front. "I'm thinking about starting a Facebook page," he said. "So I can post pictures of us in Paris."

Harvey said it was a great idea.

The maître d' who agreed to take their picture had dread-locks and a pirate beard. He told them in English there was a wait for tables, but the bar was empty.

The bartender was surprised when Harvey spoke to him in French. He showed them a list of nonalcoholic cocktails, but Jason wanted root beer. Harvey ordered white wine and the Nachopalooza to snack on.

Jason was still turning the Father's Day gift in his fingers.

"If you guess it," Harvey said, "I'll get you a Hard Rock Café Paris glass to match the New York one you have at home."

"It smells good," he said, sniffing the small package.

"That's because it's been in my pocketbook," Harvey explained. "Perfume is not a good clue for what this is, trust me."

"Is it breakable?"

When she said no, Jason pushed on the little parts, trying to discern the shape, and something jabbed through the paper and stuck in his thumb. Blood seeped from a small puncture and shone under the bright lights. Harvey waved the bartender over and asked in French for a Band-Aid. When he returned, Harvey noticed a tattoo on the bartender's arm of a human heart with the words STILL BEATING.

"You owe me a matching glass," Jason said. "It's a fishing lure." When he actually unwrapped it, the lure glittered, and there were bold colors on the shaft below the fake eye.

When their drinks came, Jason ordered the Texan burger and ribs.

"I'll take the salmon," Harvey said. "To go with your present, Dad."

The walls of the restaurant were decorated with rock-and-roll artifacts. On his way down to the restroom, Jason saw a Stone Temple Pilots jacket, and oversized platinum and silver discs signed by the members of Pearl Jam, Led Zeppelin, and Tool. "Great Balls of Fire" by Jerry Lee Lewis was playing, and after that "Cryin' Like a Bitch" by Godsmack, which Jason was surprised they would have on, as the dining area was full of families with children in high chairs.

After their food arrived, a father and son came in and sat near them at the bar. The boy, who looked like he was around eighteen, asked the bartender in French what beers they had on tap. Then he told his father in English, but the father was tired and didn't care. "Just gimme whiskey," he said. "That's all I want."

Harvey listened to their conversation as she ate. The boy talked about the history of Paris, then joked in French with the bartender. The father just stared at his glass, holding it up when he wanted another. When the father went downstairs to the restroom, Jason leaned over to the man's son and said how impressive his French was. The boy blushed. He told them he was attending school in Paris for a semester, and that his father was visiting a few days from Winnipeg, where years ago he played professional hockey.

"Well," Jason said, "you're braver than me, to come and live in another country."

The boy blushed again. "It's not that hard, really."

"Nah, c'mon," Jason said. "It's a big deal. You ought to be proud of yourself."

When the father came back from the restroom, he said he wanted to leave and took out his wallet. After they'd gone, the bartender cleared their glasses and wiped the bar down.

"It was nice of you to do that," Harvey said.

"Do what?"

"You know." She smiled. "Don't pretend."

Jason looked at the fishing lure on the counter. "I know what it is," he said, "and I can tell you how to use it. But I'm stumped as to what it means."

"Think about it, Dad."

"I'm thinking," he said. "But I can't see."

XLI

ONE SATURDAY MORNING Jason heard Harvey crying in the bathroom.

He didn't know what to do because she wouldn't tell him anything through the door. When he noticed there was blood on the handle, he told her he was going to call 911 if she didn't let him in. Harvey opened the door a crack, and Jason pushed his way through.

"There's blood on the door handle!" he said. "What's going on?"

"Jesus Christ," Harvey said, pushing past him. "Why are you so annoying?"

When she finally emerged from her room an hour later with a bundle of bedsheets, Jason jumped up from the couch.

"Are you okay? What's going on? I'm kinda freaking out here, Harvey. What was that blood on the door handle? You cut yourself?"

He followed her into the laundry room, but she screamed at him to get out, so he watched between the hinges and couldn't believe it. There was blood all over the sheets. Just as he was about to burst in, he remembered something Wanda had said, and realized what was happening.

After brewing fresh coffee, he set a mug down outside Harvey's bedroom door and knocked. "Black, Harvey—just the way you like it." But she opened the door and said she needed a ride to the drugstore.

In the car Jason told her he was sorry.

Harvey was staring straight ahead at the road. "What are you sorry for?" she said bitterly. "It's not your fault."

"I should have mentioned something. It just totally slipped my mind."

"It's none of your business, and I knew from school, anyway."

"In class?"

"Dad!"

When they got there, Jason said there was twenty dollars in the glove box. "Get some candy too, if you want, or a Polly Pocket or something."

After ten minutes, she appeared with a small shopping bag. She put the change in a cup holder.

"I think we're gonna need pizza tonight," Jason said driving home. "And you can choose the movie. Whatever you want, I'll watch, even if it's got subtitles."

Harvey just sat there holding the bag, staring straight ahead.

When they got back, she locked herself in the bathroom again. The coffee in the jug was cold, so Jason made another batch. After half an hour, he couldn't wait any longer and knocked to see if she was okay. The door unbolted and she rushed out holding a small box. But in her haste to get past her father, Harvey dropped the box, and little white things rolled all over the floor.

"Keep what you need in the bathroom cupboard if you want," Jason said. "Then you'll be ready for next month."

Harvey covered her mouth. "Next month!"

. . .

A few weeks later, Jason found a box of toys in the hall-way. "What's all this stuff?" he shouted through her bedroom door.

Harvey shouted back that she didn't need them anymore, that she was too old.

"But these are your toys!" Jason said. "It's the Polly Pockets we used to play with. And—what the hell—is that Duncan?"

Not long after, Jason started paying attention to whom Harvey was talking with on the phone, and checking her Internet browsing history. Mrs. Gonzales advised him to set a curfew and enforce it strictly—which he did, but in exchange for Harvey keeping it, Jason increased her allowance and bought her a basic cell phone.

By her next birthday, Harvey was cooking dinner a few nights a week, and Jason no longer had to wait in the parking lot with the weekend edition of *Newsday* while Harvey spent whole afternoons in the mall with her friends.

The summer before high school, Jason took some vacation time from work, and they went to Montauk for a week. One of Harvey's girlfriends came for a couple of days with her parents, and they all spent time at the beach, and had breakfast every morning at John's Pancake House.

It was the first real vacation they'd ever been able to afford. Jason had given up on his Internet business and was working full-time at the Stop and Shop, if only for the medical benefits and retirement package. The manager, Dale, rode a Harley-Davidson Electra Glide and sometimes paid Jason to help him with mechanical jobs. Jason worked mostly by himself at night, stacking shelves, listening to music through headphones.

A few weeks into Harvey's first semester of high school, she came home and went straight to her room.

When Jason called her for dinner, she shouted that she wasn't hungry. But when it was on the table, he knocked, and Harvey told him she'd come down later. Jason didn't know what to do, and so just kept knocking. When she finally opened the door a crack, he saw she had a black eye.

"I walked into something," she said. Then she started to cry. "I knew you would freak out."

"I ain't freaking out," Jason said, biting his lip. "I'm cool." Then he went downstairs and put dinner back in the oven until she was ready to eat. He had made taco pie, because Harvey loved taco pie.

An hour later when they'd finished eating, Jason grabbed the newspaper and told Harvey there was a good movie starting in twenty minutes and ice cream bars in the freezer.

For the first half hour of the film, he said nothing, then during a long commercial break, he couldn't help himself. "I know you probably don't want to talk about it—and I'm trying to be really cool—but at some point you're going to have to tell me what's going on."

"It's none of your business."

"Don't speak to me like that," Jason told her. "I would never say that to you, so don't say it to me."

"Do you even know how it feels to have a black eye? Do you?"

Jason laughed.

"But this is not your fight, Dad."

"If you don't tell me, Harvey, I'm gonna just steam into school with you tomorrow and start crackin' heads."

"Yeah, that's really cool—then I would *really* die. Look, it's not a big deal. It's just this one girl."

"A girl?" Jason couldn't believe it. "A *girl* did this?"

Harvey had always done well in the classroom, but in the past month she'd forgotten a few homework assignments and even failed a couple of tests. The lunches Jason made her were coming home uneaten, and when he confronted her, she wouldn't talk about it.

When the movie was almost over, Harvey confessed that there was actually a group of kids who were making her life miserable. They were all kids who'd been to the same middle school. Their leader was a girl named Jordan. She called Harvey names and made fun of her style, which had become Gothy in the past year, with black fingernail polish and black clothes.

"Now they're telling everyone I'm a lesbian," Harvey said.

"Are you?"

"Dad!"

"It doesn't matter if you are, I'm totally cool with it. Lesbians are awesome."

"I'm not a lesbian."

"But if you were, Harvey—"

"Dad!"

A week before, someone at lunch told Harvey that Jordan had said Harvey's *real* parents were murdered by a serial killer—that the killer was never caught, but police knew he rode motorcycles and was a cripple.

Harvey got the black eye when a door swung back that Jordan had pretended to hold for her. Everyone laughed, Harvey said. But Jordan pretended to be concerned. "Oh my God," she said, "what if Harvey's really hurt this time?"

Harvey wanted to know what her father was going to do. "Please don't go down there, Dad. *Please.*"

Jason said he was going to write to the principal. That an official, signed letter was the correct way to handle this. "What's Jordan's last name?" he asked. "Just so the principal gets the right girl."

After the movie, Harvey went out to the patio with her iPod and headphones. When Jason was certain she couldn't hear, he looked up the girl's last name online and got her phone number.

A man picked up, and Jason explained to him what had been happening.

"I can't control what my kid does," the man said. "You know what I mean, guy?"

Jason asked again, calmly, if he would speak to his daughter, because it seemed like Jordan was being a little tough.

"It's a tough world," the man said. "What can I do?"

Later on, when Harvey was in bed, Jason took a hammer into the backyard and smashed up one of the lawn chairs.

THE NEXT DAY Jordan told the whole school that Jason had called their house and cried on the phone to her dad.

Harvey came home and said she wanted to die. "I asked you not to interfere," she screamed. "I pleaded with you just to let me figure this one out by myself."

"It'll blow over," Jason said, trying to calm her down. "You'll see."

"I just want to die!" she screamed. "My whole life has

been one disaster after another!" Then she ran to her room and slammed the door.

Jason slumped into the couch and put on the TV. Harvey had said she wished to die. His daughter wanted to end her life because of a bully.

Halfway through dinner, Jason's hands were shaking so much he was unable to hold the fork. "Put your shoes on," he said.

Harvey looked at her food.

"Put your shoes on, Harvey. We're going out."

Her eyes followed him to the closet. "Why are you putting on your motorcycle jacket, Dad? It's eighty degrees."

"C'mon, Harvey, what are you waiting for? Move it."

A part of her wanted to block the door. And Jason had expected her to block the door the way women did in Westerns, when their fathers or husbands were leaving for a showdown. *We could relocate to Pennsylvania,* she might have said. *Make new friends there. We could have a bigger yard and go walking in the fields at dusk with all the lightning bugs . . .*

Jason watched his daughter put on her shoes and do up the laces. She knew where they were going but somehow couldn't bring herself to do anything to stop it, as though she were tethered to her father's will—as though, after so long together, they'd come to share a single fate.

WHEN THEY WERE in the car, Jason started the engine. For a moment they just sat there listening to the lull and tick of moving parts.

"You ready?" he said.

Harvey nodded. "I'm afraid."

"You don't have to be afraid anymore," Jason said, pulling out of the driveway. "I'm going to see to that."

There were no trees on the street where Jordan Magliano lived. The yards were all patches of lawn broken up by strips of gray concrete. It was dinnertime. Meals were being served. Televisions were being watched, and the sounds of voices and audience laughter filled each house. Iced tea in plastic cups. Garlic bread. Bits of sausage ladled onto plates with sauce. Video games on pause.

Jason didn't have to read the numbers. There was a van in the driveway with a sign on the side:

MAGLIANO HOT & COLD
BEST HVAC LONG ISLAND
(516) XXX XXXX

They parked at the curb. Jason glanced at his daughter's black eye and imagined the man he'd spoken to the night before: tall, loud, cocky—the kind of guy people call *big man* or *big guy*. Fuck up anyone he wants—makes him feel powerful. Honk at him and he'll get out of his van and fuck you up. One of *those* guys. Jason could hear his voice too, threatening Harvey, calling her white trash, a freak—a freak of nature who'd killed her parents. He could see himself revving the engine with his service van outside the school. Jordan in the passenger seat dying with laughter as her dad scares the freak girl, threatens to run her down, then pulls forward blocking her way . . .

Harvey is saying something. Jason turns to look at her but sees nothing, hears nothing, only breath rushing through his teeth and tightness in his muscles. He gets out of the car, pulls the billy club from his pant leg. With two swings, the back windows of the van shatter, the pieces falling inside. Then a few quick blows to the metal sides of the van; the panels dent easy, and the paintwork flakes onto the driveway. If Jason had his old flick-knife, he'd scalp the tires, but instead he rips off a side mirror and stamps on it with his good foot. Then he pops out the driver's-side window, spits on the steering wheel. Next come the headlights. The glass is tempered, but eventually, they give—and he crushes each bulb with a hard poke. The front grille cracks with five or six blows. As he turns to swing at the windshield, Jason glimpses a small face watching him from an upstairs window. Then the front door of the house flies open and a heavyset man appears. He is wearing blue jeans and a New York Jets T-shirt with cutoff sleeves.

"What the hell are you doing to my van?" He shouts.

Jason tosses his club to the ground. "Why don't you come over here and find out what I'm doing? You dumb mother-fucker."

The man hesitates, then moves toward Jason from the doorway. But before he can get off the porch, the face that was watching from upstairs has turned into a boy, and the child has wrapped his body around his father's leg.

"Leave my daddy alone!"

His voice is so high, it's breaking. " . . . you leave my daddy alone!"

The man shouts at the child to go back inside, but he won't let go.

Jason just stands there, staring at the boy in his pajamas. He knows those eyes, that look, the desperation to protect, the fear masquerading as courage.

Then suddenly Jason can't move, and lets his body slump down on the driveway.

By now, neighbors are out on their lawns.

Then the police come. They block the road with their cars and draw weapons.

Jason is cuffed. Harvey brushes away pieces of glass and sits with him on the concrete.

When the police lock Jason in a cruiser, Harvey asks to sit in the backseat, but they won't let her. The neighbors are staring at her black fingernail polish, her dyed black hair with red streaks, her fishnet tights and Dr. Martens boots.

Then Jordan and her mother get home. They have to park their car down the street. Jordan knows even before they get there—this is somehow her fault.

After half an hour, the police lead Jason around the back of the house, still in handcuffs. Harvey follows without saying anything. Jordan is there too, standing off to one side. The little boy is back in the house watching TV.

Mrs. Magliano makes coffee. Hands everyone a mug. Harvey asks the police several times if they'll take the handcuffs off before they agree.

"You gonna pay for the mess you made?" one of the cops says to Jason.

Jason nods. "Yes, sir. I am."

"You better, because if Mr. and Mrs. Magliano file charges, most likely you're headed back to prison. You know that, right?"

Jason nods.

"And it'll be a longer stretch than you did the first time," the cop adds.

Jason keeps his head low but then raises his eyes. "You the judge now, too, Sheriff?"

"What a piece of work," one of the other cops says, shaking his head.

Harvey is standing nearby with her arms crossed. "Please don't speak to my dad like that. Even if he is in the wrong, it's not right."

The cop apologizes. Calls her *miss*. Jason can't believe how grown up she sounds.

"No one wants anyone to go to jail," Mrs. Magliano interrupts. "Harvey, if your dad agrees here and now to pay for all the damages, then we'll consider the matter over and done with."

Harvey says how grateful she is and how sorry they are for what happened.

"I'm sure my daughter is sorry too," Mrs. Magliano says. "For whatever her part was in this."

Harvey can tell Jordan has been crying, because her makeup is ruined.

After the police leave, Mrs. Magliano sits opposite Jason in a patio chair. Mr. Magliano is there too, standing to one side with his arms crossed. It's almost dark, and insects are spinning chaotically around the outdoor lights.

"Oh my God, what a mess, huh?" Mrs. Magliano says, but in a friendly way.

"The truth is," she goes on, "Jordan is on probation right now for shoplifting and driving a motor vehicle without a license, and she's also in major frickin' trouble at school. So the deal is, in return for us not pressing charges, you pay for the damage you did to my husband's van and promise not to report this to the school."

Jason sips his coffee. Looks at his daughter's black eye. Promises he won't say a word.

"Because if one more parent makes a written complaint against Jordan at school," Mrs. Magliano continues, "she'll be expelled."

A FEW NIGHTS later, Harvey woke up in the early hours to get a glass of water, and heard noises coming from Jason's bedroom.

It wasn't the first time she'd heard him crying.

A week after that, watching her father pore over bills for the damage he had done to the Magliano van, Harvey had an idea, and spent the weekend at her computer, reading through old newspaper articles in search of a name.

Three nights later, while Jason was at work, Harvey psyched herself up and made the call.

"Yes? Hello?"

"Oh, hello," Harvey said. "May I please speak with Vincent?"

"You wanna speak with Vinnie? Who is this, please?"

"My name is Harvey."

"If you're selling something, we're not interested, okay? We don't need nothing."

"I'm not selling anything."

"What do you want to speak to my son for then?"

"Is he there?"

"Are you from the library?

"No."

"You sound like the woman from the library."

"I would like to speak to your son, if that's okay."

"What it's about?"

"I'd rather speak to him first, if that's okay."

"I hope this isn't bad news. We don't need any bad news."

"It's not bad news, but I'd like to speak with him."

"He's downstairs. I gotta call him from the basement."

"I don't mind."

"It'll take him a while to get up here."

"I can wait."

"He's blind, you know. Did you know that? Did you know my son is blind?"

XLII

THE FOLLOWING SATURDAY there was a knock on the door. Harvey looked through the peephole and saw a woman brushing her adult son's hair with one hand.

Harvey had expected him to look more dangerous. But the blind man was short, with a tight, round belly and a pock-marked face. He had on dark glasses and was steadied at the elbow by his mother.

"Who is it?" Jason shouted from the bedroom. "Mrs. Gonzales?"

Vincent's mother guided her son over the doorstep, and Harvey invited them to sit down. Jason must have heard voices, because the toilet flushed and he came rushing out with a motorcycle magazine under his arm.

"What's going on, Harvey? Who are these people?"

"You haven't told him?" Vincent's mother said. "He doesn't know we're here?"

Vincent let out a small laugh, then removed his dark glasses to reveal a delicate but quick motion under his eyelids, like small creatures fluttering under silk.

Harvey bit her lip. "This is Vincent, Dad."

"Who?"

"The guy you fought with when you were nineteen."

Jason went pale, started to back away.

"C'mon, let's go," the blind man's mother said, getting up. "This was a bad idea."

Vincent put his glasses back on, then moved his hands around in the air.

"Your daughter should have told you!" she snapped at Jason. "We're leaving, and we don't want any trouble. My son is blind."

Jason turned to Harvey. "This is the worst thing you've ever done."

But Harvey was defiant. "You need to deal, Dad," she said firmly. "Or you'll always be angry, and I love you too much to let that happen."

Jason shook his head. "What do you know? You don't know anything."

"I know a lot actually, from things I read on the Internet . . ."

Jason didn't want to hear it, but Harvey kept going. "One article said if you apologize for what happened and make up and face it head-on, you'll feel better in the long run. I'm serious. All you have to do is apologize."

The blind man turned his head slowly in the general direction of Jason. "I'm sorry," he said, fingering his dark glasses. "I'm so very sorry."

"Not you!" barked his mother. "Harvey was talking to her father!"

Then she took her son's arm to leave.

"Don't go," Harvey said. "My dad cries at night. I hear him."

Jason threw his arms in the air. "What the hell are you talking about?"

Then the blind man spoke up. "Don't be mad at her! Be mad at me if you want, but don't be mad at her. She's trying to help us. She's being a good person."

"I went to jail because of you," Jason said.

Vincent removed his glasses again, to show them what remained of his eyes. "And I haven't seen anything since that night because of you."

Everyone was quiet for a moment. Then Jason spoke. "What the hell then, I guess I'm sorry too." Then he turned to his daughter. "Satisfied now?"

"That's good, Dad," she said. "It's a great start."

"I wasn't expecting this on a Saturday morning. You should have told me they were coming."

"Well, we're here now," Vincent's mother said. "Harvey begged us to come, and we came."

When they were sitting on the couch again, Jason took a chair from the dining table and sat opposite the blind man's mother.

Harvey put out some snacks and cold drinks, and they fell naturally into conversation. Turned out Vincent had also given up drinking. His mother had gotten him treatment after he fell down the basement stairs one morning before she was up.

As Harvey refilled everyone's glass, Jason told the story of his motorcycle accident and the fruitless search for work in the city.

The blind man had not worked because there was nothing he could do. He was not married, but sometimes had dates with women, most of them divorced, whom his mother met at the beauty parlor in Bethpage. She would have to drive him there and pick him up. When they got home, she'd make hot tea, ask what the woman was like, if she had any kids, whether Vincent thought they might see each other again.

Mostly though, his life consisted of just sitting, listening to his mother or the TV. In the early days he used to cry, he said, really bawl, and move his hands around in the air, which meant he wanted to be touched.

His mother took him shopping on Wednesdays. They went to the park in the spring to hear birds, and to the beach in August when it was hot. Their most regular outing was to the library twice a week so that Vincent could socialize with other blind people and check out talking books. Around Christmas, he built doll furniture from clothes pegs, which the local Catholic church sold in the church shop with a sign that said MADE BY A BLIND PERSON.

Vincent's mother asked Harvey if she would show her the yard, give Jason and Vincent some time alone. When they were outside, she said her big dream was to see Vinny married. "I've even thought about getting him a girl from Russia. They call them mail-order brides. I ordered the catalog and everything, but all that lipstick and blond hair—Vincent wouldn't be interested."

After Harvey showed her the climbing roses and the Japanese maple, the blind man's mother said that she was actually grateful to God for sparing her son's life.

"He could have gone back to the bar with a gun," she said. "He had one, you know . . . but that's what he was like back then. You couldn't stop him from doing anything once his mind was made up."

. . .

WHEN IT CAME time to leave, Jason asked if there was anything he could do for them, now or in the future.

Vincent's mother said that if they were ever near Massapequa, they should make a point of stopping in. But then the blind man stood quickly, his body shaking. "There is something you can do," he declared.

"Vincent!" his mother said, pulling on his arm. "Sit down!"

But he wouldn't. Jason asked what it was he wanted.

"Take me fishing," he said. "I want to go fishing."

The woman shook her head. "How can you go fishing, Vincent? Tell me that."

"I want to go fishing, Ma. I'm sick of the frickin' library. I want to go fishing, and I want to catch a fish."

XLIII

THREE WEEKS LATER, Vincent stood on his mother's back porch and held up a bag of ice.

"I don't believe it," she called from an upstairs window. "Is that a fish in there?"

A month later, they took another boat out of Sayville and caught enough fluke to fill a cooler.

When winter came, the two of them bought thermal overalls at Roosevelt Field mall and took the cod boats out of Montauk. Most fleets sailed in the early hours and went fifty miles into deep water.

After a couple of years, Jason and Vincent had a routine, leaving by eleven o'clock at night, then stopping at midnight for bacon and eggs at a diner on Old Country Road.

On the first trip of their second winter season, the waitress said she recognized them from the year before. Vincent said that it must have been the tattoo on Jason's neck, but the waitress overheard and said to Vincent, "No, it's *you* I remember, not your friend." At first she thought Vincent was drunk, but then she saw him feeling around the table for salt and pepper and realized.

She asked what they were doing up at midnight, and Vincent said they were chasing a cod boat out of Montauk. The diner was quiet so she lingered awhile at the table after bringing their food, asking if they weren't cold out there on the sea, or afraid, or if it wasn't better just to buy fish at the supermarket.

In the parking lot, Jason couldn't help himself. "I personally think you look like an ape—but the waitress must like that kind of thing, 'cause she filled your coffee cup first and gave you way more home fries than me."

Vincent told him to shut up.

"C'mon, Vincent," he said. "Why would I make shit up about home fries?"

The waitress had told them her name was Bethany, and had given them pound cake for the trip—for when they got hungry on the boat.

Driving through the darkness along Southern Parkway, Vincent asked Jason to tell him what Bethany looked like. "Start with the hair," he said. "Is it long or short?"

THE FOLLOWING AFTERNOON, on their way home with seventeen pounds of cod in two coolers, Vincent wanted to stop at the diner. When they got there, Jason helped his friend out of the car and led him around to the trunk. Then he put Vincent's hand on the lid of the cooler and let him open it. The fish was already cut up in bags, ready to freeze.

"What if she doesn't like seafood?" Vincent said.

"Let me go see if she's there first."

"Wait, Jason. Wait a second, please. Jason, stop!"

A moment later, Bethany came out and Vincent handed her a bag of cod. The flesh was white with silver streaks.

"Are you serious?" she said. "You brought this for me?"

· · ·

A FEW YEARS later, when Vincent's mother passed, they put a picture of Vincent and Bethany on their wedding day in the casket under her rosary.

Vincent and Bethany had rushed the wedding so his mother could attend. At the reception, Vincent said in his speech that if it hadn't been for his best friend's daughter, Harvey, he'd still be sitting in a basement *watching* life instead of actually living it.

Vincent's mother was very sick by then and couldn't speak. In the car home, Jason said it was good that Vincent couldn't actually see how bad she was. Harvey agreed.

"Listen," he said when they were almost back. "It was going to be a surprise, but as I'm on a sugar rush from all the soda at Vinny's wedding, and so proud of all you done—I might as well tell you now: I've saved up a little money in case you want to take college classes at Nassau Community after you graduate."

Harvey had already been talking with the guidance counselor at her high school, and believed her illustration skills could turn out to be more than a hobby.

She brought home brochures for art schools in the city, and spread them out on the table for when Jason got back from work.

Over dinner, Harvey showed her father pictures of the best ones and read their course descriptions. When he asked about tuition, she was afraid to say.

Jason couldn't believe it. "You could buy a whole house for that."

"A small house, Dad. But it doesn't matter. I'm probably not good enough anyway."

"What do you mean by that?"

"They only take a select few."

Thinking about it that night in bed, Jason decided they should at least visit her favorite school and see what it was like.

Soon after, they took the Long Island Rail Road to Penn Station and had breakfast at a diner on Eighth Avenue. The restaurant was full of European tourists reading plastic menus, unable to decide what to eat.

There were so many people in the group touring the school that Jason and Harvey could hardly hear. The girl who led them around wore an Alice in Chains T-shirt. which Jason told her was collectible and would go for a lot on eBay.

The tour ended in a gallery of student work. The cost of private school could be daunting, the tour guide admitted, but there were many types of financial aid, scholarships, and loans.

By the time Harvey received the application paperwork a week later, she had already made the school website her home page and started planning what artwork to include in her portfolio. On Sunday, before Jason's shift at the supermarket, she laid her drawings on the floor, and they picked the best ones.

Harvey wanted to include some multidimensional work, like the motorcycle gas tank she'd airbrushed, but Jason told her the drawings were more than good enough.

The next day they drove to the post office together and sent the application by Priority Mail.

Jason stayed up that night doing calculations.

A MONTH LATER, a letter arrived from the school. At first Harvey couldn't open it. Jason was in the kitchen, making stew. Lumps of beef and white potato rolled at the surface.

The letter went unopened all through dinner, but Jason could tell Harvey thought it was good news because she kept putting her fork down and grinning. Finally, when Jason was in the kitchen fixing two bowls of ice cream, she ripped open the envelope and unfolded the letter.

"I didn't get in," she called out. "So that's that, end of story."

Jason rushed in, took the letter from her, and began to read it slowly. "It says they thought your portfolio was really interesting . . . and they liked your figure drawings . . ."

Harvey couldn't look at him.

"That's something," he said. "They didn't *have* to write that."

After eating they watched a movie in silence. When it was over, Harvey said good night and went to her room. Jason re-read the rejection letter, which was signed *William Reiner.*

Then on his way to bed, he noticed that Harvey's light was still on.

He stood for a moment, then went back to the kitchen, hoping the tick of the coffee machine brewing might bring her out to talk. But when the coffee was ready, he checked again and her light had been switched off. He listened at the door and couldn't hear anything but felt that she was in there crying.

Harvey had an early shift at Dairy Barn the next morning, so he wouldn't see her until late.

After drinking half a cup of coffee, Jason poured the rest out and set his mug in the sink. When he went to throw out the coffee grounds, he noticed a stack of Harvey's drawings in the trash.

XLIV

IT WAS PAST nine A.M. by the time he got to the Long Island Rail Road, but the Manhattan-bound platform was still crowded with men and women in business clothes.

When he boarded the train, it was hard to find a seat. But in the section where the seats pulled down to accommodate wheelchairs, a teenage boy with a black hoodie stood and asked Jason if he wanted to sit. The boy was with his family, who all had suitcases with them. The cases had wheels and kept moving around.

"Where are you headed?" Jason asked the father.

"Hawaii," he said.

"How long?"

"About fourteen hours, with a layover in California."

"That's awesome," Jason said. "Maybe I'll take my daughter there someday."

Jason tried to remember all the things he'd done in the summer with Harvey when she was little, like staying up to watch Alfred Hitchcock movies and going to the gardens at Westbury Mansion, and pretending to be millionaires.

On cold weekend mornings they'd loll on the couch like zoo animals, staring at the Weather Channel, wandering what earthquakes felt like or how quickly they could get to the roof to escape a tsunami or a blizzard. Once when they were playing, News 12 Long Island announced a tornado watch, and they gave themselves forty minutes to get the Polly Pockets, Duncan, Mr. & Mrs., Pink Bunny Baby, Tuesday, and Megatronus to safety by strapping them to a convoy of Hess trucks, which they rolled through the darkening house. When it was time to make lunch, Jason heated some beans on the stove, and they watched storm coverage on TV.

Aside from a few trips to Montauk and Pennsylvania, Harvey had never been on a real vacation. She had never flown on an airplane, nor stayed in a hotel that offered room service or had people carry her bags.

But on the Cross Island Ferry, when wind pushed them across the deck, how they laughed . . . and on the children's motorcycle carousel at Hershey Park in Pennsylvania, Harvey's hands on the pink grips, her babyface chiseled with seriousness . . . then her voice on the long car ride home, as she talked herself to sleep . . .

WHEN JASON GOT to the art school, a security guard asked if he had an appointment. Jason showed him a photocopy of Harvey's application and the letter they had received from the school, inviting them to visit. The guard wanted to know what was in the bag and why his daughter was not there with him.

Jason unzipped the knapsack and showed the guard one of Harvey's best drawings. "It's supposed to be album art," he said. "Like something you'd see on a CD cover. That's me right there," he said, pointing to a man in sunglasses riding a motorcycle. "And that's my daughter in the background."

"It does look like you," the guard said. "Even got the little tattoo right there on the neck."

"And check this out," Jason said as he unwrapped the fuel tank from a ragged beach towel. "My daughter actually air-brushed this. I told Professor William Reiner I'd drop it off because I was worried about it getting lost in the mail."

The guard said that Professor Reiner's office was on the fifth floor, all the way down the hall to the left.

When the elevator doors opened, there was a giant flat-screen television mounted to a back wall, tuned to cartoons. A few students stood watching. Jason watched too.

"I love this next bit," a girl said. "When the monster becomes just this giant mouth? Oh my God, it's *so* cool."

Jason imagined Harvey standing next to the girl, watching the cartoon with her friends, then going out for pizza. She'd need a new backpack for her artwork and probably some new pens and art supplies . . .

Jason tried to remember what the guard had said as he walked down a long hallway with framed posters of cartoons he recognized from TV. He wondered if students from the college had worked on them. What a dream it would be for Harvey to draw something that people saw on TV.

After studying the posters and imagining his daughter's name written at the bottom with the other credits, he found the office. On the wall outside was a sign that read:

W. REINER
ROOM 105
CARTOONING/ILLUSTRATION/ANIMATION
DEPT. CHAIR

Jason knocked lightly and waited. Then he knocked again, but nothing happened. A couple of students walked past, gesticulating and talking in loud voices. Jason felt suddenly vain and conspicuous, realizing it might be hours before the professor came back. He might even be off for the day, or the week, or the semester.

He decided to take another look at the posters and try to figure out what he was going to do. For the next hour, he studied first-year watercolor drawings that were pinned up on a yellow bulletin board. The best ones were pictures featuring animals wearing clothes, ballet dancers, a naked cannibal, a girl in a park crying, and a zombie eating someone's organ.

Farther down the corridor was a cabinet of clay figures wearing clothes cut from real fabrics.

Then a voice took him by surprise. "They're good, aren't they?"

Jason swiftly turned, knocking the man's leg with his bag.

"The guard downstairs said there was a parent waiting to see me. Might that be you?"

Jason nodded, then followed the man back to his office. "It's basically that my daughter really wants to come to the school," he said, his hands shaking. "The thing is, she's really talented, and—"

Professor Reiner offered him a seat. "Have you taken the tour?"

"Oh yeah, weeks and weeks ago. And we applied already, but it turns out she didn't get in." Jason foraged around in his bag for the letter.

Professor Reiner seemed annoyed. "We only have a certain number of seats we're allowed to put in the classroom. It's not really my decision."

"But your name is on the letter," Jason said, unfolding it.

"That's right, but it's the admission committee that makes the decisions in these cases. My name is just a formality."

"So that's not your signature?"

"Again, it's really not my decision," the professor said, but Jason had already unwrapped the airbrushed fuel tank from the towel and plonked it on his desk.

The professor put on his glasses. "This is very good," he said. "Do you ride a motorcycle, Mr. . . . ?"

"Not anymore," Jason said, and raised the hem of his pants to reveal the hard white plastic of his prosthetic limb.

"You're joking," the professor said, and quickly lifted the hem of his own pants, revealing the hard gray plastic of an almost identical prosthetic device.

ON THE TRAIN back to Long Island, Jason read over everything he'd jotted down in the meeting. Then he went over in his mind how he was going to tell Harvey.

Bursting in through the front door, he tripped over one of Harvey's shoes.

"Sorry, Dad!" Harvey said. "I thought you were working a double?"

"Forget about that!"

"Why aren't you mad? And why are you all dressed up?"

"Come with me . . ." he said. "Because you're going to freak out."

Harvey had cooked spaghetti, and there was a lot left over. Jason dragged some into his mouth with a fork. Then he sat next to his daughter on the couch and went over each detail. After he'd told her everything, Harvey got up to make coffee. Jason couldn't understand why she wasn't more excited.

"The way you told the story," she said, "I thought you were going to say I'd been accepted!"

"It's not as easy as that. I found out the process is very fair, Harvey."

"I'm just not good enough. That's what it is."

"Jesus Christ, Harvey—it was your SAT scores. I saw it right there on the frickin' computer screen with my own eyes. All you need to do is go to Nassau Community for a semester or two. I can pay for it. Take some art classes, retake the goddamn SAT, get your GPA up, and apply again. We've got someone on the inside now. This is big. We've got a contact."

"I just feel like I've failed. Other kids don't have to do all this, why do I?"

"Quit worrying about other people, for Chrissakes, Harvey."

"And we still have to pay for it, Dad, remember? Even if I do get accepted."

"What's wrong with you?" Jason said. "We have a plan—we got something to work with. You're being like one of those dementors in Harry Potter, just sucking out all the positive energy."

"Did he say I would definitely get in if I applied again? Did he say that?"

Jason shook his head passionately. "He can't say stuff like that, Harv. There's an application committee. It's the pen pushers you gotta convince."

"But I told everyone at school I was going there in the fall, and now I'm not."

"You'll get there, Harvey," Jason insisted. "Just retake the SAT and do what the professor says."

"Community college is just so depressing. I said I'd never go."

"Let's at least visit."

"I'd rather work at Dairy Barn my whole life."

But a few days later, Jason came home and found Harvey on the couch filling out Nassau Community College admission forms.

When he stood over her grinning, she gave a long sigh and closed her eyes. "Don't say it, Dad, just don't say a word."

XLV

"You got in eventually, Harvey, and look at you now. Plus, those two years at Nassau Community gave me a chance to save more money."

Harvey asked the bartender to bring their check.

"Thanks for always being on my side, Dad. Not a lot of kids can say that."

The boy and his father from Winnipeg had left their Paris guidebook on the bar. On the cover was a photo of the *Mona Lisa*.

Harvey pointed to it. "That's the most famous painting in the world."

"I saw it in a movie once. Someone stole it, but then a bunch of crazy nuns got it back."

Harvey checked the time on her phone. "Do you want to go see it?"

"The *Mona Lisa*? Sure."

"We've got an hour before they close."

Jason held up his injured thumb. "Don't you owe me something from the gift shop first?"

The taxi driver was from Poland and spoke to them in English. He said it was a good time to visit the museum, because everyone would be leaving. He had never seen it himself, but his wife had taken her sister when she came to stay from Warsaw after her divorce.

The driver stopped where the tour buses pull in. "This is the best entrance to use," he said. "But be quick, because I'm not allowed to stop here."

Harvey led her father into the glass pyramid, and they descended to an elegant spread of gift shops and cafés.

After buying tickets from a machine, a young security guard pointed them up a staircase against the flow of people.

As they moved quickly arm in arm through the galleries, Harvey realized that she'd never been in a museum with her father. "What do you think so far, Dad?"

Jason said he was thinking about where each painting had come from. Had it always been famous? Or did it once hang in some old English pub? Or in someone's house?

Harvey said *she* always thought about who made the painting, and what the weather was like, and when they stopped to eat lunch, and how, once it was finished, the artist had to carry it wrapped in cloth, through busy streets, hoping to get a good price.

"You think about that because you're an artist," her father said, stopping to glance at a small Italian panel with bold colors. "Jeez, Harvey, what's with all the naked babies?"

"Um, it's Jesus, Dad."

"Yeah, but how do they know what he looked like?"

Harvey couldn't say. "Don't all babies look the same?"

Frosted-glass ceiling panels spread light evenly through the galleries, and there were stone seats in some of the windows where you could sit and watch people outside.

"Smells like incense in here," Jason said. "Smells like a church."

When they passed paintings of Jesus as a man, Jason wanted

to stop. "Crazy how they hung him up like that," he said. "With nails through his hands and feet."

Harvey agreed. "I've always thought how strange it was that Christians use the way Jesus was killed as the symbol of their faith."

"Yeah, right." Her father nodded. "Like wearing a gun around your neck if he'd got shot."

"I don't think the Romans had guns, Dad."

"I know that, Harvey, I'm not stupid. I'm just sayin'."

Harvey said that one of the earliest memories of her first father was seeing him put a golden cross on a woman's neck at his jewelry store. "The cross came out on a cushion," she said. "A little red cushion, the kind used to carry precious things."

"It was probably Christmastime," she said. "But I was standing at the back of the shop with my mother."

THE *Mona Lisa* was in a glass case with its own security guard, a middle-aged woman with a blue blazer and a walkie-talkie. Tour guides held colored flags in the air so people knew where to congregate.

Harvey and Jason had a good view, though people kept pushing in front with their phones out.

"I must be stupid after all," Jason said. "But it doesn't look any better to me than the other pictures in here."

Then there was a surge of people, and they moved with the current to another gallery, where there were much larger paintings and a circular bench with purple velvet for people to sit on.

"So, Dad. Now you can say you've seen the *Mona Lisa*."

"To be honest, Harv, I can only relate to this stuff if it

reminds me of something from real life, like that painting of dead fish right there," he said, pointing to a shadowy canvas. "It's me and Vincent after a day on the boats."

"I think that picture means that simple things can be beautiful too," Harvey said, grabbing on to his arm. "Like a father and daughter washing the car or eating taco pie."

"Or changing the oil," Jason added. "Now that you've moved out and don't help me no more, I take it to Jiffy Lube."

"I was gonna work there, remember?"

"That's below you now, Harv."

"Nothing's below me, Dad. Don't ever think that."

As they were leaving the museum, they passed the security guard who had given them directions. He was about Harvey's age.

"So, you see it, monsieur? The *Mona Lisa*?"

Harvey said she couldn't believe how crowded it was, even at closing. The guard told them it was the most popular picture in the collection, then asked if Jason had a favorite painting. As he thought about it, Harvey noticed the guard looking at the tattoo on Jason's neck as though it were something in a gallery.

"Yeah, I do got a favorite," Jason said, finally

"Let me guess," the guard said. "*Mona Lisa*?"

"No," Jason told him. "There was a little girl with short hair sitting in a park someplace, real happy—just smiling away on a tree stump or something."

The guard was impressed. "Sounds like Raeburn. That's one of our finest pieces."

"Well, I had that for real, buddy," Jason told the guard, pointing to Harvey. "Before she grew up, of course."

"You've still got it," Harvey said, poking him in the ribs. "I'm still here."

WHEN THEY WERE outside, Jason noticed there were places to sit and said he needed to rest his leg before going any farther. Harvey followed people across the cobblestone square with her eyes, until they rounded a corner or were too small to see.

A crowd of people near the glass pyramid was taking group photos. Other people pushed bicycles, or smoked, or held hands, or read things on their phones. Children ran ahead, then stood panting in one place until their parents caught up.

Harvey reached deep into her purse and pulled out the envelope she'd been saving until his last day in Paris. "I just can't wait anymore," she said, holding it out for Jason. "I need you to know."

"What is this?

"Please, Dad, just take it."

"Should I open it?"

"Yes, Dad. Look at what's inside."

Jason removed the documents and glanced at the first page. "Is this the adoption paperwork we did with Wanda?"

"No," Harvey said. "It's adoption paperwork from when I was born."

Jason looked at her, confused.

"I know everything," she said. "Everything you've been too afraid to tell me for the last twenty years."

"What are you talking about?"

Harvey felt her life coming apart. "Please stop pretending," she said. "You don't have to pretend anymore."

But Jason just sat there with the grainy photocopies, trying to understand what she was telling him. When the papers almost blew away, Harvey grabbed them and stuffed everything back into her purse. The makeup around her eyes had smudged. "I was only a week old when your brother and sister-in-law adopted me," she said.

Jason's eyes fell upon the little stones under his feet.

"I'm not your niece after all," she said. "We don't even have the same blood."

The tip of the envelope was showing from her purse. Jason looked at it. Wanted to pull it out. Rip it to pieces. It startled him that words could have so much power over their lives.

"Are you angry?" Harvey said, wiping a sleeve across her eyes. "Are you mad that I found it out? This secret you kept for so long?"

But Jason just sat there, unable to speak.

"What I really want to know," Harvey said, her voice faltering, "what I really want to ask you, is if it ever crossed your mind to refuse. Wanda must have told you at the beginning that I was adopted. Why didn't you say no?"

When he didn't answer, Harvey tugged on the sleeve of his motorcycle jacket. "Dad?" she said. "Dad?"

He looked at her. At the woman she had become.

"You don't have to protect me from the truth anymore," she said.

"What truth?"

"That we're not even related!"

Jason closed his eyes then spoke slowly and quietly. "Remember the time you woke up screaming one night,

Harvey? And I carried you out to the driveway in your Hello Kitty pajamas, and we went all the way to the city, then drove around Times Square and opened the sunroof so the car could fill up with light? Do you remember that?"

"You let me sit in the front seat."

"That's truth, Harvey, not what's written on a piece of paper or in blood too small to see—but the memory of how it felt being together."

WHEN THE CROWDS leaving the museum had thinned to only a few, random bodies, Harvey said she was ready to go on, and they took a path through the gardens of the Tuileries, toward the Métro at Place de la Concorde.

Jason asked if the adoption papers said anything about her biological parents.

"Just my mother," Harvey said. "The space under *father* says *unknown*."

"Well, that's easy. Just write my name in there."

This made Harvey start to sob again, so Jason found an empty bench between a row of flowering trees where there was no one around. When her tissue was all used up, Jason remembered the napkin he'd saved from breakfast, with the sketch of a girl holding flowers. He gave it to her.

Then a man came toward them with a suitcase and asked if they were interested in buying designer sunglasses. When he put the case down and started getting things out, Jason stood with his fists clenched. This made Harvey laugh, and Jason watched with more gratitude than anger as the man disappeared.

He asked Harvey if she was going to try and track down her biological parents.

"If you want my help," he told her, "count on it."

HARVEY HAD LEARNED that her birth mother was dead by typing the name Rita Vega from the birth certificate into Google. She had been born in Costa Rica and died of cancer in a hospital off the Long Island Expressway. Harvey and Jason would have driven past it many times.

Harvey wondered if she had been given up because of the illness, or if there had been another reason and the disease came later. Had her mother chosen the people to adopt her? Or was the process anonymous and Harvey's life now the result of chance and circumstance?

Harvey had tried her best to find a picture, even calling the hospital to see if they had a photo on file, or if any of the nurses could remember what Rita Vega looked like.

In the weeks following her discovery, Harvey had a hard time getting used to the idea of it, and lay awake at night, unable to eat, crying in the bathroom at work—grieving for someone she couldn't even imagine.

She went online and looked up the day she died.

A Friday in April. Six minutes before one o'clock.

The other patients would have been eating lunch. Harvey would have been eating lunch, or in line at the cafeteria deciding what to eat, worried about where she might sit and the shame if she dropped her tray.

She wondered (as she would for the rest of her life) if, in those final moments, she passed over her mother's heart like the shadow of something in flight.

But more than anything, Harvey wished there was some way to get a message through. Some way to let her know about the man who became her father, and that her suffering had not been in vain, and all the love she had withheld, that was lost in death, had found its way back into the world and was undiminished.

ACKNOWLEDGMENTS

THE AUTHOR WISHES to acknowledge the following people:
Wes Anderson; Tina Andreadis; Amy Baker; Betty; Vimi Bhatia; Elona, Tammy and Joshua Bodwell; Bryan Le Boeuf; my dear brother, Darren Booy, and his wife, Raha; Joan and Stephen Booy; Theodore Bouloukos; Catrin Brace and the Welsh Assembly Government; Ken Browar; Dr. Elissa Brown and Lois Oliveira of the Child HELP Partnership; David Bruson; Michelangelo di Lodovico Buonarroti Simoni; Jonathan Burnham; Li Chow; Maria Christodoulou; Scott and Liz Cohen; Denise and James Connelly; Rejean Daigneault; Cynthia and Justin Ellis; Wolfgang Egger; Dr. Shilpi Epstein; Laurie Fink; Foxy; Dani Gill; Dr. Bruce Gelb; Gaia Grossi; Jen Hart; Dolores Henry; Gregory Henry; James Hetfield and Metallica; Nancy Horner; Mr. Howard; Professor Huang; Jig; Carlos Juarbe; David Kaplan Martial Arts; Hilary Knight; Evelyn Lehman; Mike Leigh; Sam Levinson; Filippino Lippi; Michael and Delphine Matkin; Dorit Matthews; Megatronis; Erfan Mojib; Mr. and Mrs. Samuel Morris III; Michael Morrison; Lukas Ortiz; Deborah Ory; Murat Oztaskin; Wendy and Jon Paton; Bronson Pinchot; Jonathan D. Rabinowitz; Ashwin Rattan; Tamara Rawitt; Rob; Sepultura; Lori and Ted Schultz; Alexis Shanley; Lisa Sharkey; Ivan Shaw and Lisa Von Weise Shaw; Dmitri Shostakovich; Stop & Shop supermarkets; the coaches and staff at UFC Gym, New Hyde Park; Rebecca Torrey; Tuesday; Joseph Mallord William Turner;

Violet; Virginia Stanley; Jeremy Strong; Gloria Vanderbilt; the Vilcek Foundation; Waldorf Astoria Hotels; Mojo Wang; Barbara Wersba; Sylvia Beach Whitman at Shakespeare & Company; Carol Zeitz, Ph.D.; Georgi and Sveta Zhikharev.

Special thanks to those guardians of story: librarians.

THE AMAZING INDIVIDUALS at Conville & Walsh: Jake Smith-Bosanquet, Alexander Cochran, Tracy England, Emma Finn, Alexandra McNicoll, and Dorcas Rogers.

EXTRA SPECIAL THANKS to my editor and friend, Laura Brown, for her editorial grace, integrity, and calm intelligence.

MY DEVOTED AND charming publicist, Rachel Elinsky; the incomparable Tom Hopke Jr.; and a special thank you to Cal Morgan, without whom, this book would not have been completed.

FOR CLOSE FRIENDSHIP, long walks from Mumbles to Kent Street, and poetry, Lucas Hunt.

FOR CLOSE FRIENDSHIP, strange humor, adventures on Jermyn Street, and three-hour lunches at the Wolseley, Carrie Kania (also my literary agent).

FINALLY, I WOULD like to express my deepest gratitude to Christina Daigneault and our talented, brilliant daughter, Madeleine Van Booy, for sharing their lives with me, and opening up new realms of happiness through our ongoing adventures in both the extraordinary and the everyday.

ALSO BY SIMON VAN BOOY

Everything Beautiful Began After

Simon Van Booy, winner of the prestigious Frank O'Connor International Short Story Award, brings his gift for poetic dialogue and sumptuous imagery to this debut novel of longing and discovery amidst the ruins of Ancient Greece.

'A powerful meditation on the undying nature of love and the often cruel beauty of one's own fate. This is a novel you simply must read!' **Andre Dubus III**

'Haunting.' ***Daily Mail***

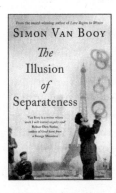

The Illusion of Separateness

A luminous story of how one man's act of mercy during WW2 changed the lives of a group of strangers, and how they each eventually discover the astonishing truth of their connection.

'A delicate, complex, moving novel, one to withstand – demand even – an instant second reading.' ***Daily Telegraph***

'There is a sustaining pleasure in wondering how the strands of the story will tie together.' ***Guardian***

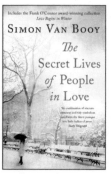

The Secret Lives of People in Love

Bringing together for the first time two short story collections from a celebrated master of the form – including the Frank O'Connor Short Story Award-winning collection *Love Begins in Winter*.

'Incurable romantics will savour Simon Van Booy's tender, Maupassant-like fables.' **New York Times**

'Its combination of staccato sentences and tidy symbolism transforms the finest passages into little haikus of prose.' **Daily Telegraph**

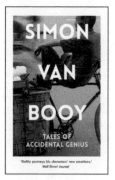

Tales of Accidental Genius

The first collection of short stories from Simon Van Booy since his Frank O'Connor Short Story Award-winning collection *Love Begins in Winter*.

'Van Booy writes with muted, unsentimental elegance about the impulses that bind us together.' **Sunday Times**

'Deftly portrays his characters' raw emotions.' **Wall Street Journal**